Labyrinth

a mythic journey

Labyrinth

a mythic journey

Rainer Neumann

Published by

landseandsky

Second Edition
Published by landseandsky in 2007

ISBN: 978-0-6151-7225-5

Copyright © 2001 by Rainer Neumann

All rights reserved. No part of this book may be reproduced or transmitted in any form or by any means, electronic or mechanical, including photocopying, recording, or by any information storage and retrieval system, without permission in writing from the copyright owner.

This is a work of fiction. Names, characters, places and incidents either are the product of the author's imagination or are used fictitiously, and any resemblance to any actual persons, living or dead, events or locales is entirely coincidental.

Cover art is a pastel drawing by the author.

This book is available through the electronic storefront of lulu.com/RNeumann.

Inquiries are also welcomed at highwayone@earthlink.net

To my mother and father whose journey is full of memories of an epic life lived... a journey not yet over...

Contents

Prologue

If an unusual memory wells up and it gives meaning to your present moment...

If a most traumatic time will not let you go...

If you've wondered about people or places that seem familiar even though it seems to be your first encounter...

If you've valued an odd thing and it becomes a part of you... If a past moment in your life is as present as a hot cup of chocolate on a cool morning...

If you've wondered what might have happened if you had not gone down a certain road or met a certain person or made a certain decision...

Path One

The Hedgerow Road

After the confrontation with his father, Twangly ran up to his room, grabbed the suitcase he had not fully unpacked, bounded down the stairs, looked around at what seemed like an alien world, walked out the front door of the estate and down the ivy-twined, tree-lined road. He could hear his mother calling, "Twangly, please don't go like this, *Twangly. Twangly!*"

As his mother's voice grew fainter he felt that this was the perfect time to take on a new name, a name that would carry him into a new life. *I don't need the legacy of my past!* he almost shouted. *I'm going to get rid of the bloody weight that's shackled to me. I'm on the road now and I'm going to take on a new character, a new name, a new...*His thoughts were ricocheting in his head, his feet were trying to keep up with the flooding words, *It's just, it's...damn! Once you've started you can't turn around. Anyway I can't. Gadfrees, I feel like an exile of my own choosing, not like Prospero who was exiled by his own brother. Maybe I'll find an island. I should let Rushdie know, or Twing. I will, when I've gotten there. There? Where's there? Where's the Island? There is one place that has islands -- I've got to go to Dover, catch the ferry to Calais and head north to Amsterdam.*

He had heard about the theater scene in Amsterdam -- on the edge theater. That was his first love. He wanted to do

Shakespeare on the edge, just as he remembered Calaban -- on the edge of being human...

This island's mine, by Sycorax my mother,
Which thou takest from me. When thou camest first,
Thou strokedst me and madest much of me, wouldst give me
Water with berries in't, and teach me how
To name the bigger light, and how the less,
That burn by day and night: and then I loved thee
And show'd thee all the qualities o' the isle,
The fresh springs, brine-pits, barren place and fertile:
Cursed be that I did so!

Calaban had traded his island for arcane knowledge. Twangly, however, wanted to find another kind of island. A place where he could trade his knowledge for experience -- *not trade*, really, but better, *add to his knowledge* -- *give it life.* He had heard about the street scenes, the hashhish, the coffee houses, Dam Square: he wanted to lose himself on the side streets of Amsterdam. He told his father he was going to take a year off before going to Oxford. He needed to. This summer had been an awakening from the last 18 years -- like a mad summer night's dream the potion had worn off and he had opened his eyes to a new world...

*I'm going to take on a new character -- maybe many, maybe, maybe...*His mind was reeling with the possibilities when a motor car honked at him. He had been walking in the middle of the road. He jumped and held up his thumb. The driver, a small, hunched-over man, barely tall enough to see over the steering wheel, looked out and saw himself, as he had walked, with the same lost urgency, many years ago. He had slowed down enough to consider stopping. He decided to stop. He had to stop -- and give his memory a ride. Twangly, however, was not the youth of the driver's memory. He was a strapping six-footer, with unruly hair that he had to water down *and* he had a strange birthmark on his neck -- a birthmark in the shape of a guitar.

4

"Where might ye be going?" the driver asked with an engaging grin.

Twangly looked at the tweed hat, plaid face and the green eyes and thought, *Where had he seen that face before?* "Oh, yes," he stammered, "ah, yes, well, I'm going to Dover to catch the ferry to Calais."

"Well, ye have a ways to go. We can take ye a little closer if you want. Climb in."

Twangly got in and very quickly felt like he had stepped into an Irish fairy tale -- with a wee leprechaun behind the wheel and magic shamrocks on the dashboard. He had just settled back when he heard the driver break into a high-pitched chuckle, *ho, ho, hay, hay, now we will take on this highway, shall we, ha, hah, hee, hee…*

The motor car picked up speed and careened from left to right until a softer voice from the left front seat said, "Watch out, dear. There's a lorry coming."

A lorry! Twangly was thinking, his eyes searching ahead of him. "HEY, WATCH IT! WATCH IT! Get over."

The driver pulled to the left. "Ahh, the thrill of it," he gasped, and began a full-voiced rendition of *On the open road*. He kept weaving and chuckling and singing. Finally, Twangly just gave up and moved his body with the curves.

"There's Willowgrave ahead of us," said the feminine voice from the front left side.

Willowgrave thought Twangly. *That sounds familiar. I think I've been there. Gadfrees, it may end up being my grave if I don't get out of this car.*

"I just realized I've got to make a phone call," he almost yelled out. "Can you drop me off here?"

We've just begun, came the driver's response as he caroused through Willowgrave.

On the other end of the village stood a young woman holding up a sign that read: RIDE NEEDED.

"Shall we pick up the young lass?" the driver asked.

"Why not?" said the woman. "We already have one, why not another? Who knows, they may get to know each other."

The driver stopped the car. The young lass jumped into the back seat.

"Hello, everyone."

Hello, and hang on! came a warning from the driver, as she fell back into the seat and let go.

"Where are you going?" she finally asked. Twangly was close enough to feel the heat of her voice. It was like fire breathing out.

Was she a circus performer? he wondered. *A fire eater? Why hadn't he gotten out when they stopped?* Now his apprehension turned into curiosity or even chivalry. *Could he save this woman from the fate of this mad driver, this wild man at the wheel?*

"Okay, where are you going?" She asked again, sensing the situation was a little unusual, even though unusual situations is what she thrived on.

We're on our way to make hay, came the driver's response. *Ha, hah, ho, ho, hee, hee. We'll throw away the key...*

"Now, dear, watch out for the next turn. It's a hairpin."

Before they could look out, the motor car was on two wheels, screeching, screaming, scraping the hedgerow. The fire woman was thrown onto Twangly and lay all over him. He was engulfed in hair and sweat and arms trying to hold on while her hot breath was barely screaming, WATCH OOOOUT! The driver's companion, whose face Twangly had not yet seen and whose voice carried an atmosphere of calmness and imperturbability, said, "Hold on." While the plaid-faced leprechaun, the wild man behind the wheel, was in a white-knuckle mode, giddy with excitement. Finally, however, the scraping of the hedgerow brought some awareness of danger to him and his instinct -- tempered by years of driving -- brought back some control, until he ended up in the middle of the road, whistling a sigh of relief, with a sly smile on his face -- as if he had planned it all and it had gone off splendidly.

In the back seat *hot breath* was still in Twangly's arms and he allowed himself a chance to look into her eyes, *Gadfrees, what dark, placid pools,* he thought, *surrounded by an aching redness. Who is this strange girl?*

6

"Are you all right?" he asked.

She had settled into a trance and just looked at him, this childboyman. She felt his arms. "Let me stay here?" she whispered.

He smiled and felt a swaying lilt come over the motor car. The driver had settled into the turns of the road and his companion was humming, *Oh, Britannia*, while this strange girl had eased into his lap and lay sleeping. He was enjoying the ride, watching the hedgerows, feeling this soft, dormant body use him as a pillow.

"We're here," came a calm announcement from the driver's companion. "We're here. Please dear, do stop the car and let us roam about a bit. It is the tor of Terra Grandeur. We must stop to climb it. The view is effervescent. It is history...It is..."

The soft dragon on Twangly's lap moved and in a startled voice said, "Terra Grandeur! Oh, let's go. Let's go, mister, Mister Driver. Come, beautiful boy, let's walk up to the tor of Terra Grandeur -- It's a labyrinth, you know..."

The car was parked. A break in the hedgerow was found. A path, many had taken, had walked, had pressed their footprints into, was again pressed into and deepened. They scrambled through the hedges. The girl led the way, holding Twangly's hand, pulling with exuberance. Her eyes lit up. He could feel her pulse. His head was pounding as they curved around the hill, along a path carved eons ago. The driver and his companion were following at their own pace, wandering without hurrying. As the path turned higher, Twangly ventured to ask, "What is your name?"

With a movement of her shoulders, indicating a slight gesture of mystery, she said, "My name's not important, but my roots are here. This is where I shot up and curled around. I'm from the old bridal paths and I've met a young stranger. Where are you from?"

Twangly didn't know what to say, wasn't sure what to say. He finally spoke, as the ruins of Terra Grandeur came into view. "I was brought up here, also, but I'm not originally from around here," he told her.

7

"What's your name?" she asked.

Hesitating for a minute, he finally said, "At school they called me T-Rex."

"T-Rex," she repeated, "T-Rex, Oedipus Rex, Rex the King -- the King who's climbing to claim his throne. This, the ruins of Terra Grandeur, will be infused with your youth, my young King, and I'll be your *Lady*, your *Earth Lady*...The one who has brought you through the hedges and thickets and a wild, death-defying car ride -- Hey, we lived through that to climb this path...*Look, here, now, feel these old stones, go on, up, climb the old stairs, look, look at your fabled kingdom, look around you, you are the young King these stones have called out to...*"

She went on and on...until he looked through her to the undulating fields and verdant, grassy greens, outlined by hedgerows and the wall-like, rocky remnants of those who had ordered and organized this place throughout time and memory.

"Who are you?" he silently asked himself.

Ha, ha, came the strident cry of the driver, *ha, hah, ho, ha, ach, whee, wheeze.*

"Now slow down," came the insistent advice from his companion.

There they are and here we are, at the top of the world. Look out, ha, hah, ho, ho, hee, hee, as far as the eye can see.

As he heard the enthusiastic exhortations from their driver, Twangly could only smile at the woman next to him -- this *earth lady*. "He's a real eccentric, isn't he?" he finally said to her. "I wonder where they're from?"

She, however, was caught up in reverie and possibility...*Come here, my boy King*, she whispered to him, *Here, to where the knights of Terra Grandeur looked out on the fields of valor, where they tested each other's strengths and weaknesses, see, they still wait with their plumes of gold and green and their velvet tunics of reds and blues, the gleam of their armor blinding in the afternoon sun. Hear the snorting of their horses, the pawing of the ground. Can you hear them? Listen to the clash of swords echoing off the surrounding hills. There, there! Look at the multicolored tents and banners...*

He let his imagination soar with her words, expand and soar...Her hot breath gushed like some ancient volcano and exuded a story she had heard and possibly lived...onceuponatime...Now, he was next to her and she, she had a willing vessel to fill...again...upon this time...*Do you see? There? -- A shield -- Glistening in the sun?*

In the sun -- out of the spewing dust -- breaking out of the banners encrested with the symbols of lions and bears and falcons came a rider with a shield on his arm and a flowing, velvet cloak of dark forest-green over his shoulder with a matching forest-green plume on his helmet. His head was held high. Even from the heights of the tor of Terra Grandeur, Twangly could see fire in his eyes. The rider rode up the hill as close as he could.

He called to Twangly. I HAVE COME AS YOU HAVE ASKED, MY KING!

Twangly's flesh ran with excitement. *Earth Lady*, the ancient story teller, took on a royal glory. Even the driver, now in jester's clothes, and his companion, the Lady in Waiting, stood in silence. The evening sun glistened off the Knight's armor, giving him a golden sheen that temporarily blinded all who looked in his direction.

YOU CALLED ME...the Knight spoke again and his voice broke through the stabs of light.

Twangly, the youthful King, gasped and grasped the solid stone archway around him and peered into the distance, his eyes half shut, his mouth open...Before he could answer or make any kind of sound there were cries from the encampment. A young child was running out from between the tents, and behind him a long-haired, rugged-looking man in red underclothes was cursing and running after him.

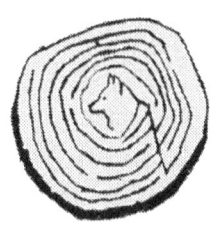

Path Two

Nicholas

*Wait till I get my hands on you! I'll...I'll skin you alive! I'll tie rocks on your feet and throw you in a well! I'll, I'll...*He kept cursing after the boy, but his feet were giving out. The ground was rough and he had not taken the time to put his boots on.

The boy ran up the hill towards the reflecting sunlight. He was quick to jump and take the shortcuts of the labyrinthine pathway. Finally, he came close to the Knight with the forest-green plume. "Oh sir, please, please protect me from that man. He's taken me as a servant and beats me! For no reason! Look at my welts, my bruises. I try. I'm a good worker but he isn't satisfied with anything I do..." The cries and words kept coming out of the child.

"Let me see?" the Knight asked. The child stood in front of him, in some pain. With eyes that turned to anger he saw the blue bruises on the child's arms and around his eyes.

"Who is this man?" he asked the child.

"He took me from my uncle last year when he came through our village."

"Where are your parents?"

"They are dead and I was living with my uncle, but we did not have much to eat last year. It was such a long winter that our crops went in too late and my uncle said it would be better for me if I went with this man, as his servant…*but I think my uncle just needed the money.*"

By the time these words were spoken the rugged man had closed in on where the child stood. Enraged and cursing he ran towards the boy but the boy just evaded him again.

The Knight rode his horse in front of the man.

"Why do you beat the boy?"

The man was in no condition to answer reasonably and just cursed him, *Get out of my way, you! Don't meddle in my affairs.*

"You did not answer me," the Knight replied and cornered the man between a rock and the hedges.

With a fury the man grabbed the reins and tried to maneuver the horse. The Knight grabbed him by his long hair, pulled him and half dragged him, until he lost his balance and fell into the bramble hedges. The cursing and yelling could be heard throughout the valley. The Knight dismounted and pinned the man in the hedges.

"You have done enough damage. What did you pay for this child?"

The man sputtered, *ten shillings.*

"Here are your ten shillings. He threw them into the brambles. If you are ever seen near this child again it will go bad for you"

The Knight went over to the child, "Let us find another place for you. If you are willing to work, I think there is someone who is willing to take you in."

"Thank you, thank you," the boy answered.

While they talked, the rugged man slithered away and lost himself in the din of the encampment. The Knight remounted and let the boy take his hand. With one jump he was on the back of his horse.

"Take me to your tent and we will get your belongings."

"I don't have anything."

"Nothing?"

"Well, I have a pack of clothes in his tent but I have everything I want in this pouch. I always have it tied around my wrist. It's the one thing he didn't take."

12

"What do you have in your leather pouch?"

"Secret things."

"Let us keep them secret and find a place for you"

"Can I stay with you? I could take care of your horse. I could shine your armor."

"I have come to answer the King's summons. There is to be a grand feast in a few days, the Festival of Songs. I don't know what my journey will be after that"

"I could start the fire in the morning and make hot drinks for you."

The Knight smiled. He was beginning to like this child's willingness, his insistence. He kept him on his horse and rode into Terra Grandeur with him. He rode up to the balcony of the King. The young King was waiting for them.

"Ahh, finally, you have found your way here. And whom do you have riding with you?"

"A boy, who was sold by his uncle to a scoundrel. I've paid for him and now he needs a place to stay. I think he will be a good worker."

"I will send him to the scullery or to the baker. I will see that he is taken care of and put to work."

"But, but, sire, I want to go with you. I will serve you well."

"I am sure you would, but you are still too young to take on a knight's wandering path. I have saved you from a scoundrel, now be grateful to the King."

As he said these words a huge, round man with a cook's hat came out. He had heard the King's pronouncement and bellowed loudly enough for all to hear, "Well, now, what have we here -- another strong, young lad for the bakery. Come, boy, and I'll show you where you will find a new home." With a rolling voice the baker took him by the arm and began to walk him into the bakery.

The boy turned around, meeting the eyes of the greenplumed knight. He spoke loudly, but with a touch of sadness said, "Thank you, sire," and, bowing to the King, added, "Thank you, your Highness."

"I will see you before I go," the Knight answered back.

"So, what are we going to call you?" the baker inquired.

"I'm not sure what my parents named me. I don't remember them, but my uncle said I was born on December 6 so he called me Nicholas, after a saint he had heard about."

"Well, that's a fine name. Tell me, do you sing, Nicholas?"

"Well, I think I've forgotten the few songs my uncle taught me and I was, when I did sing, that man...His eyes filled with tears...

The baker put his arms around him. "A song will help you in your work here. I'm going to put you to work kneading the dough for the bread of the King's household. It's best with a song, *Come on, join in, take a stand,* the baker began with his full-bellied voice, *knead the dough with your heart and hand.*"

Other voices soon came out of the stones, around corners, out of the crackling of a massive stone oven, *We'll put it in the oven, we'll put it in the oven, and it's aroma a ah, will rule the land.*

The voices echoed around the room -- over and over the words were sung, *and its aroma a ah, will rule the land.*

Over and over the dough was pushed and pulled and pounded, over and over the words were sung until the dough was done and a hundred loaves were ready for the oven's heat.

Nicholas, too, had gone to a marble table piled high with dough. He, too, had joined in the song as he kneaded, becoming one with the dough and the voices and the crackling warmth. He was also needed until his arms and hands ached, until the ovens were filled with the raised dough, now brown-crusted, and an aroma wafted throughout the kitchen, out the doors and into the courtyard. A baking day had come into his world, so different from where he had come from.

Our Jolly Baker, as he was sometimes called by the King, showed him where he would sleep and told the other boys to help him find his way around the bakery and the castle, where they ate, where they peed, where they slept and when they had time to hide. That night his muscles ached but for the first time he felt good. For the first time, in a long time, he felt good. His muscles did not ache with bruises from beatings but from work that was filled with songs and smells and a taste that stayed in

14

his mouth. He lay on a hard wooden cot with his clothes on and a blanket to cover him and it felt like the most comfortable bed he had ever slept in. His hand felt the warmth of stones beneath him, stones that kept the heat of the day in them and slowly let it out to night.

As his arm dangled over the cot, the pouch around his wrist fell and clinked as it landed on the hard floor. In the dark he opened it and put his fingers around a flat metal coin with incised lines. His fingers followed the lines from the outside to the center. He knew the center -- a secret out of his past -- a symbol that had been his father's and his father's before him. Three small bones were also a part of his possessions and when his uncle had shown him how to write letters, he carved his own name into one of them.

Clutching his secret things, he thought about the day that had transpired. He had met a Knight, a Knight, with a green, forestgreen plume and his overwhelming desire was to ride with him. Half hoping, half wishing, he saw himself as his squire. He saw himself, now, faintly, projected on the stone walls, with this Knight, riding together, taking part in a grand pageant, a pageant that started ages ago and now, he, he wanted to be a part of it, to ride to the shores of this rolling green land, to follow the paths of wanderers, to ride into the songs of minstrels, to, to…With this vision his eyes shut and his soul moved in the realms of the stars…

Path Three

Street Corner Singer

Amsterdam was cool in the morning. The North Sea air was brisk and followed the canals into the city. That is why he liked getting up early, before the bustling sounds of the waking city overwhelmed his senses and obscured his contact with the sea. He walked along the Oz achterburgwal and, in the diffused light, turned onto a bridge that crossed the canal. In the middle of the bridge he looked down on the moving, flowing water and thought about his life -- thought about the world. He wanted this North Sea air to blow on him -- in him. *He wanted to be reminded -- at the turning of this century -- he desperately wanted to be reminded of being -- just being alive.* His head had been spinning and his body turning for too many nights now. Somehow he couldn't shake the thoughts that had clung to him.

"Why?" he asked, almost out loud. *Why? Why were people going on -- blindly building weapons so powerful that they could destroy a whole city? -- city after city? -- until, until...GODTHESUFFERING, the...*

He could not even finish his thoughts, he was angry and shaking inside and kept wondering why he was coming into a time and a world that could be taken from him in an instant. He could not understand it, did not want to understand it. And it was not just the people in the governments, who had control of these weapons, that he was worried about but also the

17

disenchanted, the extremists, the suicide terrorists, those who may not build the weapons but who wouldcould hold the world hostage if they, if they...

He had been obsessed with these thoughts and his frustration and anger had grown so much lately that he had to get up early in the morning, to walk those streets, to feel the sea air, to remind him of what it meant to be alive. He needed an outlet for these feelings and thoughts, and he had begun, again, to write in his small notebook, to write out his frustrations. This morning he was shaking when he took out his notebook and his pen. Standing on the bridge, he quickly jotted down a few words...

Where is the voice that speaks for truth?

He wanted to shout it into the air, along the street, over the canals.

Where is the voice that speaks for all?

He looked around. No one was out. A light turned on at the bakery cafe where he usually had a hard roll and coffee for breakfast. On the wall was fresh paint -- spray-painted letters that looked like L. O. V. E...*Sure,* he said in a cynical voice and he continued to write in his notebook:

Is it just a morning...a twilight shadow

He crossed out *morning. Shadows, twilight shadows, before the darkness,* went through his head until he wrote,

Is it just a twilight shadow?
No more than writing on the wall?

That's it, he thought and continued to let his words flow...

18

Inside the minds of desperation/devastation

He crossed out devastation.

Inside the minds of desperation,
Is the threat to all we know.
I'd like to think it's an illusion,
But they build, to bring our fall

He looked over to the doors of the bakery cafe again and continued to write,

Where is the love that takes in life?
Where is the love that takes in all?
Is it just a twilight shadow?
No more than writing on the wall?

"I've got it…"

As I stand beside the canals…the river

He crossed out *canals. Rivers flow with the eternal water*, he thought and continued,

As I stand beside the river,
And watch the ancient water flow.
It seems as though I'm moving,
And change is all I know.

Where is the voice that speaks for truth?
Where is the voice that speaks for all?
Is it just a twilight shadow?
No more than writing on the wall?

He sang it over and over,

No more than writing on the wall?

No more than writing on the wall...

He sang it until the morning light struck him and he became aware of people crossing the bridge, walking on the sidewalks, the ringing of bicycle bells. He walked to the graffiti wall and door and opened the letter "O". The aroma of fresh baked bread and hard rolls as well as fresh brewed coffee filled his nostrils. *Couldn't life just be like this,* he thought, *Why do I, why do I even have to know about these ffffed up people? Why? Why? Why?*

"What would you like?"

Momentarily startled, he shook his head and ordered a hard roll and coffee, poured some sugar in the saucer, dipped his hard roll in the coffee, sucked on it, dipped it into the sugar and took a bite. The Adler Bakery Cafe or L O V E cafe, as it had been christened during the night, had become his morning routine since he settled in Amsterdam. He had taken a room in the Hotel Europa, a student pension on Warmoesstraat. In his youthful despair and frustration he had come to Amsterdam again, thinking the move could change things. For him *love* was still written all over the city. He was in love with the canals and the alleys that held mysterious doorways -- sometimes a club or a coffee house; the cobblestone streets, the sometimes stoned, leftover hippies asking if he wanted to buy some hashhish from Morocco. *It's all right,* they seemed to say, here in this port city, this world city, this place of embarkation for the exotic ports of the world, it was all right, for here, you spoke, at least, three languages.

He had come to the city years ago, during the summer, when the park was full of traveling kids, like himself, looking for a *happening*. He could leave his backpack leaning against a tree in the park, walk around the city square and it would still be there when he returned. Such was the city of Amsterdam when he had come the first time. This time he decided to stay for a while writing his songs and performing on the street corners. He had even taken on the moniker of Street Corner Singer and his friends had shortened it to SC. He found out that some clubs had 'open mikes'. Someone told him about a club named the Cat's Cradle, named after the famous book or maybe just named after the string game. Now it was a *blues* club. Instead of intertwining string it was intertwining notes. On Monday nights they had 'open mike' and if you got there early enough and put your name on the list or stayed late enough you could get on stage for about fifteen minutes. If the audience liked your show you could stay on for ten more minutes. This was one late night place he had heard about. It was word-of-mouth only and someone told him about it the first day he sang on the square.

You go down Kloveniersburgwal towards Nieuwmarkt, turn left at an antique store, go down the alley under an archway to the right, go under it, into a phone booth, go in, dial S O S, tell them you're a singer, tell them Vango sent you -- Don't write this down -- Remember it.

He found the antique store the night a blues singer was on stage, the sound of her harsh, plaintive voice could be heard down the alley even before he got to the archway, before he found the phone booth…

I'm a honky tonk woman.
I'm a honky tonk woman.

He went under the arch way,

Every Saturday night,
when you're feeling blue,
and you long to be happy

He walked into the phone booth,

I know what you can do…

Her voice was like a siren, urging him on, pulling him in. He dialed S O S.

21

"Hello"

"Vango told me about this place"

"Who are you?"

"SC, I was singing on the square"

"Hold on"

The back door of the telephone booth opened…He stepped down into an underground cavern. The eccentric looking place was half-filled with people of all ages, from street people to mop tops to *ravers* in black to Dutch men with lean faces. He looked around and found a seat at a long table. Several people were sitting at it and he could hear several languages. One man with a ruddy face and a fisherman's cap welcomed him by making eye contact and nodding. He smiled back. He wasn't sure what to expect. Slowly, his eyes adjusted to the dim light and the sight of the cavernous club began to mix with the sound of the blues, the *boom boom boom* of a standup base, the tinned beat of the cymbals and the husky, fullthroated sound of a big mama. Eventually, these sounds became a background to the oddities surrounding him. It was like a museum inside. He was surrounded by the remnants of someone's wild collecting mania. A faded newspaper clipping was staring at him when he turned to his left. On it was the headline, FIVE SURVIVED, with a picture of five emaciated young men hanging onto a boat. Across from him was a stuffed weasel-like animal, maybe a mongoose, baring its fangs at a cobra ready to strike. There were old posters and signs everywhere, including pictures of singers like Billie Holiday.

Where am I? he wondered, words and thoughts wandering through his reverie…

A Spy in the Mist

"Where am I?" he asked again, realizing he had just come back from an inner journey, his mind swirling with the images around him.

Looks like you're deep in thought. A voice came out of the smoky air.

It brought him back to the underground museum, to the posters and exhibits.

"Ah, huh, I'm sorry. Were you talking to me?" He looked around but all he could identify was a poster with a black and white image of a woman in the shadows of a narrow, cobblestone street. Written on the bottom of this poster was, *Speak softly, there are spies everywhere.* It was a World War I poster from England, most likely, or America.

Well, what were you thinking about?

He turned all around but saw no one looking at him, talking to him. As the poster came in sight again he thought he saw some movement.

Was it a draft from a door? he wondered. *Was it the smoky, hazy air?*

Come here. Let's have a chat shall we? The voice seemed to come from the woman in the shadows on the cobblestone street.

"What is going on?" he blurted out. He looked around but no one seemed to notice, to hear him or her.

"Are you speaking to me?" he couldn't believe he was saying what he was saying.

Yes, you, I'm whispering to you, handsome. Come here. Let's go for a walk. It's a wonderful, hazy…

"What, but, I don't even know…oh, man, you're a picture, a poster."

Not so fast, Mr. Songwriter! Come here and take a walk with me. We have a few things to talk about.

Before he could say anymore he was standing beside her. In the dim light he noticed her black beret covering the upper part of her face and the collar of a black trench coat covering most of the lower half; red lipstick lips moved in between.

There, now, that wasn't so hard was it?

"No, ahh, no…But how did I get here? Who are you? What do you want with me?"

You looked distressed. I thought I could help you. I heard way too many 'whys'.

"What do you mean you heard too many 'whys'? I was just thinking about…"

That's what I want to talk to you about, what you were thinking.

"What do you mean?"

Well, didn't you ask why, why, why there was this continued development of these weapons, these grotesque weapons?

"Yes, but how did you know that?"

Let's just say that I know and let's talk about your 'whys'.

"What do you want to know?"

Well, what is it that is actually bothering you?

"Are you a spy?" SC suddenly asked.

A smile -- a red-lipped smile answered him. *I'm just interested. Is it a secret? Do you think I'll use it against you or something like that.*

"I don't know and maybe it doesn't matter anyway. It's just that I'm..."

You're what?

"I'm just damned angry, angry and frustrated in so many ways. Even while I talk about my anger, I'm thinking, how can I be angry at abstractions? I mean...here I am -- talking about things, angry at things I've only read about, or seen pictures of, or studied. That's already incongruous, but still, that's what *becoming aware* is all about, isn't it? -- Or getting to know something? I mean most people know something about their family, their backyard, their job, and kind of accept the rest. I can't even accept my anger without questioning it. Sometimes I just want to destroy something so that I can start over and then I can start over..." He caught himself, as she questioned him again.

So, you want a clear-cut right and wrong answer? Right or wrong way to live?

"Come on, I just want to know how I can live with the world as I see it and still do something. What do I do, forget about what's going on around me and do crossword puzzles? Play bridge? In other words -- does doing something, some little thing, even -- *you know* -- to use that old cliche -- *to light one candle in the darkness* -- kind of thing, matter? Damn it!"

Well, does it?

There was silence. For a long while, walking slowly, there was silence. Her collar was still turned up. Her face was still

24

shadowed. Finally, the blood-red of her lips moved to break the soundless sound.

*Let me show you something. Not too far from here is a field, a field of crosses, simple white crosses. Under each cross lie the remains of a man who was sent out in a gray uniform, wearing a steel helmet, holding a rifle with a bayonet attached to it. On this field, in the mud and trenches that once were...*She turned to him. *I'm sure you've seen pictures of these nightmare battlefields. Not even Delacroix could take away their horrors and romanticize them in a painting. Maybe you've read 'All Quiet on the Western Front'? It was just yesterday that thousands of men, young men, like yourself were lying in mud and blood and agonizing on these fields. Dante's lowest circle of hell could not describe their tragic reality. Death was a welcome relief from their agonies of pain, the deafening explosions and wailing horror.*

They walked out of the alleyway, past the houses and walked along the hedgerows until they traversed a small field and walked up a small hill. As they slowly climbed up, they began to see a mist-filled field. From somewhere a soft light illuminated one white cross after another, one white cross after another, one white cross...

Listen, she said. *Listen to a bereaved voice -- calling out...looking for her husband, her loved one...*

Ay, Marieke, Marieke,
The Flanders sun burns the sky
Since you are gone.
Ay, Marieke, Marieke,
In Flanders field the poppies die
Since you are gone.

Ay, Marieke, Marieke,
The bells have rung, the echoes sound
The day is gone.
Ay, Marieke, Marieke,
In Flanders field the echoes sound
The day is gone.

25

The songwriter, Jacques Brel, who wrote those words, left afterthoughts in the air, if we listen, we can hear, if we listen…if we listen…they can touch our hearts…

"How do you know all this?" he asked her. His voice was drifting through the mist.

I have spent my time spying in these very hearts. Listen again…beyond this field…in a valley not too far away…do you hear the faint sound of hammering?

The Man in the Black, Frock Coat

He strained his ears. Yes, he could hear the faint tapping of hammers and voices speaking in several languages, and laughter. *Laughter? Don't they know what's happened here?* He was incredulous. In his wounded mind he strained to hear more.

"What are they doing?" he asked her.

Come with me…

In a moment they were looking up toward a hilltop. Rising up from a cement foundation, which seemed to have grown out of the very rocks of the Alps, were the curves of a wooden building being covered by two cupolas on which many young men were hammering, nailing on wooden shingles to cover what looked like two breasts upon the land. The voices were louder now. The same languages that lay entombed in Flanders field were being used to build a sanctuary between the sky and the earth, a structure, a building, a temple…

Look around you, she said, as they walked into the midst of the activity within the temple itself.

Between the two domes, underneath the cupolas, straddling their spheres, stood an austere, finely honed man in a black, frock coat, *Guten Morgen,* Herr Steiner said, to a worker nearby.

Morgen, a man sweeping up wood chips answered back.

Geht's gut?

Ja. Pointing to a column, the sweeper held his broom and said to him, *Wir sind fertig.*

"What did he say?"

26

He said: *They have finished.*

Another man came by and with obvious satisfaction answered also, *oui*.

All three rested their eyes on one curved, carved column after another. Each column representing a planet and the influences they exert on the earth. As if circling the sun, these columns circled the smaller of the two rotundas.

Come. The man in the black, frock coat suddenly spoke and gestured for us to follow him.

My guide turned and practically whispered to me: *This is one of my contacts. You've come at the right time. You're really privileged today. He's taking the time to get us up to date on his work.*

We walked through the hammering and sawing of the larger hall, around a flurry of people trying to keep up with his long strides. A young man with wood chips in his hair and a birthmark on his neck glanced over, smiled and met the penetrating eyes of this *contact* in the black, frock coat. With a wooden mallet and a chisel in his hands, the youth asked nervously, "Do you have a minute?"

The man stopped and with a conscious engagement answered back, *More than a minute! Fredrick. I always have time for a question, especially a question that comes from the heart.*

Fredrick smiled and, almost in embarrassment added, "I'm not sure if my question is that important, but several of us have wondered what the first performance or ritual or..." He stammered, not sure which word seemed right.

The man in the black, frock coat put his arm around him. *My dear Fredrick -- You are right in wondering -- your hesitancy in finding the right word...the right description of our work is especially telling. We, Fredrick, are working on the manifestation of a new world. It is not always easy to know what to call it -- Between these two domes, that you,* all of you," he gestured to those standing around him, "*are helping to build is the meeting place of our human consciousness at this time in our history: the beginning of our modern era, the fifth post-Atlantean cultural epoch in our long, long history. In that space we will, all of us, will bring forth many manifestations. Among them will be an art of movement, through music and words, veiled in colors. The impulse for this movement is here. It will take form from the movements around us, the sounds of words, the sounds of music, wandering through us, working through us…*

As his words flowed into me, I looked around. A crowd of workers had gathered to hear his words, to hear him speak.

Come, he said. We walked toward the front of the larger hall, towards the doors. He took both his arms and hands and pushed on the large doors, opening them to the late afternoon light, to the expansive rounded hills and the fertile valley in front of us. We saw a row of apple trees blossoming in pinks and whites, softening the verdant greens of the valley. *You see the renewal of our land, our garden, even as the sounds of destruction can still be heard from miles away.*

We gazed in wonder at the beauty of this spring day and slowly walked after him, with a sizable crowd, which by this time had gathered around him. There was a sense of anticipation in the very air we were breathing. Hushed voices mixed with the crunching of stones on the path. We came to his atelier in the carpenter's house. The door was opened, as many that could, walked in after him to a nook where a large wooden statue was being worked on. Out of the wood, emerging from the grain and knots and heart of an old ash or oak tree -- I couldn't tell which -- out of an old gnarled tree, a human figure was emerging: with one hand stretching to the sky and the other pointing to the earth.

This, he said, *is a representation of our new consciousness, our new human consciousness, reaching for the cosmic realms and pointing to the very earth we call home…Living within the forces of spiritual striving and material grounding -- between Luciferic and Ahrimanic forces. We, all of us, are helping to bring this new consciousness into the world. We are on the threshold of a threefold path; where our thinking and willing is tempered by our feeling, our heart forces. This is a path taught by the great teachers throughout our human existence. Remember, who you have the potential to be; from the universal spirit, which permeates our universe to the material substance of our bodies, our living, life bodies as they have evolved on the earth. We are now in the midst of another war, this one, more terrible than any we have known, with an increased human ability to*

28

destroy faster...Our intellect and our will, have again, outrun our feelings -- our heart forces. Whatever we do here, in these surroundings, with people like you, we will begin, again. We will balance our great intellectual abilities with our will to act. We will permeate this union, from the very core, with our feelings, our heart, our compassion, our love. Now, colleagues, we have work to do. The bombs will soon be quiet. Then, the sound of our voices will waft over the dying fields to sow the seeds of renewal...of love...

We walked slowly away as the others dispersed to go back to their endeavors. I took one last look at the wooden, sculpted incarnation of this *new consciousness*. Its image seared into me as his words resonated in the air.

As if she was reading my mind, the red lips opened and spoke quietly, *Remember this moment when you are in the throes of your 'whys'. Do not write it down -- Let it live in your soul. Let it live while you live. -- These are the secrets that can take you out of despair.*

With these words I opened my eyes only to see the vague mist-filled shadows of a poster not too far from me. A figure in a black beret and a high collared trench coat looked back at me, holding one finger over her blood red lips.

The sound of throaty blues spread out around the room...

Every Saturday night
I'm alone most every Saturday night
You don't come home
You don't come by
You don't care if I live or die

Every Saturday night...

He got up and left the smoke-filled cavern, wound his way past the tables and the habitues, out through the telephone booth, and into the night air, the North Sea air, along the canal streets, back to his room, back to his songs, filled with purpose...

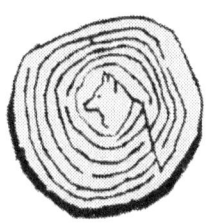

Path Four

The Boys of Terra Grandeur

"He wanted to be a part of it -- to ride into the songs of minstrels..." She repeated and settled into a grass-grown nook made from the leftover stones of the onceuponatime castle of Terra Grandeur. Her eyes wandered over the remaining standing walls that might have held a child's dream..."And you, my young King, it was you, who let him into the bakery, who let him dream...Even if the morning did come too soon...

Whoa oo, wha, whut, what is going on! Nicholas could hardly contain himself.

He vaguely heard snickering, *Douse him again. Douse the sleeping beauty.*

Ice cold water was trickling down his face. He grabbed a ladle, pulled, grabbed an arm, with laughter, around him he finally opened his eyes enough to see several boys he had worked with the day before -- What a way to wake up. His anger gave way to surprise, to a slight smile, to a feeling of camaraderie. He held an arm, went for the ladle and started laughing also. They tussled, and he, along with several of them, fell off the cot onto the stone floor.

"Ooh, that's hard," one of the boys said.

"And cold in the morning," Nicholas added.

"What's your name?" he was asked.

"Nicholas. And yours?"

31

"They call me Haystack," said one whose hair had a resemblance to the harvested mounds in the fields.

"Mine is Richard."

"I'm known as Roland," said a tall boy with a ringing voice.

"What's all the noise about?" roared a centerion voice. The morning baker had entered the room. Like a door, his huge body covered the entrance and gave them all cause to quiet down and get ready for their chores. He was generally in a good mood but he was also sharp and quick with discipline if any one of them did not fall into line. Chores were to be done. They all knew they were privileged to be working in the bakery of the King's household.

There were soon put to work lighting the fires in the ovens, getting the pans out and carrying in the ingredients for the day's baking. By the time they sat down for hot oatmeal, milk and bread, Nicholas was ready go back to sleep. The oatmeal tasted good, especially with sugar and milk on it, and the bread, bread they had baked the day before, had butter and marmalade with it.

"Well, Nicholas," Haystack said, through his sounds of chewing and gulping, "What do you think of our *jolly kingdom*? It's a lot of work, heh?"

"Yeah" is all Nicholas could say, while his head nodded.

"Hey, don't you think we should really initiate Nicholas into the secrets of Terra Grandeur?" Roland said and asked the boy across from him, "What do you think, Whirling?"

A long-haired, deep-eyed boy looked up at Nicholas. Their eyes met. For a moment, something swept through them, then it was gone.

Whirling nodded and said, "After supper."

Nicholas could only wonder what he meant, what they meant, by *real initiation*? Even after they went back to the baking room his mind was on the days end, after supper, he kept thinking -- *after supper...*

Jewels

Today was cake day and the bellowing Baker was in his element. "Come around boys" he sang, and gathered his crew of youthful energy around the baking table. "Today we are executing a grand spectacle of garish delight," he said with a wink and a sly smile. "The King has requested ten cakes of enormous proportions each imbedded with a jewel, that, by the way, only I am entrusted with."

With this he took out a royal blue satin bag that he opened and slowly emptied. It's contents fell on the table. Red, blue and white stones fell out on the marble table with clicks and clunks - - *Ahhs*, filled the room. "Now, who knows what this is?" He picked up a deep red gem.

"A ruby" came from several voices.

"Yes. And this?" No one answered.

"This? This is the most rare," he answered. "It is an amethyst with a star inside." He let them all see the tiny glittering star inside the gem. *Ohhs and ahhs...*followed their eyes. "The rest are also precious," he continued. "The King wants us to put one in each cake -- wrapped up, of course. The cakes will be decorated to emulate the symbols of the honored guests coming to the Festival of Songs. Now, there are ten jewels, so we will bake ten cakes. When the barons and the princes and the various knights and all the rest of the exalted," he winked before he went on, "guests arrive, including the Cardinal, of course, they would eventually be served a slice of the cake. Believe me, this will be the most carefully enjoyed cake we have ever baked."

The boys' eyes widened and filled with the reflections of a thousand facets. Nicholas finally turned his gaze from them and looked at Whirling. Whirling's eyes were fixed on the jewels. Suddenly, the morning sun streamed through a high window, onto the table strewn with the 10 beautifully cut gems. Born in the hot cauldrons that formed them, they were now imbued with this cosmic light, reflecting, echoing, redirecting the secrets of the very earth they had sprung from. Whirling's face was bathed in the light that transformed these jewels. Whirling looked at Nicholas. Their eyes met again. For a moment the connection of their seeing went deeper. It seemed to Nicholas that Whirling was much older than he looked, his gaze deeper. Whirling, too, wondered who this boy was. He could feel a pain in Nicholas' eyes -- maybe from his life, maybe more. Just as suddenly, the stream of light changed and moved away from them. The booming voice of the giant baker brought them all back to the hard marble table and the work ahead of them.

"What are we waiting for?" His voice bounced off the stone walls. "We have cakes to bake and jewels to..." He gathered up the jewels, put them into the satin pouch and started the process of mixing the ingredients. Vats were brought to the table as well as flour, yeast and nuts. Orders were given and the boys scattered like mice to all the corners of the room, rounding up the ingredients.

Whirling took Nicholas with him. He showed him where the spices were kept, some from far-off lands: vanilla beans and cloves. "Here. Smell these." He told Nicholas.

Ahhh, that is heaven, Nicholas responded with a huge intake of aroma.

They all came together in the circle of the singing baker. They measured and mixed and kneaded and when all was ready the satin bag was opened again, the jewels were poured out like an iridescent waterfall of color. He began to wrap each one in parchment, each one in a separate parchment container big enough to bite on. He did not want anyone swallowing these precious jewels. They wrapped seven, eight, nine of them. Where was the tenth? There was one missing. He unwrapped them. They looked at them all.

The star amethyst is missing! shouted Roland. A hush fell over them.

The scowling baker's face grew long. "We must find it," he said, slowly.

They all looked around themselves, over, under, inside, wherever a small precious gem might be hiding. Nothing. The star amethyst was not to be found. What could he tell the King? He was entrusted with these wondrous gems. Now they would come to haunt him. He was silent for a while. Slowly he began to re-wrap the rest of the jewels. "Let us put them in the cakes," he said, "There will be no more talk of jewels."

With a hesitancy they continued and, by day's end, ten beautiful nut-filled, spiced cakes were cooling on the stone counters. Their aromas had brought many noses to the door of the bakery.

"Ahh, ohh...What has our aromanic baker concocted this time?" They seemed to ask.

But for all the attention it was surprisingly still in the bakery. For once, it was from other parts of the kitchen that the excitement of preparation resounded around the stone walls. Tomorrow was the feast. Tomorrow, the knights would come into the Great Hall and the princes and the princesses would be announced. It would be the Festival of Songs, the feast of the birds, the telling of tales, the singing of ballads. Every village and every castle would send a singer of ballads, for it was the ballads, the telling of heroic journeys and tragic stories that the court was waiting for.

Uhralt

The air was filled with excitement. Everywhere the boys walked -- from the courtyard out to the Grand Gate to the jousting meadow -- there was an air of anticipation. Colored tents were set up, banners were blowing in the wind.

Was there a green banner flying somewhere in this crowd of colors? Nicholas wondered. *Was his savior coming to the feast? Was he a singer?* He couldn't even remember his name. All he remembered was the forest-green plume and his face -- *Is that why he was here? Did he come for the feast?*

"Come on, Nicholas," Whirling shouted. "Roland and Haystack and I are going to see Uhralt. Maybe he can help us find the jewel. We've got to help the *gemless* baker."

35

Will I see him again? Nicholas wondered as he turned to catch up with them.

They headed back up the hill, jumping over stumps, climbing over outcrops of rocks, winding along the old paths, back to the first gate of the castle defenses.

"Who is this *Uhralt*?" Nicholas asked.

"He's the oldest man in the land. I think he uses magic potions to stay alive."

"Wait till you see his room. He's got a wobble solver. He's got bottles all over -- some of them filled with animals."

"A skeleton hanging in the corner..."

"Orbs turning around a star..."

"Glass that can make fire."

"A round crystal ball that he looks into."

"What you do mean?" Nicholas asked with a maze ment.

"It's a crystal ball," Whirling responded. "He looks into it and he can see the future."

"He can see the future!" they all repeated.

"Can he find the jewel?"

"Maybe he can tell us what happened to it."

Whirling led the way. It was not a well-kept path. The castle had been built over the ruins of an old church. Some of the old church walls were still standing. At least, they thought they were the walls of an old church. Some walls looked like they were carved right from the limestone of the tor. The path, these ancient structures created, had become a labyrinth of corners and tunnels.

"How do you know which way to go?" Nicholas asked.

"You have to observe the signs," Whirling answered.

"What signs?"

"The signs along the way..."

Nicholas looked at the walls, at the floor. He couldn't see any signs.

"You have to see things differently. Look at that stone wall. See the lines carved into it. He took his finger and followed the grooves until a fish-like symbol appeared. Now look about ten feet *farther* along the wall, another vaguely similar outline."

36

"But what about the corners? Here? This corner? Do we go right or left?"

Whirling pointed to the floor, to stones covered with dust and dirt. He took his hand and wiped away some of the dirt. This time a circle with a wolf-like image revealed itself. The wolf's head looked like it was pointing to the left.

"Now do you see the signs?" Whirling asked Nicholas. Nicholas' eyes widened, he remembered the coin in his pouch, he wanted to say something but held his tongue. Instead, he was determined to look differently.

"You see the old man is teaching me," Whirling added.

They finally came to an old wooden door. Whirling took hold of the clacker. *Bang*, BANG! It resounded and echoed down the corridor. They felt goose bumps on their skin.

"I think I want to go back," Haystack whispered.

"Come on," Roland answered him. "You'll never find your way out again. We'll have to come looking for you."

Whirling struck the clacker again. Again the steel on steel echoed around them. A lock sounded. The door slowly opened to a dark room. An old long-bearded man squinted out at them.

Who is it? he rasped.

"It's Whirling and these are friends of mine. We want to see you. We have a special request."

"We need to find a jewel," Roland said.

"Can you help us?"

"We have to save…"

Slowdown, youngsters, came the rasping voice. What's this about a jewel?

"We were baking and…"

"The baker brought out a satin bag…"

"We were going to put a jewel…"

They all talked a once.

Wait, slow down youngsters. Let's have one of you…How about you, Whirling.

Whirling told him what happened. "So you can see we've got to help the poor baker. He's in trouble."

At this, Uhralt's face turned into a smile. *That is the first requirement in the search for knowledge. If it is your concern to help someone, the elementals are at your service.*

"Elementals?" several questioned, "What do you mean? What are the elementals?"

They are the forces of nature that flow like the streams, like the rivers. When you reach out to them, in the right way, you can use them. They will help you become stronger in your search and your quest.

At this, he beckoned them in. When their eyes started to adjust to the dim light one strange image after another came into focus. Haystack's eyes widened, a hideous fatty face, enclosed in a jar, stared at him.

Eye eee, he gasped.

Several of them reeled about. In a corner they saw the dangling bones of some human remains with its skull cracked open. In another corner was the curling smoke from a bubbling cauldron, letting a putrid smell permeate the room. In the middle of the room was a red glow. Over the red glow, Nicholas' eyes took in the outline of a perfect sphere.

"Is that the crystal?" he asked.

They all turned to the eerie, red glow, with a crystal ball, seemingly hovering, within it.

Yes, lads, that is the teller of the future. The old wizened, bearded man rasped to them all.

They gathered around. He sat down and intoned a low chanting sound. The red glow increased, throwing a red aura on the inhabitants of the room. Shadows emphasized their character. In this light, even their youthful faces showed their age-old souls.

"What do you see?" asked Haystack, breaking the silence.

Hush! a stern look came with the raspy reply.

They all looked into the crystal. Slowly, slowly, gray walls of stone appeared. A beam of light flashed from the gray mass. A star shape formed.

Hey and ahh, they gasped, *the star amethyst.*

The gray masses changed, breaking down, falling, building up again, falling, breaking apart again until...fallen, tumbled down stones were left with broken walls. The star beam flickered. A hand came into view. A hand going down, reaching down, to pick up the star jewel they had all seen. A young man held the gem. He looked like Nicholas.

"Nicholas, is that you? asked Whirling.

Nicholas didn't know what to say.

"I'm here," he barely spoke.

There was a young woman with him. They had strange clothes on. He had picked up the beaming jewel and held it up to the light. Through the broken walls they all looked upon the green hills vaguely familiar to them. But here, not a tent was pitched, not a pig was being roasted, not a banner was unfurled.

That is the future the old man rasped.

Not a sound was heard from the visitors to this distant world.

"What about our future?" Haystack finally asked.

The crystal ball clouded up. The green hills faded.

Concentrate, Uhralt told them.

Whirling gazed into the mist. Slowly vague forms could be seen. A bearded man much like Uhralt came into view, only this time his robe of stars was tailored in a three-piece suit and the sheen of his shined leather shoes was reflected in the mirrored walls and the ceiling of a grand foyer, a hundred suits of stars moved when he moved his arm, beckoning them to follow him. After they had snaked their way through a tunnel hallway they came to a room in which they could see a large oak desk, behind the desk sat a waxen figure in royal dress -- Next to him stood a knight and a friar. The faces looked familiar to the faces looking in. A jester with wild hair and a plaid dress bounced into view, *back and forth*, as if on a spring, *back and forth...*

They smiled and began to laugh at their future friend.

"And who is that bearded man" another voice wondered out loud.

Their eyes focused on the man, now reflected in the mirrors, surrounding the occupants of the room, wearing the sun and the moon and the stars?

"Could that be? Was that Whirling?" They asked quietly.

The crystal ball clouded again. This time the glow waned until all images faded from their eyes. The room they were in came back to them.

You've seen enough for one night Uhralt spoke.Slowly they left his presence and walked out of this curious world, back to the labyrinth of halls and tunnels, back to the familiar places, back to their beds and to enchanted sleep.

Nicholas lay on his wooden bed still wondering about the things he had seen, his head full of the red mist and the crystal images. "What did they mean?" he wondered...Until he drifted away, until he saw himself looking through the same opening of ruined walls...

Nicholas, Nicholas, someone called.

It was Twangly, the reborn King of Terra Grandeur.

Look what I've found.

He showed him a tiny jewel.

Look into it. See the star in it. I found it in a crack close to where you're standing. I'll bet it's been there for a long time.

"No, it was just yesterday, just yesterday..." Nicholas answered out loud -- *I think it was...*

The Festival of Songs

Nicholas woke up, jostled and rolled his eyes. Whirling gave him another push. "Come on, sleepy head. It's the day of songs. We've got to get ready. The big-bellied baker will be here anytime."

A feeling of excitement began to permeate the room. Other boys were waking and the sounds of feet on stone stairs, yawns and rushing about all combined to create a stir in the air. Nicholas got up and joined his new friends.

"I had a strange dream," he said to Whirling.

"What was it?"

"I dreamed I was looking out the window of a broken down castle, much like the one in the crystal. Someone called to me, called me by my name and said something about finding a jewel. I woke up then. It seemed so real. You think it had to do with the lost jewel?"

"Dreams are our connection to the cosmos. That's what Uhralt has told me. *They are like a crystal ball*, he said, *and every one of us can gaze into it. The past and the future are all in there. It's just being able to tell their meaning.* Uhralt can. He's teaching me, but he asks more questions than he gives me answers."

"I wonder what he would say to my dream?" Nicholas questioned and was interrupted by a booming voice.

"All right, fellow bakers -- if you get your work done and if you're not seen, you can probably go and watch the festivities."

He had not mentioned cakes since the loss of the jewel and he hoped it would somehow be overlooked, but an anxious feeling still tugged hard at his gut and hung over the cavernous room.

The King is young and sometimes lets others influence him the philosophical baker pondered, *particularly when the Friar puts a fly in his ear.* He had seen it happen before. Not too long ago the King's ire was raised when one of his young bakery apprentices was accused of stealing a silver candlestick from the sanctuary. Of course it was the Friar who accused him and even though the youth claimed he was innocent, the King gave him over to the Friar who proceeded to make an example out of him. When he finally came back to the bakery he had red welts across his back. He would not talk to me of his time with the Friar but it was rumored that some strange things -- even unspeakable things -- had happened to him. He became reclusive and one morning he was gone. One of the boys said he had seen him in the great church a day's journey from the castle.

But this was not a day to think of unspeakable things, it was to be a day of celebration, of *speakable* things. Stories and tales of heroes were to be heard, adventures were to be recalled and unknown lands were to be imagined through their song. Even the bakery would present its finest work at the end of the feast.

This was to be their contribution to the Festival of Songs -- a sweet touch of icing and beauty. Stories told through the palate and gullet, inward not outward from the throat. The sweetest nightingale was to be found in their concoctions of pastries and cakes. *And what of the cakes?* The boys would carry them in with the intrepid Baker leading the way, followed by Whirling, Haystack, Richard, Roland and finally Nicholas, the newest apprentice.

But apprehension and several bad dreams accompanied the baleful Baker as their time came. The feast had progressed into the afternoon. In grand style the King had requested a song after every course. A knight, from the white, snow- filled forests of the North, was reciting a song from the great saga of the *Kalevala*. They heard his sonorous voice...

They want to drink from Louhi's fountain
Bridesmaid of the forest spirit
Turner of the milling stone
And drain the blood from glowing features
Dry the rivers with their damning
Sing the Goddess into serving
Hungry weapons of the smithy
Her golden tresses torn to pieces
Like the fragments of our knowing
From a former Age of Wisdom.
Louhi gazes deep.

The revelers listened in anticipation, almost in reverence, to the last lines of the defiant tale of Louhi...

And she knows: she will not do it
Won't surrender precious Star Mill
Will not lay down without fight
Won't hand over Juice of Heaven
To those who drink not with their hearts.
Louhi gazes deep.

When his voice was still, stems were raised, flagons were emptied and a great shout went out from all, from all those, who had become a part of this saga.

In the midst of this clinking and boisterous upheaval, in the midst of this most colorful crowd, the King slowly stood and, like a receding wave, a hush fell over the Great Hall...

"We have partaken of our field and game and our hunters' and farmers' pride has been set before us...Grand stories have been sung by the Great Finn from the Land of the Midnight Sun, by Wycliff of the Isle of Weight and McHeath of the Eastern Moors. We've even listened to the ribald songs of Tony Belch from the Village of Rye." He smiled and flagons were raised again. Ale and mead flowed amidst the laughter. The King let it flow, until it all subsided again, and he was able to proceed with his announcement, "Now, it is time for our bountiful baker's entrance with his sweet breads and pastries and cakes baked in our ovens and hearths. This sweetness will sing in your mouths. Today, they will be especially sweet, for in each cake is a rare gem. This is the finest work the earth and our artist's can fashion. Chew gently, lest you swallow a precious gem. Those who bite gently and find one will have a rare reminder of this grand day; this celebration; this Feast of Songs."

The hush was perceptible as we walked into the room carrying our treasures. I followed Roland and put my anise-crusted, plume-shaped cake on the table next to his table. Carefully, I set it in the middle, not noticing anything or anyone until it was set down. Finally I could breathe again and looked up, up into the very face of the forest-green, plumed Knight. There, across the table, a smile gathered on his face and his hand gestured for me to come around to him.

"Well, my wayward apprentice, it looks like you have settled in, even learned the rudiments of your craft. Is this some of your work?"

"I kneaded the dough," Nicholas said with a proud grin.

Did you hear that, he kneaded the dough, a bearded, boisterous reveler added to the conversation, *he kneaded the dough, well, we all need to be needed,* he continued, setting off a round of laughter.

Nicholas was a little uncomfortable with all the attention but, with the arm of the Knight around him, felt protected, letting the raucous laughter run off of him.

Are you going to tell us a tale today?" Nicholas asked his protector.

"Yes, I'm going to recite the story of my forefathers across the north sea, from the regions of *Silesia*. It is a tale sung to me by my grandfather when I was just a child."

"When, when?" Nicholas asked in anticipation.

"When we have eaten of your sweet concoctions, my young apprentice"

At this Nicholas realized he had stayed too long. The hall was quiet. The baker was irritatingly gesturing from the side hall.

"I have to go," he quickly said and ran off to join the others, peering out of the crannies and corners.

As he went back, he realized Whirling had brought in his second cake and decided it was best to stay out of the baker's sight.

On each table the cakes were cut and split up until each and everyone at the table had a piece. With admiring anticipation they began to bite gently and chew gently, tasting, feeling every crumb. Never was a cake so good, so fulfilling, so potentially enriching.

What, what's this! A cry came from somewhere in the room, *A small package, a wrapped package.* A lean and highbrowed man opened it to find the blood red ruby. *It is incredible!* he shrieked. *It is the worth of all my opponents' blood.*

From another table came a resounding cry of painful joy, *I have just bitten into something. My tooth has chipped away. It is a hard, hard rock that is wrapped up in my mouth. What a gift!* He opened it to find a faceted crystal reflecting all the torches around him.

One by one a rousing, startled cry of delight resounded about the huge hall -- the Great Hall, where stately ceremonies and grave consequences were usually played out. But this, this was the Festival of Songs and in the midst of its' revelry came the stuff of more songs. What was to become of the grand jewels passed out in such a strange manner? What stories would ensue and pursue them. Eventually the King rose and the hall hushed with another abating wave. "We have heard from nine of our ten banquet tables. Is there not another fortunate fine-plumed finder of a rare gem?"

The room stayed silent, while slow chewing could be heard. Slow chewing, slower, slower until all the cakes were consumed. A few burps could be heard but no cry of surprise, elation, jeweled success.

The King rose again. "Do I understand that no one has found the last rare gem -- at least not yet? -- I think there will be some searching in unpleasant places tomorrow," he half chuckled. "But it is also possible that there was not a tenth gem to be found? Maybe it was consumed before it was baked."

He took a quick glance over to the scarce baker or where he thought the baker was standing, but it was Nicholas his eyes fell on. It was Nicholas, who caught the glimpse of his eyes; Nicholas, who felt the penetrating doubts of the King.

It was not me! He wanted to scream. *I had nothing to do with the disappearance of the star amethyst. Why do you look at me like that?*

It was a look that had often made him feel guilty, even though he had not been directly involved. Somehow, he felt a sense of guilt whenever a transgression had occurred. If a friend of his had stolen something or lied, he felt one with the guilty. He did not ask why, he just felt it; an inner connection with everyone. He felt joy when others were happy, he felt pain when others were hurt. It was from this interconnection that the King's eyes of doubt and question penetrated him.

He wanted to shout out, *No! It wasn't me. It wasn't me who took the jewel. I was just there when the gems were tossed on the table. I saw them but I would not take one. I would…*

He turned his face, avoided the King's eyes and wanted to crawl into the very stones that surrounded him.

Still the King was not satisfied. He looked for the hidden baker and peered around the room. Not a baker's hat could be seen.

"Well," he finally stated in his most royal voice. "We must have a rare gem in the bowels of a great knight. Is this not the stuff of legends."

At this, he broke into a smile that was slowly noticed from the front table to the successive tables around the room. A slow, slight, mirthful laughter began growing, rolling, becoming louder until it seemed to lift the ceiling higher. Even the jolly one showed his face and he could be heard among the loudest. When did it die down? -- This feast of laughter. It ebbed, finally, when each and every one of them had been sated with this outpouring of laughter, which had, at some point, continued for its own sake, until a heave of relief was felt; a deep breath of relief.

Finally, the King, again, directed the great hall in another direction and stated, "We have amongst us a troubadour of the highest caliber, whose stories have ridden on eagles' wings and whose beginnings have plumbed the deepest well. We have the great green-plumed knight from the far eastern lands, Sir Waldundstein."

At that, the hall seemed to be one gaze, a gaze that came upon a center table, a gaze that seemed to have its own life. The great Knight rose from his chair and Nicholas was swept up in the feelings he had for him.

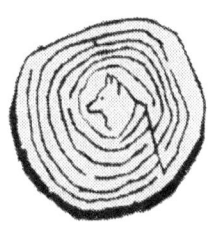

Path Five

A Fabled Story

"Will you honor us with a fabled story from your lands and your history?" the King announced, as he gestured to the Knight's table...

Slowly Sir Waldundstein rose and the anticipation rose with him, for his reputation had swept the paths he had traveled and the room he was now standing in. He seemed to gather strength as he took a deep breath and began to speak and sing the song of his ancestors...

From the barren fields of winter snow
from the land of morning breath
from a land where fruit trees used to grow
where now is found the stench of death.

This is where my story is from
this is where the seeds were sown
this is where the past lies wounded
this is were the blood has flown.

From this place a man named Aimless
wandered west to find a home
where he could settle down and prosper
where his dog could gnaw a bone

47

In due time he came upon a river,
and asked a man with a boat beside him
"Tell me sir, is that land settled?
And what kind of people live within?"

"What kind of place have you set out from?"
he answered with a questioning look
"I come from a worn and barren place
where people have lost hope and laughter,"

"But don't give me questions for my questions
just row me over to the other side
it looks green and lush on yonder bank
take me over or I'll break your pride

Sir, you will find the same in these lands
unless you change your grievous tone
and see the same with a heart that's open
to the child, the fields and a home

Row me over, row me over
I can hear the clarion call
row me over, row me over
Let me cross this watery wall

They were soon upon the water
when the ferry man grew pale and old
"I sense my time in this earthly body
is close to changing, growing cold."

He gave the man his rowing stick
from hand to hand without a fight
he lay down for the final crossing
when heaven's portal was in sight

The man in instinct pushed the boat
as a storm woke up the waves
the craft tossed and heaved and lifted

into the light the lightning made

The man looked on in amazement
as the ferryman rose in the sky
on spirit wings he was so carried
while on earth he was to die

The Knight's voice ascended and descended weaving a tapestry upon the stone walls, interspersed with the flickering light of a thousand candles glowing and cascading from the chandeliers of the Great Hall.

Row me over, row me over
I can hear the clarion call
row me over, row me over
until I've crossed this watery wall

When Aimless woke from this strange crossing
he was lying near a home
bequeathed to him through circumstance
as well the rowing stick and bone

He settled down and was soon married
out of their love a child came
a boy who knew the currents of the water,
the clouds and all that he could name

And in winter of this western land
when frost and snow befell them all
From the river's flow the boy could hear
the plaintive cry of a ferryman's call

Nicholas waited…and listened…letting the 'plaintive cry' resound around and through him, letting himself be swept up in the story…

Row me over, row me over
I can hear the clarion call
row me over, row me over
Let me cross this watery wall

This is where he wanted to be; to be in that story, to hear the ferryman's call; to grow up like the Knight who saved him. He wanted to cross a river...He wanted to overcome the terrible bullies, like the man who bought him and beat him. He wanted to go into the world and save others like the Knight had saved him...But more than that, he also wanted adventure; he wanted to see the world Sir Waldundstein had seen; the world Sir Waldundstein was singing about and unfolding for him...

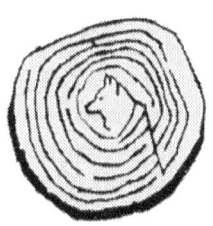

Path Six

The Nose of the Dog

"This is incredible," Twangly said, "I mean, how long do you think this has been here? It really looks like a shift in the stones, in the floor, in this area of the old castle. I wonder where it was. I mean, if this is a jewel, is it possible that this is a jewel from the time when this place was occupied. It was probably the queen's or the king's room. No, this is on a lower floor, a Nobles maybe, or maybe someone had stolen it and they hid it here. I wonder what its history is? In any case, I'm going to take it with me, as a good omen."

"Where are you going, anyway?" *Earth Lady* finally got in the question she'd been wanting to ask.

"I'm heading to Amsterdam. I was, anyway, until these two characters picked me up."

"They do seem a bit eccentric, at least in their driving, and coming from me, that's a lot. I think they're quaint."

"They seemed to be on holiday or something, just out for a jolly ride."

"Maybe, we can get them to drive us over to the constellations."

"What do you mean? -- The *constellations*?"

"It is an area of the west country that conforms to some of the stars that we can see in the northern hemisphere. An actual topographic land area that seems to resemble the star patterns

51

of various constellations, some say, even the signs of the Zodiac. For example, I have a friend who lives in a cottage that is located on the *nose of the dog*, the constellation of the big dog. The connections of these topographic landmarks to the stars was made by someone who, apparently, was looking for ley lines."

Ley lines? He questioned.

"Yeah, many of the old paths, when they became worn and walked-on paths, were along energy lines, on *ley lines* that underlie the country. They continue onto the continent and around the world. A lot of the standing-stone centers were built along the lines and churches were built over them or along them. I've traveled on some of these, camped along them. They're also called *bridal paths*."

"You know I've gone to school here and I've never heard about these things."

"Surely, you've been to *Stonehenge?*"

"Well, we drove to it -- as close as we could. My father never let me do too much traveling or sightseeing. I was either at school or at home."

"It's about time you walked the paths, slept by the stones. Come...with me."

Twangly was not quite sure what to say. Here was his chance to take on something new...his thoughts were reeling...

Hey, you two royal lovers, came a strident voice from the bottom of the hill. *Are you coming with us? We've just begun, you know, and we have a terribly long way to go,* which echoed over the surrounding hills...*to go...to go...*

Twangly looked at her. She touched his cheek with her hand. It was electric. It was like sparks flying. He didn't want to move...

Well, lad and lassie, we're waiting for you...for you...for you...

Earth Lady took Twangly's hand and they started running down the path, "We're coming."

Running and tripping and laughing, falling, running again, "We're coming, we're coming"

I say…You're quite the wild ramblers. Now, what do you say, shall we continue on our journey to the coast?

"Now, dear, perhaps they don't want to continue with us?" came a comment from the driver's reasoning counterpart.

"What! I say! They don't want to come with us?"

"Well, actually," Twangly interjected, "we were just talking and this beautiful, *crazy* woman here has enticed me into seeing some of the country…following a *ley line*?…visiting the *nose of the dog.*"

"I say! Following a ley line, did you hear that dear?"

"Yes, children, we've been following ley lines for years."

Actually, I rather consider myself an expert on the paths and some of the stone circles that pop up on them, but the nose of the dog, that's a new one.

Earth Lady told him about her friend who lives in the land of the constellations. "He has a cottage on the *nose of the dog.*"

The nose of the dog? By Jove, I know about Canis Major, the hunting dog of Orion, but that's a constellation in the heavens. I didn't know there was a constellation on the land. What do you mean? the driver asked quixotically, and yet, there was a look in his eye, as he winked to his companion, that he knew more than his a maze ment showed.

"It's one of the secrets of the land around here, probably not known to a lot of people, different topographic spots that seem to correspond to the patterns of stars that make up several of the constellations. Some say you could find the Zodiac, if you knew where to look."

"The Chinese also have a year of the dog." His companion reminded him. "You, dear, were born in the year of the monkey."

Twangly smiled slightly and thought to himself, *That could explain this wild character.*

"Well, I was born in the year of the dog," *Earth Lady* answered. "Maybe that's why I've had such an attraction to Aiden and his cottage." And with a touch of insight, added, "The nose is just above the star *Sirius*, one of the brightest stars in the sky."

I say! What are we waiting for, head us in the right direction. We must pay your friend a visit.

They piled in the back seat and the front seat -- this time with an air of anticipation.

"Take the first road west -- we're heading for the *nose of the dog*," the driver's companion directed.

He closed his door. *Everyone in?*

Yes. *SLAM!* Yes.

Splendid.

He started the engine, gunned it for effect, put it in gear and let dirt fly ten feet behind them.

"Now dear, we have all afternoon. You needn't race to this protuberance."

But he was not to be dissuaded. *Hang on,* he shouted, *I know these roads well, ha, ha, hee, hee, We're on our way to the windward sea, Ho, ho, he, he.*

Earth Lady and Twangly settled back and let him fly. They made themselves cozy in the back seat. This time they were not as apprehensive as on their initial encounter.

"He must know what he's doing," Twangly whispered to her. "After all he's lived this long."

"Yeah, but will we?"

Twangly smiled, maybe we should get to know each other before it happens?"

"What am I going to call you?" She asked.

Twangly thought for a second, *It's now or never. I have to make a break.* "I'm Jules."

"Sounds French."

"Ahh...yes, my mother has a fondness for the Gaelic."

"The garlic!"

He smiled, "the Gaelic, the French. And you...what is your name?"

"I told you, I've been following the *ley lines*, you can call me whatever you want."

"Well, I could call you *Leyline*. Yea! How about *Sophie Leyline*?"

She laughed and a volcano erupted...

"Don't go overboard! *Ley ley ley lani*...how about *Leylani?*"

"Sounds nice"

"I like it. *Jules and Leylani*

They had lost track of the maniacal driver and his companion.

"*Jules and Leylani!* Hey! What do you think of us?" *Earth Lady* suddenly blurted out. "*Jul es and Leylani* The woman turned around and repeated, "*Jules and Leylani* What beautiful names, we have exotic travelers in the back seat, my dear."

The driver, however, was careening down the narrow road, turning left and right whenever the direction was given and did not give much thought to exotic names. The land began to open up and become flatter, in some places, pancake flat, as if rolled out on a baker's table, as if it would wash right into the sea, until, in some places, there was hardly any distinguishing distinction between the long, low land and the ever-present sea except for a few outcroppings of rocks and small hills, which made them all the more noticeable. They opened their windows and let the air fill them.

I say, this is invigorating, the driver said as he took in a deep breath, and exhaled with a long *ahhhhhhhh,* which turned into a song,

I'm as happy as a clam, I am, I am. And I don't give a damn, you see, you see,

He stopped the car.

I'll sink into the sand, the sand...

They waited for him to finish.

And you'll be rid of me, ho, ho, hee hee.

They opened the doors. Jules and Leylani jumped out and ran to the sea like kids on a holiday.

"My dear, shall we bring the umbrella?" his companion said. "We must be careful of radiation."

It was one of those evenings when the slightest opening in the overcast sky was like the prologue of a new saga, a new play on the stage of the old world. Streaming shafts of light spotlighted the quartet of wanderers and brought them into a Turner landscape. A blend of subtle changes in clouds and mist and gentle shifts of grays hinted at the possibility of color carousing through and following them. From this blended landscape, from this space between the sea and sky, these invigorated travelers took time, *yes*, the very idea of time to task. As if to ask, *What makes you think we have to move as fast as you want us to? We'll decide our tempo on this panoramic stage...*

And when the light settled on this isolated strand, a vision of a cowled figure came into view, playing chess with a different kind of knight, a cynical crusader who had just returned from an unholy quest. This vision, slowly, manifested itself to the four timeless wanderers. It was a moving picture etched into the visual world by the great twentieth-century film maker, Ingmar Bergman. They surrounded the two world-weary characters and watched the game.

I say! Don't let him take your queen. Watch the trap. The driver couldn't help kibitzing the game as he was trying to aid the crusader in his death match.

The grim reaper slowly turned his cowled head. Nothing but the void could be seen. Slowly, a voice from the eternal crypt graveled out, *Your turn will also come...*

Egad! He screamed.

"Hey, our eccentric has found something,"

"What is it? Jules inquired.

The driver's face was white next to the rocks and debris scattered about.

I, I, I've just talked to the grim reaper, I don't play chess well, my death is imminent, imminent, I say.

"My dear, don't excite yourself. Remember your heart."

Let us go! I must go. I've got to get away from here.

A voice as gravelly as before -- carried in on the sea wind - - resounded over the strand...*You cannot get away...No matter where you go...*

Egad! The driver turned and ran up the beach, falling in the sand, getting up, turning every which way. Jules and Leylani, silhouetted against the evening sun, just watched him run. The third figure, his companion, attempted to catch up.

Path Seven

Tragic Encounter

Jules smiled and shook his head. Leylani found a round rock to sit on. "They'll be back," she said and pulled on Jules' pant leg. He looked at her, sat down, lay down on the sand, plucked a strand of grass, put it in his mouth, took it out again and sat up. He put his hand in his shirt pocket and pulled out the star amethyst, turning it in the evening sun until its staccato streams of light penetrated him…until a thousand candles flickered in front of him, lighting up a great hall. He imagined Nicholas, lost in the words of the saga sung by the minstrel-knight…*What happened to him?* he wondered…As Leylani's voice crept into his reverie and brought back the Knight's refrain…

Row me over, row me over
I can hear the clarion call…
Row me over, row me over
I want to cross that watery wall

Again and again, Nicholas heard the words…letting them fill his hopes and dreams, letting the lilt of the voice, like the drifts of a winter's snow, build inside him, until…until he was with him, riding, riding along side him, on a sturdy steed through fields as wide as the sea, flowing with the wind-swept waves of spring-green grasses. The voices had stilled. The sound around him was like bated breath -- waiting. Their ears were cocked to the gentle rhythms of the swells of grass.

All was right in the world, he thought. *All is as it should be.*

He was lost in the epiphany of the moment.

Hark! Waldundstein spoke and stopped abruptly.

Nicholas broke out of his reverie.

Hark! Waldundstein said again, this time with a greater urgency. "*Look*, in the direction of the East."

A plume of smoke was beginning to rise in the distance. They turned their horses and rode towards it.

"Is it a fire?" Nicholas asked him.

The smoke was beginning to darken the horizon, smothering the clarity of his clear grass-grown horizon.

"It is a fire." Nicholas stated this time, while they quickly rode in its direction.

The Knight had been silent. Nicholas, looking over, felt that he was sniffing the air, looking intensely at the gathering storm.

Help! Help us, help us! A struggling voice came out of the smoke-filled air, billowing, wafting over the fields. *Oh, help us, help us,* a voice unlike anything Nicholas had heard came out of the grays of smoke.

They listened and went deeper into the acrid air, now holding tunics over their mouths and noses.

Help us, a quieter, aching voice drifted towards them once again, very close, seemingly underneath them, around them, fleeting…

Waldundstein stopped Windward, held his reins, dismounted, walked towards the voice, parted the grass, there, in abject terror lay a woman, eyes frozen in fear, her voice growing weaker.

He bent down, "Woman…woman…Can you hear me?"

Only a moan came from her lips.

"Woman can you hear me?"

*Mmmm, help us…*came a faint and frightened sound, *There was no where to run, our Lord, his house, we thought, we would be safe in his house, they broke the door, like animals they came, they…"*

58

My master was holding her head, gently holding her head, until those terrified eyes closed and there was silence from her.

Quietly he spoke, "She is now in the sanctuary she sought." He laid her head down on the pillows of grass.

"We must see if we can help," he continued, "but be forewarned, these are not men of honor we are going to encounter. This, you will learn, as you have already seen the results of their brutality. We must take care and consider what and where our strength lies. Make sure your sword is ready and if we die in this search, we will die with honor."

Nicholas felt calmed and also imbued with a sense of purpose. His fears seemed to be overcome with the words and emotions and the strength, his teacher, his master, had brought to him, out of the tragic reality of the woman.

They tethered their horses and walked slowly through the high grass in the fateful, terrible direction the girl had come from. The grass lay bowed where she had fallen and her life blood had deepened the yellow browns of the stalks. The closer they came, the darker the sky became and the nearer the sounds of moaning. Crackling in the near distance, the flames silhouetted a steeple and the stone walls left standing. With smoke searing their lungs they saw the remains of the devastation and looked for human movement amidst the flickering shadows.

"Stay here," the Knight urgently spoke to Nicholas, as he continued towards the smoke and flames.

Nicholas crouched down, looking, watching him go into the smoke. Suddenly a figure loomed out of the grass and lunged towards him. With a gleam and a glint of silver caught in the firefilled air, a figure -- a grotesque figure with eyes bulging, hairy and bearded with the glint of saliva and madness on its teeth -- loomed over him.

Nicholas froze in fear, his mouth unable to utter a sound -- no words came to him. It was all too sudden. The glint of saliva and silver, all he had ever imagined in his worst nightmares was confronting him. In a moment, a split-second moment, he was engulfed, and yet, in this same moment, he brought in this monster, this grotesque apparition. He moved and responded to its very thrust and charge. He let it come into him. He moved with its gleaming, silvery metal talons. He held it in all its repugnant horror, its odor of sulfur springs, its grating, grizzly hair, its bulging eyes. All this he held until they tumbled and turned in the grass with the smoke and glints of fire. Finally, after an eternity, they lapsed into the earth; the very earth took them in and Nicholas lay upon it, spent, his fears, his worst fears transformed into a bed of grass.

He slowly opened his eyes to the fire light. *No! It was not fire light.* It was the morning light, a beam of sunlight. It came to him like a golden figure, a beautiful golden figure within a field of growing light. Now each stalk of grass was beginning to come alive -- their transparency was beginning to fill with the streams of morning light. It was as if each had its own aura of life.

He beheld them and barely asked, "*Why? Why, why? Why am I alive?*...After such a horror filled darkness -- as dark as the darkest cave. How can I, now, be surrounded by...surrounded by this light..."

He could not describe what he had felt, because he felt something else, something soft, fingers soft on his cheeks, the brightness of the moment momentarily shaded by the outline of a face.

Are you, are you, alive? came a faint voice.

Slowly, his eyes found the sound...his cheeks felt the touch of someone, *someone* -- a girl -- kneeling next to him. He slowly realized he had rolled into a ball as if he was ready to be born.

Can you hear me? She asked in a strange language.

He looked at her and his mouth began to show a faint smile.

Can you see me? She asked in the same language.

He looked more intensely and began to speak, "Who are you?" he whispered.

Shh, shh, she said, and put her fingers on his lips.

He slowly uncurled. All the while he looked at the girl. Now he could see a worn and ragged dress...Now he could see her face, her young face covered with the black soot of smoke, her hair singed.

"Who are you?" he whispered again, but she just put her finger on his lips and pointed with her other hand, in the direction of the smoke.

Now he remembered -- But what had happened? Where was he? Where was his master? He was alive. He did not die in the darkness. He had lived through a terrible struggle. Here, now, he was alive with this girl who had wakened him. It seemed like nothing could stop him now. He was given a second chance. He was still alive. He wanted to find his master, the Knight who had gone into the smoldering, moaning ruins.

He took the girl by the hand and this time he gestured with his fingers to move in silence. They half crept and crouched closer to the lingering smoke. They listened. There was just the occasional crackle of a dying ember, no sound of human voices.

They crept closer until they could see the remains of the church. The steeple was still standing in the midst of the darkened rubble and the remaining stone walls. There was an eerie stillness. They stood up and walked slowly, carefully to the front of the church and looked inside. The girl hid her eyes and wanted to run and did run from him. Nicholas looked deeper into the charred remains. Here and there, he could see, still, lifeless people, some blackened by the fire and smoke, some dried in blood, a mother and a child holding on in dying hope and agony, an older woman, mouth open and eyes shrieking in terror. All this Nicholas saw. His nightmare returned, he saw it in their faces, only they were not waking up, they had crossed a threshold, they would never wake-up from the nightmare that had befallen them.

Nicholas felt like, he, too, had crossed a threshold, but he had come back. He could see what happened here, be a part of it, yet he felt free of the suffering. He wanted the girl to see this -- in the same way. But she had turned away…run away. It was too much for her to take in. Nicholas found her sobbing in a grassy bed, her tear's flowing softly into the ground around her. She had wakened him. Now it was his turn to bring her back. He helped her up. He pointed to the ruins of the church and made motions of digging into the ground. She nodded with anxious eyes, waiting…

For a moment they stood there, waiting. Nicholas looked around and listened. There was no sound. They were alone with the dead. He looked around and uttered, "Where was Waldundstein? What had happened to his teacher, his master?"

His eyes widened. He pulled at the girl and uttered with anxiety.

Where is Waldundstein? he uttered in anxiousness. *Two of us came here,* he told the girl -- gesturing with his hands, trying to make her understand -- *Two of us came here…*

"Come," he finally said, his eyes fanning the ground looking for signs. Horse's hoof prints were all-around, bits of clothing, here and there. There, in the direction of the rising sun was a broken lance with a forest-green plume still attached.

He ran to it.

THIS IS WALDUNDSTEINS! he yelled, breaking the stillness. "He was here. He was here…"

He looked further. Only the horizon met his gaze, his intent gaze, looking, looking for another sign. Remembering Whirling's words, his eyes followed the road away from the church over to the leftover village houses, some still smoldering.

All he could say to himself was, *Where had he gone?* What had happened to him? Where was he? He had to find him."

"Come," he said to the girl, but she held back.

She pointed to the church…She started towards it. He let her go and went looking for other signs, hoping for another sign from his master, while at the same time dreading that he would find him…*dead, dead, like the others.*

Aah, eeaa…a wail-like scream came from the church. He ran to it as if possessed.

"Where are you?"

He tumbled over the burned timbers.

Aah, she moaned.

She was bent over a woman.

Mama, he heard her say, *Mama, Mama*

She was kneeling over the woman he had seen lying in stillness with blood drying on her breast. He stood there with the girl, one with her grief. She cried until she was exhausted and fell asleep.

Nicholas looked around. Somewhere there must be a shovel, a spade to begin the burial. No one else was coming to help.

They must be either dead or were taken away, he thought.

He wanted to look for Waldundstein. In his search around the charred remains his eyes caught the glint of a gold-like object. He picked up a charred board, black with the glint of gold in a half circle. He wiped off the soot and smoke. It shone like the sunrise, a face could barely be seen under this halo of gold, one eye had a black hole in it, the other held a star. He cleared it. It looked like colored glass with a star in it -- glowing -- as if to see into him. He was transfixed by the gaze of this eye, this jewel of starlight.

He held it up, this charred piece of wood, he held it against the sky, against the bright noon day sun and still the star sparkled, while all around it was black. Even the golden halo had turned black against the sun but the star shone from within like a beacon on the dark sea. In his desperation for his lost master he gazed at it, looking deeper. It turned a forest-green, the color of Waldundstein's plume. *It must be*, he thought, *I must find him.*

With a new resolve he went to the girl. He woke her from her reverie of sorrow. She looked dazed and worn with tears. He tried to tell her, with gestures, that he had to leave. She seemed to understand but held onto the dress of her mother. Nicholas gestured that he would help bury her. She followed, looking, in all directions, for the garden of the dead. It was next to the church, behind the church, where small monuments broke the ground.

This will become the place of peace for her mother, he thought, *and eventually for all those unfortunate people who had succumbed to the hands and swords and spears and flames of this conflagration.*

"Let us take her into the garden," he spoke to her, as they both awkwardly lifted the body. Slowly, they carried her over the charred wood. The necessity of the task took their thoughts away from the tragedy. Flaxen helped Nicholas dig a shallow grave and helped him lower the body into it. With deliberate movements they filled the space around her with dirt, the soil of the Steppes, soil imbued with the potential of renewed growth. Only after they had a small mound showing above the ground did Flaxen let her tears flow, moistening her mother's last bed.

"I must go" Nicholas said and gestured -- pointing to himself and then towards the direction of the green-plumed knight's broken lance, "I must go."

She grabbed his arm, held on to his tunic and just shook her head, telling him she would go with him.

At first he objected but soon realized he could not dissuade her. They took what they could in clothes and blankets and food and tied it all on their backs. With a finality they turned towards the East, away from the setting sun. Only once did they turn around and in that moment Nicholas thought he saw green shoots springing from the mound of death, green shoots, moistened by Flaxen's tears, breaking forth, growing…

They walked, lightly at first, along the trodden path that had been marked by the broken lance and the green plume. They could see the results of many horse's in the grass and turned over soil. The hoof-prints, in the dry path, were like a continual warning of the danger they might face, as well as signs showing them the way. They walked slowly and in silence, Nicholas leading his horse, Pathfinder, until the sunlight waned and shadows started to take over. He gestured that they should find a place to sleep for the night and went into the grass, put his pack down, unfolded a blanket and made a place for them.

She, too, put down her pack, took out some bread and water and offered it to him. They sat, eating in the quiet of the twilight's unfolding. They finished their meager meal and lay down looking up at a heaven of awakening stars, one after another, glistening and glittering and gladdening their hearts, touching their own souls, transforming them into children of the earth, being warmed by the kneading earth and touched by the pulsing light. She lay her head on his shoulder. He put his arm ever so gently around her. She snuggled next to him, fitting into his warmth. They lay there -- bathed in star light -- until sleep came to them…came to them…like a mantra of the surrounding night…until their souls hovered and mingled in the realms of dreams…

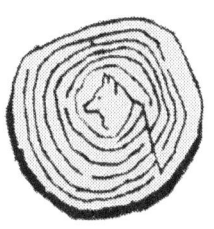

Path Eight

The Ikon Painter

As they wandered on this dream-filled path, a voice came to them and slowed them down. They stopped and waited, opening their ears and their hearts. Out of the past, from beyond their sight, came the voice...

Imagine...imagine a man, in a time gone by, who lived in relative security, yet, his soul churned with doubt. Imagine a small room lit by a candle, which was almost out, and a man who had worked late into the night, his thoughts resounding in the mist...

How long can I continue to carry on this obsession? he asked himself again. *Hadn't he found his calling? Hadn't he gotten over interminable questions? Would he never find contentment?* In this state of agitation and ferment, he loaded up his brush and continued to let the liquid gold flow onto and into the image in front of him. In his feverish movements, he recalled the extraordinary experience that had driven him to paint these images.

It was during the solstice time, during the darkest night of his 33rd year. It was during that night that he ventured out into the courtyard to fill his bucket with water. He needed water. He would bring back ice water from the well. He had been fasting. Wrapped in a bear skin over his tunic and leggings, he opened the door. It was bitter cold in his mountain monastery, isolated from the nearest village and the warmth of the fires being set by the people celebrating this longest of nights. This isolation he had learned to live with over the years. It was another kind of isolation that had driven him to fast in this winter's cold, an isolation that came from a question,

"Was he on the right path?"

After all these years of meditation and dedication and the routine of stillness and conscious activity in the garden and the distillery, after all these years the question of what he was doing should not have bothered him, in fact, should not have come up. This was his life, the path he had chosen.

*This was...*he thought. And yet the question had dared to come up, to encroach his routines and his stillness and would not let him alone.

It was in this state he went out into the courtyard that night, wanting to fill his bucket with the ice water, life giving water. In the darkness of this star-less night he groped his way along a worn and weary path, he felt the stone setting of the well, all was frozen, he wanted to break some ice. He took the ax. *One blow cracked the night.* A light from somewhere broke through the overcast sky, moonlight bathed the very spot he stood on and its wonder filled him with awe. Reflecting from the ice was a golden halo surrounding a face. His skin crawled with emotion, his eyes widened, the face was everything he had ever meditated on. Its beauty overwhelmed him. He was transfixed by its emanating beauty and wonder. He could not move. Inwardly, he seemed to be everywhere and in all time, he felt...he wanted to bring this image into the world, he felt a part of that light, as if he was the sky itself, the heavens he had prayed to, and the God of the heavens was here, now, in the face and it's surrounding glow. That was his vision, that was what stayed with him...

In the morning Brother Benedictine walked out into the courtyard. He saw his Brother kneeling by the well.

"Brother Rubens," he called out, but Brother Rubens did not move.

He walked up to him, felt his body and touched his face of ice.

"Rubens!" he screamed and slapped his face. "Help me, help me, brothers, Rubens, Brother Rubens is frozen, help me?"

He slapped his blue, icy face again and looked into it -- into his eyes. His eyes glowed. They were wide open, glowing like moonlight.

The brothers came and carried him back into the monastery, into the warmth of their fire-lit room. They placed him near the fire and stood around him, holding him, breathing on him, warm hands touching his face, his hands, his feet. For three hours they held him, warming him with their bodies and their prayers.

His eyes were still glowing with a life they could feel. Slowly, as if awakening from a long sleep, the cold body of brother Rubens began to turn warm, the color flowed into his face, flushed with the warmed blood of life.

"Brother Rubens, Brother Rubens," several of the monks whispered. "It is a miracle, a miracle."

With his eyes, now, wide-open, his mouth began to turn slightly upward into a beatific smile. It was the smile of one who had seen something beyond his own life, who had gone into another world, a world he had, many times, meditated on and had only imagined. Now his face emanated a serenity that his brothers could only wonder at.

"Brother Rubens, it is a miracle that you are alive," one of them whispered to him.

Rubens spoke with a slow assurance, "Brother, I am back from the dead and I have touched the face of our Savior." They could only gaze in amazement at his words.

"Brothers, I have seen the face of our savior in its golden beauty, it is rarer than and more beautiful than anything we can imagine."

"What was it like?" one of them ventured to ask.

"It is like the rays of the sun in a morning sunrise. It is like the glow of the moon when it is full. It radiates with a light that comes from the farthest star."

"How can we experience this wonder?" asked another. "With this beatific vision I have found my life, brothers. I'll paint the beauty of that face in all its glory over and over again. I will try to bring into the world what I have experienced.

"How will you do this?"

"When I am able and with your help I will gather the hair of the sable to make brushes, I will gather gold dust and lapis lazuli and rose attar and all manner of hallowed materials to make the colors, I will dry the wood of our sacred tree, the ash, to make the base of the painting. All this I will do to bring this vision of beauty to the world, so that all may begin, just begin, to glimpse the world that is possible, that I was witness to."

From the day he spoke those words to his brothers, Rubens lived them. One painting after another had been painted by him, each time he had hoped to come closer to the image in his vision. None were ever adequate for him, but he had come to be known outside his monastery as a painter of extraordinary insight. Visitors had seen his work, and marveled at it, had come to sit in the presence of these images, had come to be healed by their colors, their beauty, had come to meditate on them. Rubens had allowed some of the paintings to be taken to other monasteries and on occasion to churches in the area.

This was how one golden, hallowed painting found its place in the chapel that Nicholas tragically walked into many years later. Out of the charred remains of the chapel and the tragic deaths of those inside, an image of healing and beauty had found its way into Nicholas' hands. It went with him and Flaxen as they traveled farther east to find his master, the green-plumed knight, Sir Waldundstein.

Path Nine

Moonlight Grace

When Flaxen woke, she heard noises in the vicinity -- horses neighing and strange voices. She nudged Nicholas and held her hand over his mouth. He opened his eyes and glared at her.

"*Ssh, ssh,*" she voiced, and, wanting to hear every sound, held her hand to her ear.

They both looked above their grassy lair and saw in the near distance five or six horsemen with someone…Nicholas squinted and tried to focus on the person walking behind them. "Could it be? Could it be, Sir Waldundstein?"

With trepidation, they both watched the boisterous procession. "We must follow them," Nicholas said, and took Flaxen's hand. They crouched and walked and followed them from a distance, always watching the wild horsemen.

Were these the killers of Flaxen's mother?…and the other innocents in the church? he wondered as he watched them pull the Knight behind them -- his hands tied to a long rope, held by the last one in the procession.

They followed them all day, picking up their horse-hoof trail and the soft but dragging footprints of their prisoner knight. When the evening came on and they no longer saw them, the thin wisp of smoke from their fire guided them.

All day Nicholas was thinking about how he could free his master. He knew they were brutal and any failure on his part would mean death, probably for Flaxen and the Knight also. He did not want to fail, but he also had to dare to try. He had thought of one approach after another but all seemed fraught with more risk that he wanted. They had only seen six horsemen all day and had no idea if there were more to come. When they saw the rough and ragged men sitting around a campfire Nicholas looked at Flaxen. "One at a time," he said, quietly and held up one finger that became two fingers walking away until his fist crushed them.

Flaxen nodded and pointed in the direction of the horses.

"Yes, yes," Nicholas responded. "We have to take the horses. I don't know how much time we'll have. They may kill the Knight. They may walk him until he drops from exhaustion. They may..."

He began to get anxious. She could see it. She touched his lips and calmed him.

"Tonight," he said to her. "I will see if I can free him. I must try."

He proceeded to try and show her with his hands.

"You," pointing to her, "will help let the horses go when we come back."

He did not know if she understood but he decided to undertake the first part of his plan. They let the night fall on them. The darkness covered the view around them and, by hiding behind high clouds, even the stars were helping. All they could see was a soft reddish glow and a dying trickle of smoke. Nicholas took his sword and slowly crawled toward their camp. It was quiet. As he got closer to the remaining life of the fire, he could see that one of the horsemen was sitting with his hands on his sword, the hilt under his chin. The others seemed to be sleeping around the fire. Now he could clearly see the Knight. He had been tied to a tree some ten feet away from the fire.

Could he get close enough without being seen or heard? he wondered. The answer resounded within him -- *He had to. He felt he had no choice. This was a moment he had to face* as he had faced the nightmare demon. He had crossed the threshold and come back. He had come back to save his master; to change the course of the green-plumed Knight's destiny. *What was in this moment's meaning that compelled him to act?* he wondered, *Was it something larger than himself, larger than the horsemen and their dark brutality, larger than Waldundstein's honor and life, larger than his own fears of death?*

He had no more time to dwell on any questions of meaning, he had crossed the threshold and he had come back. He took the sword from its sheath, held it with a steady hand and let the blade point forward. From his sack he took the blackened wood, with the image of a face on it, surrounded by a golden halo, and put it inside his tunic. Flaxen looked into his eyes and saw both fear and bravery. She gently touched his cheek with her hardened hand, a hand that had known plowing, threshing and the swing of an axe. From her touch he could feel a strength come into him. He looked into her eyes, his heart was pounding, blood was surging through him...What could stop him? He had the strength that youth and love could give him. *Now -- if his wits could only keep up with his new found strength.* He closed his eyes, breathed in and smiled -- *if he died right now*, he thought, *this must be what it would be like, to be in a timeless state, to be in a heavenly state.* He did not want to come back. He felt her touch...He did not want to leave her touch...He did not want to come back...

*Whoo...who...*the night owl called. He awoke to find himself crawling in darkness -- feeling the ground -- his eyes becoming accustomed to the feel of the soil and the stubble of grass. His eyes caught the gentle streams of light from the dying embers of their fire, the only warmth the horsemen's brutality could hang onto, and, it seemed, even that was a dying, waning effort.

Nicholas continued crawling, feeling his way. He felt his heart beating -- *too loud*, he thought, *too loud.* He slowed down and just listened. He was not sure of his plans. He just knew he had to contact his master. If he could wake him, let him know he was there. Slowly, very slowly, he continued until he was behind the tree they had tied the Knight to. Nicholas heard his belabored breathing. He looked at the guard sitting not too far away. His head had drooped. He was asleep. Nicholas put his hand slowly around the tree. At the same time he was whispering, "Master, master, don't make a sound. It is I, Nicholas. It is I, Nicholas,"

But no sound came from the man, only a slight, very slight tug at the rope, a tightening, a pull.

Had he heard? he wondered.

Again, there was a slight pull at the rope.

Yes, yes! thought Nicholas. He whispered, *Master, master, I will cut the ropes. Do not move.*

At that Nicholas cut away at the several ropes binding him to the tree. His sword moving slowly and deliberately -- slowly the ropes frayed, slowly they came apart. His master sensed the loosening. Finally the ropes parted, like the sea, many years, before them, the ropes parted and his master, the green-plumed Knight felt the freedom...But they were not free, until they were free from the waves of brutality about them, they needed to move, with moonlight grace, through these waves.

They moved and not a soul woke to their moving. The sentry, the guard, the drooping head, all slept in stillness, lost in the night.

They moved back from the flickering, dying embers, back into the darkest dark of the night, back to where Flaxen was waiting. In silence they met each other. In silence they held each other. In silence they breathed the breath of freedom. The waves of brutality and death had held back and they had moved through them.

In a hushed and grateful voice, the knight reminded him that his captors would soon wake. He spoke with urgency,

"We must prepare."

Flaxen moved her fingers and pointed to the horses.

"Yes, yes" both Waldundstein and Nicholas nodded.

Quickly, they grabbed what they could see of the blankets and food and quickly they found their way close to where the horses were tethered. Waldundstein immediately began to cut one of the ropes with Nicholas' sword while Flaxen untied another. Nicholas held on to Windward and Pathfinder.

Almost done, he thought. The other horses whinnied, *Too loud*, he thought. "Hurry," he said, under his breath, but this time it was too late. He heard commotion from the fire direction. He knew that their loss had been discovered.

"Get on," he heard Waldundstein say. He helped Flaxen get on one of the horses. He got on Pathfinder. Waldundstein jumped onto Windward and gave the other horses a smack with the blanket.

The horsemen came. First, the guard in blazing anger ran towards Flaxen.

RIDE! shouted Nicholas, but the crazed horsemen yelled at the horse, slowing it enough to get within reach. Waldundstein saw two others come. He took the sword and rode towards them. Nicholas rode towards the guard who, by now, had grabbed the reins of Flaxen's horse.

It was now that he had to act. He rode towards the horseman. Howling, shrieking, filling the night's silence with his pent-up fury, he rode straight at the horseman, who let the reins go and turned in terror. He tried to avoid the horse but was knocked down. Hoofs cracked his ribs. He cried out in pain.

Nicholas and Flaxen looked into the waning darkness, listened for sounds. A great clash of metal violated the silence and vibrated in the distance, in the ground, in the very air, the very breath they took...

Waldundstein! Nicholas wailed more than yelled, *Waldundstein!*

He rode towards the clashing sounds -- taking the icon from underneath his tunic -- he rode in the direction of the heaving of metal and muscle and breathing. He saw them, he saw the knight falling on his back, on his elbow, his sword broken...He saw the horsemen over him with sword raised. He saw them and hailed with an inner might. He held the shield, his image of gold and rode towards them...

The final clash of metal was still ringing, all around them ringing, with a sound that set the hallowed gold singing, shining...

The horseman was overcome, was blinded by the singing, ringing, shining gold. He fell backwards holding his eyes.

I am blind, I am blind, he convulsed in fear.

Waldundstein rose at the momentary miracle that had saved his life. He picked up the fallen sword of the horseman, whose strength was of no use to him now. The horseman groped in circles. His eyes had turned him inward. There was to be no morning light for his eyes. Waldundstein let him convulse in his darkness. They also knew there was still danger -- only one horseman had fallen under the hooves of Nicholas' horse...Two had fallen to Waldundstein's sword and one was blinded.

The knight shouted into the breaking dawn, COME AND SHOW YOURSELF, COWARDS! DESPICABLE COWARDS OF BRUTALITY! YOU ARE AN AFFRONT TO GOD! His voice resounded with the coming light, with the morning light and shook the very shadows left behind, within which two remaining horsemen were rapidly disappearing.

Waldundstein looked at Nicholas and saw the golden sun of the shield in his hand. It was his savior. "Where did you get such a wondrous shield?" He asked him.

"I found it in the charred remains of the church. It is made of wood, very old and was covered with the soot of the fire. I rubbed the blackness off and this picture -- this sainted image -- shown with a radiance I had never seen before. I brought it with us and, and..."

He ran towards his master, *I'm overjoyed to see you,"* he stammered, *"I thought we would not see you, find you, I thought you were...*

He could not bring himself to say it. His eyes were filled with joy.

Waldundstein put his arm around him and walked him over to the young girl awaiting, still sitting on the horse, watching all that had transpired.

"And who is this?" he wanted to know.

"This is Flaxen. At least I call her that. She does not speak our language. I found her at the church. Her mother died there...She has no home."

"Then we will take her with us. We will leave the sorrow of this land and travel back to our mist-filled valley -- back to the heart of my father's home, the castle of Waldundstein."

Towards the West they rode. They left what they could for the two horsemen -- each needing each other. Now they would learn what it means to care and to live in vulnerability. One blinded and one unable to move. The eyes of one would guide the movement of the other.

After their stories had been told to each other, they rode in silence, until the land opened up again in seemingly endless, billowing grass. The horses stopped by a fresh stream. They all drank from the rippling water and ate the dark bread that Flaxen had packed. The horses grazed on the grass. When they finally mounted, the sun was moving deeper into the western sky. Nicholas rode next to Flaxen and encouraged her horse to run. Flaxen laughed and made no attempt to stop. Nicholas rode after her. They rode like the wind over the sea...

Path Ten

Ironic Radiance

"They rode like the wind over the sea," she repeated. "They rode for days...through fields and forests...they rode in the timeless, adventures of not so innocent youth...they rode until the morning found him..."

"Hey, look. It's Nicholas. He's riding in his sleep."

What, hoy!

"Nicholas, Nicholas? Where are you? Where have you been?"

"Where have I been? Where have I been? Where am I?" His half-opened eyes gazed in amazement, trying to adjust to the candlelight surroundings. He turned his head slowly from one side to another.

"The knights have sung, Nicholas" and the night has turned to morning"

"You've slept it well away."

"Well, well," the booming voice of the waking Baker broke through the din of the voices. "Where did our apprentice go last night? Did you get lost in the sounds of the songs and the crevasses of the castle?"

This voice finally woke him out of his dream.

"Where have I been? This I can rightly tell you. I was traveling on the grassy fields of the East with my master, the Knight Waldundstein..."

You were dreaming," said one of the boys.

I was traveling in the direction of the East when this great plume of smoke showed itself in the distance...I saw the smoldering ruins of God's house. I saw the terrible deaths of mother and child and mother."

"You were dreaming," said another.

"We buried the mother and the daughter came with me. The Knight was captured and we rode to find him. We fought his captors and freed the Knight, then we rode like the wind towards the West.

"You were dreaming" said the booming voice of the now busy Baker.

"No, I was there. I was there. We rode like the wind and came to other villages, other towns on our way to Waldundstein's castle."

"And what did you see?" added another boy.

"That's for another time. I'm awake now and I remember Waldundstein singing in the great Hall."

"Yes, he was and he is long gone. You imagined you were with him from the sounds of your dreams."

"I was, I was...Wait, look, I'll show you. Look under my tunic, a shield"

He opened up his tunic and there, in its gleaming glory was the golden halo of the saint on the charred board.

"Look, see. I was not dreaming"

They looked in a maze ment and out of the corner, over the heads of the boys gazed the eyes of the giant baker.

"What is that in the eye of the saint?"

"It looks like a jewel," said one.

"Yes, a jewel with a star in it."

"Could it be the lost jewel?" another asked.

The group grew silent. The astonished baker took the shield from Nicholas.

"This is the lost jewel," he explained. "*You, Nicholas*, took it and put it in the eye of that face. See, see...There is only one."

His voice was becoming harsh.

"No, I tell you. I found in the smoldering ruins of the church."

You are coming with me, you young thief! The baker ordered, and took Nicholas by the arm and half carried him to the chambers of the King.

"Your Highness, *your Highness*! I know it is early, but I have some news of the lost jewel. I found it in the eye of this picture, this wooden shield…"

The King looked at the golden halo and into the eyes of the saint. He saw one star-like jewel gazing back at him.

"It is the jewel," he said in amazement, "What have you to say for yourself?"

"I…I found this wooden shield. It only had one jewel in one eye. I did not take the…you see, sire, it's missing one eye…"

For once the King was not in the mood for explanations. He had stayed up too long, drunk too much. It had been too many nights of reverie ending with the Festival of Songs. Oh, he had been in grand spirits throughout the festivities but now, this soon after, this early in the morning, all he could say was, "Take him away, into the dungeon. Let us deal with him some other time."

The baker understood and the guards took Nicholas down, down the stairs, down, down…until they opened a door to darkness. The guards shoved him in and, with a horrid clang, shut the door behind him.

Path Eleven

The Sound of Hammering

By the time SC had wound his way down one canal street and up another, by the time he reached the Hotel Europa, he was sweating, late and sweating. His mind was reeling with words and images, rolling in the aftermath of his experience in the Cat's Cradle. "What had become of all the *hammering*?" he kept asking himself. What had become of..."

"SC," a voice from the cushioned corner of the lobby called out to him. "SC, you're SC? Aren't you?"

SC looked in the direction of the voice. "Yes," he said as he put down his guitar.

"Do you have a minute?"

"Yes, I guess. Who are you?"

"Let's just say I've been traveling a lot and I decided to stop in Amsterdam for a while. I heard you singing in the square. I overheard you tell someone that you were staying in this hotel. You probably don't remember me listening to you. Anyway, I've been waiting for you. The desk clerk said I could wait for you. You're called SC, the Street Corner Singer, right?"

"Yes, that's right."

"Well, I like your songs, at least the ones I've heard. But I'll get right to the point, I'm starting a club with a new idea. It's going to connect to other clubs -- there'll be video connections -- digital images -- sounds -- a singer, like yourself, could be seen in Munich or Paris or San Francisco. But that's not the main point. The point is: people, singers, songwriters, theater people, poets will be able to see each other, hear each other. You, *they*, can become a force- become catalysts through clubs that are connected -- *live* -- do you see?

"Ah, yea, I, I'm not sure?"

"I'm thinking of satellites, satellite clubs...you see... Now, we have stationary satellites over different spots of the earth, right? But these, these will be satellite spots on the earth, *satelites* with one *el*. Can you imagine it, first major cities, then in smaller towns, then anywhere someone can pick up the digital video transmissions. It could come from someone's home. I know someone who has an old castle in Silesia. I mean, he lives in this place. He sent me pictures of it. There's a huge room where he wants to set up live video exchange. Are you beginning to see?"

"Why me? What have I got to do with this?"

"What do you mean? What do you have to do with this? You're going to be one of the catalysts. You spread the word around here...When you're singing or whatever...We need a ground swell of voices."

He was trying to convince SC in ways he would see and would, hopefully, agree with. "All the technology isn't worth the wire it travels on or even the air it comes through, if there's no story to tell, nothing to take into the gut. That's why I, *we*, need to...You've got things to say. I've heard you...What do you think?"

"It's an intriguing idea. You mean someone goes into one of these clubs -- these places set up for this -- and what? They see someone performing *live* and there are screens around, from other clubs to watch this?"

"That's just the beginning. It could be two, three, four or more screens that have live transmissions and connections to the other clubs. Eventually it could be three dimensional, in front of you, holograms. It could be like going to hear your favorite local band, feel the beat and have them heard and seen in San Francisco where it's eight hours later or in Paris. Twenty-four hours worldwide words and music and theater, etc, etc.

Can you imagine not being able to sleep, go to a club at four in the morning and be with a live show from Tokyo?"

"But we can get TV broadcasts from other countries already."

"Sure, sure, but this is live, simultaneous and, and..." He was getting excited, getting closer. "You're with others, your friends, new friends. Can you imagine singing your songs to a worldwide audience -- *live* -- It is mind-boggling isn't it?"

They both just stood there for a moment. Finally, SC ventured to speak, "I would like to see a kind of place for social commentary...you know...where words and music... where a kind of theater...short works dealing with social issues..."

"I could definitely see that. The intimacy of the club, or space, could lend itself to a cabaret atmosphere."

"Social cabaret, not necessarily decadent or nihilistic, we have enough of that."

"Yes, yes, but don't restrain it...there are enough conservative elements around, even in Amsterdam."

"I've had a dream...I can't tell you too much about it, but it was a kind of mind transforming dream, an answer to things I was thinking about, but it's set me in a direction...It's got me, I want to, I have to try to..."

"To...What?"

"I'll put it this way. I want to...I want to hear the *hammering*."

"Hear the *hammering*?"

"Yes, I think that's it. I think you've been a kind of revelation. You've described a possibility for a dream I had. I want to help create a place, *even better*, a *consciousness*, where people are hammering; where they are creating places, that can be heard by more and more people."

The stranger let the words sink into the room and into himself.

"If you put it that way, I want to set up the *hammers* and you'll do the *hammering*."

SC smiled. The stranger smiled. They started to laugh until they were caught up in an outburst of laughter. They laughed until the tears ran. They hugged each other. It was an unusual meeting of souls, of beating hearts, a pact made out of the stranger's knowledge and...SC's hope...They finally had to sit down. They were exhausted.

"It's a quarter after five," the stranger said.

"Yea, I'm ready for bed. Let's meet at the Adler Bakery Cafe - - it's off the Oz Achterburgwal -- tomorrow, I mean later, today, this afternoon.

"Yes, today."

In a moment the stranger was gone. SC could not remember him leaving.

Path Twelve

Darkness

The darkness, at first, was overwhelming. No matter how much Nicholas blinked the darkness continued. Blind, he felt blind - - not a sliver of light. *Wait...*His eyes were adjusting -- down on the floor -- there -- there was a crack, under the door behind him. He sat down. The stench of urine and mold penetrated his nostrils. His hands and fingers felt the floor, slimy in places, hard rock in others. Now that his eyes were gone, his sense of smell was acute, overwhelming him with a foreboding world. His ears were cocked for every possible sound as he sat motionlessly on his knees, but all he could hear was his heart throbbing. His initial terror started to subside into questions,

Where was he? How big was this room? Would he get fed?

His questions were still couched in hope. Over all, he felt he would be rescued, that the truth would come out. Waldundstein would save him and the King would realize he was telling the truth.

All of these thoughts took turns in his head. Over and over he thought of these things as he sat in the dark, wondering, listening for any sound that might break the stillness.

Would Waldundstein rescue him? Would anyone? he asked himself. The time seemed endless. He felt like he had been in this world forever. Night and day became one long night. He had to feel his way around the room. Standing up, and with his arms outstretched, he slowly walked forward, slowly, until he felt the hard surface of crusted rock. He moved his fingers on the surface -- to the right -- farther -- feeling a vertical edge, he followed it around and finally felt around it. *The door*, he thought, as he felt a warmer surface with grooves and round rivets of metal patterns over it -- *Never had wood felt so good.* He put his face against it, smelled it, followed it around the edges with every finger until he got to the bottom. There…a crack of reflected light, brighter now, now that his eyes were open to any possibility of deliverance.

CLICK. A *sound,* he thought heard a sound.

CLICK. CLICK. CLICK. The huge door clicked and creaked open. The soft, almost negligible light of the catacombs was blinding to his eyes; eyes that were straining for light. The door opened enough to let a wooden bowl come in with a thick slice of bread over it.

HEY! he shouted. *Hey! I want to talk to Waldundstein, Sir Waldundstein, a knight, the green-plumed…"*

The door shut as suddenly and yet, as slowly as it had opened.

WAIT! he shouted, but it was silent again. He groped for the bowl and took the bread. He had forgotten how hungry he was until he bit into the bread.

Bread, from our ovens, he thought, as his eyes began to water. He was overcome by feelings of despair -- his betrayal was too much to bear. This was no nightmare or dream that he would wake up from, *or was it?* He put his hands together and looked into the darkness,

God, in heaven, please let me wake up from this dream. I did not take the jewel. I don't know how I ever got the shield with the golden halo. At the moment I thought it was a miracle. You gave me a miracle and now I have been thrown into darkness. Why, dear God, why?

He waited in silence for an answer, for a sign…But none came. He waited in silence and darkness…for a day, two days, three…until he lost track of the days…

With Jules listening intently, Leylani repeated, quietly, and with a sadness that only time could heal, "Until he lost track of the days…"

Path Thirteen

Adler Bakery Café

With half-closed eyes SC wandered up to the door of the Adler. This time, barely noticing the leftover, spray-painted letters of L O V E…He opened the letter 'O' again and walked in, ordered a cappuccino and found a seat. He let the cup warm his hands while he smelled the aroma of the French roast. He began to look around…

"SC," a voice beckoned. Turning his head and from almost out of nowhere, the stranger appeared.

"SC," he said again and held out his hand.

"Did you get some sleep?"

"Yes, Europa is relatively quiet during the day."

"Well, I put in a couple of hours but I saw someone who is also excited about the satelite project."

"Who?"

"Jeannette, she has a restaurant on Warmoestraat. I was in there a few days ago. We talked and for some reason I asked her what was happening? She said business had been slow. So, while I was eating, I thought her place would be a perfect spot for a satelite connection. Anyway to make a short story shorter, I saw her today. She's interested in the idea. Her place has a kind of *DeStijl* look -- you know, bare brick, high ceilings, bare industrial look. They call it an attitude."

"You're going a bit fast for me. What's *DeStijl?*"

"That was a '1920's artist's group. They were a kind of Dutch Modernist movement, you know, get rid of unneeded decoration, go to right angles, get to the materials themselves, where ever, whatever the materials are, glass, metal, etc. It could be a way of focusing on the performer, the story teller, the images…"

"The messages?"

"Of course, dialogue night."

"Or visionary night."

"I like that. A kind of futurist…Remember the Italian *Futurists?*"

"Maybe?"

"They were into *speed* before *speed* became a drug -- fast cars, trains, planes -- of course, speed is relative -- thirty miles per hour was fast then."

"I wonder what they would think of the Concorde? Or the Bullet train?"

"Or video speed, light speed, digital speed? I mean this is going to be *live* around the world…"

"Hey, we're taking off again. Let's concentrate on the *hammer* for a minute."

"Yea, sure…well…I'll talk to her, but there's also a video group that we should see. They put on shorts at a gallery that I've gone to, around the corner from the Cat's Cradle."

"They put on shorts?" SC shot back. "What are they, tennis players?"

"I see you have a sense of humor. Shorts, short videos, up to 30 minutes or so, they crank them out, trying all kinds, the cameras go everywhere, they follow the cops…I've seen them around…video…it's a new world."

"It's a new world," SC repeated, as he pulled out his note pad. "Any room for songwriters?"

"What do mean? You've got to fill them with something…A car is metal and gas until we get into it. Take a walk through the Van Gogh museum. The canvas was just canvas until he put his soul into it. Music can be notes or it can move us."

SC jotted down a few words as the stranger talked on…

Hello, hello,
Hello stranger
You are all the rage
Hello stranger,
It's the dawn of an age.

You've seen the world of video
You know what it can do
The sorcerers of olden time
have nothing over you you you you...

"You know what I mean," said the stranger. Have you heard of the German *Lieder* of a hundred years ago or more -- the whole nineteenth century -- poetry set in motion, with piano accompaniment, now it's guitar, guitar, guitar...

SC repeated, "poetry set in motion..." and wrote quickly,

Bye, bye Shakespeare,
You've come a long way
Bye, bye Shakespeare
You've had a long day

You've seen the world of Gutenburg
and cracked Rosette stone
Now it's time to
Bring it all back ho, ho, ho, home...

"Poetry slams, cowboy poetry...what we could use is walking, talking poetry, remember the 'exquisite corpse', the beatitude of the beats, refined chaos, poetry of the theater, in your void poetry, hip hop, rip rap, rap rap...I'm tired of waiting for Godot, let's go....

Hello Bowie, Hello Jackson
you are all the rage
Hello stranger
It's the dawn of an age

you're in the air and in my life
the world won't be the same
if I don't get it fixed today
I swear I'll go insa yea yea yea yeane...

"Video, Romeo, metaphoro," SC intoned and continued to write in his note book,

"Metaphoro...I like that. Do you know *Carmina Burana*?"

"No, what is it?"

"Karl Orff wrote music to these Latin songs, in the 30's, to these old medieval songs about love and drinking and life and fortune and it's -- the combination of music, words, voice, the relationship is so incredible. It moves me...remember Elvis' *Milk Cow Blues Boogie* -- well he's singing the song, slow like, right, like it was probably done before and he says on the record, *It don't move. Let's get real gone for a change*...Yea, yea, that's it. Orff's music gets real gone for a change, man, It stands by itself, like Stravinsky's *Rite of Spring*..."

"Hey, we're not getting ahead of ourselves, are we? Or is the past catching up..."

"No, no, we're in and out of the whole 20th century, early on there was a Russian composer, Scriabin, I think, was his name, who wrote music with colors related to the tones, the first tone paintings. Can you imagine the tone of C, middle C, being a certain color, make it viridian green, other colors move around it, higher tones in front of the light, yellow, vermilion and lower tones behind the light, turquoise, cobalt blue, you can make chords out of colors..."

"Yes, yes, tones, chords...a whole composition..."

"Do you know Kandinsky's works?"

"Some of them, *abstractions*, I like his earlier *compositions*..."

"Yes, that's what I mean. Even he called his paintings, *compositions* because of the relationship between color and music. He also wrote a theater piece called, *The Yellow Sound*. It was published in the *Blue Rider Almanac* in 1911...Seven scenes were created in a theater setting -- each one having a predominant color -- color became sound, tone and color..."

"*The Yellow Sound*…Let's do it. Let's do an updated version with voices, poetry, songs to bring out the abstract. It could be the first satelite performance."

"Why not?"

"It could be…"

"It could be…"

"You have to meet Jeannette. She's the owner of the restaurant I was telling you about. What a character…There's a menagerie of birds flying around her, people from all over, circling around her, coming in and out. If something's happening, she'll know about it. The problem is they don't always have the money to keep the business going, more often than not they need money and she stakes them, when she has it."

"OK, tomorrow, I need to make some money myself. I'm also working on new songs, Where is her place exactly?"

"Warmoestraat, around number 40."

"OK…Tomorrow…dinner time."

Path Fourteen

Storm

"Hey, mister, Mister Driver," *Leylani* yelled through the sea wind. "Do you think we can get going? The cottage is down the road from here?"

"I do think we can still take them," the driver's companion said. "Don't you think, dear?"

He had run as far as he could, then walked, until he was exhausted…His momentary despondency -- from his encounter with the chess player, the grim reaper -- had worn itself out. Now, he had been sitting quietly, letting the sea air fill him up again. With renewed vigor, he suddenly jumped up. *Yes, yes, even if we have to cross a bog, we'll find that nose of a dog. I say…Let's motor on, ho, ho, hee, hee, break away from the sea.*

Jules and Leylani clamored into the back seat waiting for their final amusement ride of the day. The driver did not disappoint them. *Hold on, whee, hey, hey, we're on our way…*The motor car lurched down the road, off and on the road, until he lost track of the road on the flat of the expansive lowland.

"There it is." Leylani pointed. "There's the *nose of the dog.* See the cottage, in the mist…There, over there…"

"*By Jove,*"

"It is, dear. It is a cottage. Let's motor over."

But a quick turn and a revving of the engine shattered their dream world. They were struck in the marshy, sandy strand.

By Jove, I do believe we are stuck. I say... Can you put your shoulders into it and get us out of here?

Jules and Leylani got out and pushed -- to no avail. The wheels just went deeper into the sucking sand. "Well, looks like we're stuck," Jules finally said with a worn-out look, as he leaned over the trunk of the car.

"Let's walk over to the cottage. Aiden can probably help us.

"I think she has a point. Don't you think, dear?"

By Jove, this is an adventure, ha, ha, ho, ho, hee, hee, we're stuck beside the sea. He pushed a button, and with a loud *hoo bah, hoo bah* resounding in the air, joined them. They left the forlorn motor car with it's tires half buried in the graying sand. From there the quartet of intrepid, slow-moving silhouettes slogged towards the fabled cottage. Spirits were still high, with adventure beckoning. Shelter was in sight. Even the wind seemed to pick up on their excited state. As they continued, however, the air began to change. Blowing lightly at first, the invigorating wind had brought in the coastal clouds that, now, created shadows over them. Sunlight disappeared into the western sea. With sudden cracks of lightning the heavens, suddenly, yielded up a pent up fury that fell on them, dousing them -- soaking them. They quickened their steps, almost running, then running, their feet sinking deeper into this marsh-like, bog-like land, the ghosts of history squishing beneath them, their feet squishing and churning with the elementals of this land and the remains of the age old wanderers who had looked for shelter 5,000 years ago, steeped in the mists and storms...

Path Fifteen

Sign of the Wolf

With their animal skins wet and the storm beginning to turn on them they were going to set up shelter for the night but Ng would not have it. He grabbed their arms, pulled them forward, urged them on, towards a shelter he knew was close by. *Come. Hurry. Shelter!* he said in staccato sounds.

He took the weight of the wood off the old woman. In stinging rain they followed him, walked, trod, walking with belabored steps, continuing until he stopped, *Here. Shelter.* But all they saw was more rain and felt the hard surface of a rock wall.

Come. They touched the rock and followed him around and around, until the rock wall opened into darkness. Ng stepped in with wary trepidation. His pulse was pounding. His senses acutely tuned to any danger. This was a place of refuge for other living things. He knew it and listened for breathing, smelling the air. He took his great wooden stick and pounded on the wall.

Bats fluttered in profusion around the ceiling and out the opening. From a deeper darkness came the yelps and yaps of young wolves, no grown wolf was heard over their high-pitched sounds.

Wolf! Ng said, as he placed himself in the entrance. His eyes were beginning to adjust to the storm's overcast grays and the black of the cavern.

Lightning, suddenly, lit up the sky and in that split second he saw the wolf pups in a corner. No mother could be seen. Again, he called out, WOLF and waited for the mother to return. With his club in his hand, he listened intently for the sound of padded feet or a snarling mouth. He knew this could be a fight to the death. He had no choice. They needed shelter and the mother wolf was going to protect her pups. They all waited and hoped for lightning to light up the night, to let them...

Wolf, he pointed.

Sniffing and sensing something was wrong. The mother wolf heeded the danger. A low guttural, snarling sound sent shivers to the group.

Ng banged on the side of the entrance, the snarling increased, the yelps could be heard crying in the darkness, the snarling become furious and Ng feared she would attack.

Lightning lit up the sky. In one fearsome, fang-bearing charge the mother wolf was in the air and ready to tear the throat of Ng. With all his muscles taut he sensed the moment and brought up his stick. In the darkness, between the lightning bolts, he swung with every muscle. The club found its mark. The dull thud of his stick on the head of the wolf brought a shriek and a lifeless thump to the ground in front of him. He had survived and two pups were now without a mother, but Ng would not worry about them tonight. Now they would sleep and wait for the storm to abate, for the morning to find them.

The storm, slowly, moved over the sand and the occasional outcrops of rocks, until the rosy mist of dawn found them sleeping, huddled together in the confines of this natural dwelling. A few yips woke Ng up and he saw the two pups trying to suckle at their dead mother's teats. He picked one up, looked in its face and held its warm body, *wolf*, he said, with a warmth that conveyed his intentions. He would help them and the grown pups would extend their noses and their eyes.

Turning to the others, who were also waking up, he said, *shelter* and proceeded to gather wood to erect a door for the entrance. All day they worked on the door and by evening they felt the security of their cavern. Now they tore apart the mother wolf's body for they had grown hungry in their search for shelter. After their mouths tasted blood and liver and heart, Ng picked up a pointed rock and scraped an outline of a wolf onto the side of their cavern.

Wolf. He said to them...*Wolf shelter.*

Path Sixteen

A Hammering Place

"Aiden, are you home? Aiden…"

The night air shivered with Leylani's voice. A light came on and shone through an upstairs window. It creaked open.

"Who is it?"

"It's Leylani

"Who?"

"It's Annie, Aiden."

"Annie, why didn't you say so. What are you doing here? I'll be right down."

"We got stuck in the marsh. We were on our way to…" But he had already closed the window and was on his way to the front door.

"Annie."

"Aiden, God, it's good to see you."

They embraced and she opened her arms to let him see Jules and the chauffeur and his companion. He greeted them and led them inside.

"These are new found friends of mine," Annie said. "We were on our way to see you when we got caught in this weird storm. The car is stuck in the marsh. We could see your cottage and then we lost it, walked around in circles, heard all kinds of noises, finally found it again."

"How could you lose this place?"

It was eerie, for a while there, it seemed like I, or we, lost track of where we were. The rain just gushed down on us. We couldn't see anything. We're soaked.

"Sit down. Sit down. I'll start a fire. I went to bed early tonight. It was also a bit strange. I felt like I was going to have visitors and here you are. I also heard these echoing, kind of gravelly sounds. I thought it was the storm but I still looked around. I even went outside. Anyway, we'll find a place for all of you to stay. Sit down. Make yourself comfortable."

"These are our motor car friends," Annie said, "They've been driving us and this is Jules, a king from Terra Grandeur."

I say, this is a comfortable old place, the driver interjected, *I mean, since it is the nose of the dog, as your friend Annie has pointed out, I guess you would expect it to be wet here, hey hey.*

"Now, dear, don't be rude."

"I'll get this fire going and then we'll have some hot toddies"

Jolly good idea. Why...I believe we could warm up to this young friend, the driver said, as he eased himself into a worn out, cushioned chair in the living room.

"What's this about a king from Terra Grandeur?" Aiden asked, looking over at Jules."

"She's kidding, Jules said. We climbed Terra Grandeur today and your friend Leylani err, sorry, Annie, has a wild imagination."

"Oh, but he found a gem, Aiden. It was probably from a King's crown."

"Yea."

"Show him, Annie insisted."

Jules brought out the star amethyst and handed it to Aiden.

He whistled and said, "Hey, this looks like the real thing."

Aiden took it over to the light and let the star shine, sending flickering reflections around the room, like a strobe light from bygone dance floors. He let it continue...

"So, what do you think."

"I think we should get those hot toddies going."

Jolly good idea.

With the fire warming the inside of the cottage and the hot toddy's warming their spirits they settled in and replayed the events of the day. After much back and forth Aiden finally asked where they were off to?

"I was on my way to Amsterdam," Jules opened up, "and then I met Annie."

"Leylani to you, Jules," Annie chimed in.

"Well, I met *Leylani* in the back seat of a wild ride -- I mean a very interesting ride, with our generous chauffeurs."

"It has been an adventure," the woman sitting to the right of the driver stated.

Yes, by Jove, we've made the most of it, ha, ha, ho, ho...

"Get your flute, Aiden. They would love it."

"A flute."

"Well, I have a penny whistle."

A penny whistle then, by Jove, let's have it then. I know a jig or two. That will warm up the blood.

"Now, dear, you know what happened last time."

"Last time?" Annie asked.

"Oh, he put his back out and was laid up for weeks," his companion answered. But Aiden had already started a lively tune and the leprechaun was lifting his legs double time. Annie joined in and took Jules by the hand until all three were tearing up the rug, or stones in this case, even the voice of reason was moving with the tune.

Wha, ho, whee, hee, this is the place to be...

Another tune and another and one after the other collapsed in a chair. Only the wild driver was still going, dancing with glee. Finally Aiden slowed the high pitched sounds down to a more familiar tune. Annie's voice picked up the call and filled the room with the words of an ancient story,

By the shore of Lake Eden
my love was in flight.
He had chosen to leave me,
he had chosen to fight;

fight for his father,
who had broken his word,
taken land from his brother,
with a treacherous sword.

My love's heart was aching.
He knew it was wrong,
but for the love of his father
he put his sword on.

It was then I decided
by the shore of that lake,
if he fell in the battle
my own life I would take.

wah oh oh ah oh aaa
wah oh oh ah aaa
wah oo ooo ooo
wah oh oh ah aaa

By the shore of Lake Eden
I saw my love fall.
From the spear of his uncle,
who had resisted the call.

It was then that I ventured
into the water and sank.
Only moonlight shone on me
lying dead on the bank.

When his father had heard this,
his heart it did break.
The agony in him
made mortal souls shake.

Well, they played the flute lowly,
and the mothers they cried,
for a son mortally wounded,

and his love who had died.

wah oh oh ah oh aaa
wah oh oh ah aaa
wah oo ooo ooo
wah oh oh ah aaa

Annie's plaintive voice carried the young girl's yearning and sadness and loss into their hearts; where every connection to loss is found; where every sadness is harbored. Her voice and Aiden's evoking accompaniment filled up the room, went out the windows, went out the door and between the stones. Like a single pebble thrown into a surrounding sea, the ripples of loss emanated outward, until the ages sang with her and the wolf pups howled in the graying sky.

When Aiden stopped playing his bittersweet tones, and Annie's last howl came from her mouth, the plaintive sounds continued to resonate through the air and vibrate outward, outward, throughout the very rooms where *hammering* was to be heard.

Even the stranger had stopped checking cable connections and sound levels and stood with SC, watching and letting the sound come over him. Slowly, and without anyone wanting this beautiful sadness to end, a hush fell...A hush fell on Jeanette's place in Amsterdam, her place of *hammering* and a hush fell on Alfred's castle in Silesia and a group known as the *geary gathering* in San Francisco and Monet's Cafe in Paris and the Blue Rider Kneipe in Schwabing and other satelites, other *hammering* places around the world. A dreamlike awakening swept over them, momentary, yet lasting. Momentary, yet with a stillness that seemed forever. Then slowly, one hand clapped, then another and another, the minotaur had succumbed to the swelling waves of applause, a crescendo of appreciation from one place on the earth to another to another to another to another until the string, the yarn, the rope was woven throughout them all and there was no need to find their way out, they were out and they were in at the same time, they were in Amsterdam and they were on the *nose of the dog,* they were in San Francisco and they were in Schwabing, they were out and they were in, they were out and they were in, at the same time...

Aiden pulled back the drapes along a wall. What might have been a window, in fact, in front of a window, was a screen, a relatively thin screen that had four separate video images. He turned up the volume and the sound of many hands clapping, of whistling, of cheers was coming from people on each screen, in different settings. They were living into the last plaintive, woeful sounds coming from Aiden's cottage, the *nose of the dog.*

Leylani had the first startled response, "Aiden, what is going on here?" Jules looked and listened. The driver settled down and his lady friend simply said, "My word, dear, there are people on the wall -- a virtual crowd. What are they all excited about?"

"They are clapping for Annie," Aiden announced modestly.

"How? What?"

"What?"

"How did they hear?"

"They not only heard but they saw. Do you see the camera, that small camera in the corner of the room?"

An announcement came from the screens, *That was an impromptu performance from a 'hammering' place out west. Aiden are you there? Who was that lady?*

"Aiden," Annie said. "Are we on TV? You should have told us."

"I hoped it wouldn't be a problem, but I just turned the camera on when I started to play the flute. Other places -- they call them satelites, *hammering* places -- can tune in or turn on if they want to. Sometimes there may be ten screens on the wall. That means at least ten places have simultaneously connected. I can choose which places to tune into and they can choose to tune into us, if they like what we're doing. I'm usually tuned into 4 different satelites. I don't always know who's going to join in. *Hello, where are you from? Anybody?* he inquired, as he looked into the camera.

"We are in the Blue Rider in Schwabing, that was incredible! Gut, mensch!"

"And this is SC at Jeannette's in Amsterdam. Who was that singer with you, Aiden? That song really got to me, and a lot of other people. As you can see, they're still wanting more."

Annie winked at Aiden and mouthed, Ley Lan ee.

"That was Leylani, SC. She knows some of the old songs from around here."

"Leylani, when can we hear more?"

"Actually, this has been a surprise for me, I, we, we've been on a kind of tor, the kind you climb and we got lost in a thunderstorm and here we are. Actually, I feel lucky to have survived. We've been traveling with these two wild adventurers."

"Yes, and this is the wildest of it all, don't you think, dear?"

What, by Jove, this is extraordinary, we are on TV, you can see me, and I can see you, ha, ha, who, who...

"Who, who, who are you?"

"We are on an occasional motor tour, taking in the country, and sometimes, some very interesting people. I am Moira and this...this is..." She was just about to introduce the dancer and the driver of their wild odyssey when he piped up,

I am a rambler from the old country, as you can see, ha, ha, ho, ho, hee, hee...And who, by the way, are you?

"Well, I was singing in Dam Square, when our *hammer* here, putting his arm around the stranger, enticed me into this satelite project, I wanted places for, what I called *hammering*, where people could tell their stories and connect up to others. He made the portable video...digital video connections possible in these places, where we could hear voices from around the world. Jeannette saw the potential and let us start here. Aiden's place is also one of the first. We're still giving birth."

"And we have been feeling the pains here in Silesia. We just got wired up. We've been trying to tune into other satelites when we heard the last howling sounds of Ley Laa nee. We thought we had tuned into Siberia. Please excuse us. It was was...it was a haunting howl. There, finally we are getting other transmissions. Hello. This is great. Ausgezeichend! Actually," the excited voice continued, "Alfred, the ancestral owner of this castle and also the local poet-philosopher, would like to read something for the occasion. Hello, hello. Are you there?"

"Yes, yes, we hear you and see you. It looks like a big room, an old room. Are you sitting in front of a painting or..."

"It is a tapestry," came the voice of Alfred, as he rose to let the camera view it. "It is at least 600 years old, woven in remembrance of the owner of the castle -- a famous Knight of the time. From what I know, he had quite a reputation as a singer of sagas, particularly of stories from around here."

"Alfred, before you continue with this history lesson, maybe you should inaugurate your satelite and do some *hammering*"

"Yes, I will do that. I would like to read a short poem, one of my first attempts in English. I hope it fits into your vision, SC?"

What do I really care about?

His voice carried the words in such a way that the images on the screens slowed down, as if, in slow motion they listened,

What do I really care about?
As I live here, as I learn and strive?
Is it knowledge, faith or doubt?
Or do I just fight to stay alive?
Is it the soul? My inner being?
That other people end up seeing?

Or do I just care for myself, alone
and not at all for others?
Is it important that it's known
what I am doing? Here and there?
Can I be a generous donor
without proclaiming: I'm the owner?

Do the opinions of others count?
Or do they have more influence
on me, on how, and what; than when
my conscience and intelligence

speaks out loud? Or do I surrender
to superstition and become it's defender?

Do I still care, even when I'm rich,
about the sick and poor around me?
Or do I behave selfishly
and always take a quick detour,
so that I don't get well acquainted
with the misery that real life has painted?

Do I like to read and hear
how other people have to live?
Am I sincere in my belief?
When help is needed, do I give?
Or do I only find satisfaction
when I gain from a transaction?

Do I care enough for truth,
or only what others may think
or believe? Does dishonesty
make me suffer? And even on the brink
of war, with our world close to destruction,
do I seek a gain in war production?

It always matters how I care,
for what, and what I do with pride.
How much am I willing to share?
Will I be quiet or loud
when there's wrong done in any place,
to anyone of any race?

There was rapt silence for a moment over which a polite clapping began and grew as the meaning of the words deepened.

"Hey, your words don't just fit, they practically define the dream of this endeavor," SC announced to everyone tuned in.

"Thank you," Alfred said, and let the room come back into focus.

"Oui."

"Alfred, what was going on behind you? It looked like a yellow light that was flickering."

"You mean in the tapestry? *It is strange.* I have seen colors shining on occasion. There is a fire woven into it. Here, can you see this?"

"I'm not sure."

"It's faded but I believe it's a church that is on fire. It is just one of the incidents in the Knight's life. You must remember that tapestries were not just visual allegories of the time but may have included family incidents -- except that only a few people could afford to have them...to have their lives documented in a weaving of this size."

"Do you know the stories behind the rest of the images or weavings?"

"Some, but I would have to look at some very old books to elaborate."

Beautiful Hands

I say, this has been a very interesting evening, but Mister SC, you are the hammering boy, the founder of this visionary medusa, are you able to add a song to this gathering, or what is the protocol for that?

"Ah, we're working on that, it's pretty loose so far, but I would love to do a song, if I can take the floor here or the camera."

"Yes. Hear, hear, SC."

The simple arpeggio of an E chord began to hush the people around him and the others tuned into Jeannette's place, "I'd like to dedicate this song to someone I met in a strange dream. He had gathered people together from all walks of life; people who spoke many different languages. They were working on his vision of the future; a great building, a modern temple. These people were hammering shingles onto the two domes of the building, carving the columns that held the domes up, etching the colored glass, while, not too far away, they could hear exploding bombs and the horrible cries of men dying."

The tones continued until he began to sing,

The rulers of mediocrity
can darken the world that you see
and close off the joy that can be
if you go too far you'll see
they will be detain you
they will restrain you
they will then chain you
to the weight of all their fears...

Like vultures with blood in the air
that circle and live in despair
and dive for the beauty that's rare
if you stay too long you'll see
they will then tear you
they'll strip and then bear you
then they will swear that
they're doing it all for your very own good...

2000 years of pain
does it have to happen again
they put another joyful man in chains
if you spread your arms you'll see
they will not heed you
they will not believe you
they will just bleed you
then they will feed you to a page of tragedy...

radiant one
can it be? can it be?
radiant one
can it be? can it be?
that no one can live with what you've become

that no one can live with what you've become
beautiful hands
don't they see? don't they see?
beautiful hands
don't they see? don't they see?
that you have achieved what they could become
that you have achieved what they could become
radiant sun
in your face, in your eyes
light the way, touch my eyes
radiant sun…
radiant one…

They let the words and the music continue until they found a place for them in their own hearts…Until their weariness overtook them and the night let them rest.

Aiden had found a place for all of them. The driver and his companion were sleeping in his bed while he was lying on an old cot in the attic. Jules and Leylani had been left in the main room with the smoldering fire. He had given them a few blankets and an extra mattress. As they watched the fire slowly die out Leylani said softly to Jules, "Jules, I could barely hold myself back when I heard Alfred talking about the Knight on that tapestry…It's really a bit much, don't you think. The story of Terra Grandeur just came out of me…I mean…I was just letting it spout out of me…Where did it come from? And here…out of nowhere…out of some new techno world connection with Alfred's castle comes a story of a knight who sings ballads, sagas…and to top it off, there's an image of a church that's on fire…"

"Leylani, there are many stories of singing minstrels from those days, that's how the news was spread…it's in the tradition of the storytellers…*you…are…in…that…tradition*…

Before he was finished with his words she had closed her eyes to the long day and lay softly next to him…

Morning

Morning reminded them of the motor car stuck in the marsh but no one ventured out until they had all, again, investigated the wall-hanging of video screens.

Incredible! The driver opined.

His companion felt the material between her fingers, "It just rolls down," she said in astonishment. "How do you get the transmission? How do you send them?"

"There's an antenna attached to them. I can take them ...that is...I can take the camera and the screens, practically anywhere, like a wireless phone. These satelite places, these *hammering* places, that SC calls them, have a connection to stationary satelites in orbit. I actually have two cameras. One is in the kitchen. That's where the *kaffee klatsches* take place... It's usually more open to discussion, or, as someone suggested, it's more like the *speakers' corner* at Hyde Park, in London, where anyone can get on a soapbox and spout off for a while... until people stop listening. Here...they can tune out, turn off, drop in somewhere else. They can see who else is *hammering*."

By Jove, this is a breakthrough, ha, ha, ho, ho, ha who...

"Now dear, let's use our energy to get the motor car out of the mud."

Let's, but we will need the strength of our whistler. Hey, what say, Aiden?

"Let's go."

The troupe of hardy souls finally ended up in on the marsh, pushing, pulling, cursing and eventually extracting the car from the previous night's ooze and succeeded in getting it on the roadway to the cottage.

"You know dear, I believe we should motor on and let these young people continue with their visit and their videos and their *hammering* and God knows what else."

Yes, yes, it's been a very interesting ride, ho, ho. I've enjoyed it immensely.

"Well then, let us motor off and let these children be,"

The doors closed, the engine revved, the sand and pebbles flew. They were off in a cloud of dust and a hearty *hi, ho, hi, ho, hoo, hoo, hee, hee.*

"Where did you find those two?" Aiden asked Leylani

"You know, I never even asked where they're from."

"Maybe they just travel around," Jules added, "And find people to add to their little adventures."

"What a life."

"Actually, Jules, it's not much different from the kind of life Annie and I were living when I met her...way back when. Whenever something was happening, kind of like the satelite connections, we actually just ran into each other at one party after another...

"Or one protest after another."

"Right, we would just drive and pick someone up, or go to a pub, open our ears and eyes and off we went to another...Remember Lord Sexton and how we just happened in on his revitalized arts and crafts movement."

"You ended up staying on the estate for a while. I still have one of your hilltop breasts. Aiden was doing ceramic sculptures of breasts."

"Yes, well..."

"You were really into breasts, I mean, Jules, he made hills out of breasts with small people holding on, nursing or climbing on -- what a fetish."

"It was ages ago, Jules, we were lovers then and have been friends ever since. We just don't see each other very often anymore."

"Well, it looks like you two may have some catching up to do. I'd like to explore the area -- take a walk around. It just feels so old here."

He stepped into the softness of the surrounding land, spongy from the rain and the nearness to the sea. He felt like he could sink into the land here, go a foot down, feel, not only the earth, the marsh, the loam, but, in the sinking, feel it's history.

Imagine, he thought, *I am standing or sinking into the ages here, meeting those who have walked here, lived here and died here, to be ground into the soil, the earth, again, over and over and over…God, it's been an incredible journey since I left home, Leylani is a rather strange and, I must say, alluring woman…She sent me and a lot of other people into another world with her song last night, then there was SC and Alfred in his medieval castle with his poetic anthem for the world and then the tapestry…Now I'm the King of Terra Grandeur, that is ironic, my, so-called, royal past is following me around and I end up being a King on the ruins of another past; a past, Leylani, effortlessly created, without my knowing -- what a story, the festival of songs, the minstrel Knight and the tragic irony of Nicholas. I'm sinking into it; into this history…it's almost like I was there, I had lived it…I started out, wanting to do Shakespeare on the edge…it almost feels like I'm living into a creation of his…Is he still a part of this? Can I bring him into the present, into this simultaneous world, can I get him hammering…that's it, I think, that would be a great outlet for his plays, at least excerpts of them, on the edge? yes, at least the medium certainly is, now, it just needs the right kind of hammering…maybe I could get Leylani interested in being in the stories, not just creating them, or…*

He was reeling with ideas when he turned back towards the cottage. As he surveyed the horizon, he wondered about the other indicators on the land that would represent this mythological *nose of the dog.* It seemed impossible to tell -- there were outgrowths of rocks here and there and small hills in the cottage area but putting them together, you would have to be above them…

Why not, he thought, *Let's fly. I want to see these connections for myself."*

When he was back, he told them of his desire to see the country from the air, make the connections himself, see this *dog* from the air.

"Do you want to come?"

"I'd love to, I've never really seen them from above," Leylani spouted, "Let's do it! When? Where can we hire a plane, Aiden?"

"Actually they have hot air balloons about five miles or so north of the village. Occasionally I'll see one floating over."

"Hot air balloons, *By Jove,* as our friend would say."

115

"That'll do it," Leylani said and was already off the ground and beginning to float to the door.

"I'll pass," Aiden said, "but you two go for it. I've got to work on the foundation here -- I've let it go too long. The cottage is sinking on the west side -- the rain has been relentless. I'm sinking. See the cracks on the ceiling."

"All right."

"You can use my car."

"OK, let's go for it." She grabbed Jules and they were off.

Path Seventeen

White Mushrooms

"Ben, I'm a little anxious, what do I say? I mean...I don't know them. Geez, this is crazy, I don't wanna do this..."

"Come on, Twing, you'll do fine," Betsy tried to reassure him. "You're a California boy."

"They are probably as anxious as you are," Big Ben added. "Remember, this was as much of a shock to your father as it was to you."

"My father," he repeated and sang to himself, *oh, oh, my father, mm mm ma mmm mmm...*

"There they are," Big Ben shouted as he pointed to a silver Mercedes. *Tiger, Tiger.*

"Ben, it is good to see you and this...This is remarkable...This must be Twing. He even has the same birthmark. Remarkable, it is like seeing Twangly. How are you?"

"I'm OK. I...This is all pretty new to me."

"And you must be Betsy?"

"Yes, well..."

"Ben, she looks like a fine lady, but I fear you have come at a very bad time, I am afraid..."

"Afraid? Afraid of what?" Ben asked.

"I am afraid I have bad news."

"Bad news? What?"

"Twing, your father has had a stroke. It was just too much, these last two weeks. We tried to calm him down but it went on and on with your mother and then Twangly left after a big fight. Your father is not one to let things go."

"How bad is he?" Twing asked.

"He is at home. They have moved much equipment in. He has been unconscious, in a coma, they said, and then he woke up speaking in the old language."

"Old language?"

"Yes, anyway, that is what Euphrates thinks."

"Can we see him?"

"I think we should talk to the doctor first."

There was a palpable quiet in the car as Tiger drove them back to the estate of Twangly's upbringing. Twing and Betsy were enthralled but now held back their enthusiasm for the English countryside. Now it had taken on a melancholic tone and yet Twing, in an almost vacant gaze out of the window, could not help saying to himself, "So green, *wow*, it must rain a lot, so green...greenfields...*greensleeves is my delight, greensleeves is my heart of gold...aww but my lay a dee greensleeves. Alas, my love, I have longed for you, I miss you too, Angelina, if you could see these fields, if you could see them now*...a sweet memory merged with the green meandering fields until he thought he heard her voice -- Angelina...the daughter of Mariah -- whose farm he had worked on and where they had met -- Angelina....he could hear her voice...

I see them, Twing. I want to run over them, through them, come on, and she took his hand.

Hey, Angel, Angel, wow, OK, let's go...running, jumping, running through verdant fields, falling, just letting themselves fall into the grass, laughing, feeling the grass, seeing the round, white mounds of mushrooms around them, their hands touching the soft, spongy roundness of white mushrooms, ready to be plucked from the garden.

"Are these poisonous?" Twing asked, gently following the outline of Angelina's fingers around one.

"No, I don't think so. They're field mushrooms, like we get in Washington after a rain. Momma made great soup from them. You can eat them raw."

She picked one up, wiped it and took a bite. "Here," she held it in front of him.

He touched her lightly, pulling her hand towards him. The aroma of mushroom and earth, the closeness of her fingers, the touch of her hand…He bit into the mushroom, touching her finger tips. It was all too much for him, his head was swimming around her, he was off the ground, floating around her, she, around him, grass and green and sky and blue were one, they floated to the entrance of the woods, through the encircling fingers of oak trees.

Come in, pass through the ten ticles of time, and the dimensions of ree al i teeeee…hah, hah, hah, hah, hah, hah, hah have a noth er ap pull my dear Adam, "a damn," you say I say we say we all sway in this dim en sion my dear Angels from the heavenly hosts…hosts…hosts…

"Twing, where are *weeeeeeeeeeeee…*" "We are *heeeeeeeeeeeeeere*…Don't let goooooooooooo…"

Their sounds did not stop but echoed and continued. Where ever they were, the long *eees* and *ooos* and *uuus* did not stop, where ever they were, the sounds continued to float in and around them, until they, too, were floating in and out of radiant life, transparent and pulsing with light, trees glowed, poppies bloomed and closed and bloomed, the ground was not ground but shimmering mist, they touched not ground but floated into and through and over…holding hands they softly settled in the vermilion mist while light forms grew around them, colors streaming in through openings all around them, they settled into the vermilion mist and gazed outward, outward until sleep took them into a leaf-covered, root-covered cavern inside the earth.

After a lifetime, someone called, breaking the silence, *Twing, Twingly, where are you?*

His ears heard the faint sound of a far away voice. His eyes opened into darkness, yet, not darkness, for in front of him, seemingly suspended in midair was a face with a golden halo, like a vision out of the ages. Before him was a light; a golden, radiating light…He felt like it was coming into him. *Where was he? Where was Angelina? What was he doing here?*

Slowly, a raspy, mostly hollow, almost hallowed, voice drifted through the light. *Twing? Did I hear Twing? Twingly? Is that you?*

This time he clearly heard it, sat up and reached out for the radiant face. In his a maze ment, the face came to him and spoke with an echoing sound that seemed to echo not just between hills or mountains but between…the present and times gone by.

Twing, I have been waiting for you.

"What! Where? Who are you? How do you know my name?"

I have been waiting for you.

"What are you talking about? Let me out of this. Please, where is Angelina?"

She brought you here.

"Yes, but, what do you mean here? Where is here?"

Back to the earth, the roots of your past. Look around you. This was your home. This is your story buried over and over again. Take a look at your humble home, simple, yet there is a purpose behind it.

Twing got up, slowly walked over to the hearth where the smoldering remains of a fire threw shadows around the room. For a moment he thought he saw the shadow of a bent-over, bearded old man. He was talking. He had been talking all along.

What was this radiance? Who is this? Twing wondered.

Put another log on, for we must continue what was begun eons ago, the shadowed-face said. *Then sit and pour yourself a drink of mead, from my own honey. The story I want to tell you has much yearning in it and it has not yet been resolved.*

"But, who are you?"

That, you will find out in due time, but for now, drink and break some bread, for that, too, comes from my oven, you see, I learned the art of baking when I was younger than you. I came here, into this place, in the latter part of my life, after much traveling and searching. Let me begin with the time I rode over the steppes of the eastern lands. Next to me was a woman, a young woman then, whose hair was the color of flax and it flowed like rivulets behind her, whose laughter could touch the sky. We rode like the wind. We were in the very spring time of our lives and yet we had both known the pain of loss and senseless brutality. She wanted to ride by my side. I wrote songs for her; songs I still remember...

I sing a song of love for you, sweet Flaxen,
Born in the ashes of the night.
You are my dawn and you clothe me in sunlight,
I will be yours where ever we are, where ever we ride.

She fills my heart here and now, as if it were yesterday. He let his melancholic reverie fill the corners of the room.

With the strings of a lute
I want to play for you
the longing of my heart.

Twing's eyes closed and he saw Angelina floating in the vermilion mist, reaching out to him, but the voice of the shadowedface brought him back to the root-covered room...

We were traveling with a Knight to his home in Silesia. I had saved his life with a golden shield that I had found in the ashes of a church, I had saved his life and in gratitude he was going to give us, Flaxen and me, a forested land upon which we could build a home. But before we reached the land of his forefathers I woke from this youthful adventure. My first and only love became a memory that I pursued....that I pursued for many years. It was her fingertip touch on my lips -- Ssssshhhh, she said -- that kept me alive through a terrible ordeal, the memory of her touch lightened the heavy darkness I came to find myself in. By some strange miracle I carried this golden shield back with me. It had the most radiant face painted on it surrounded by a golden halo. It was like looking into the face of God.

"Yes, yes!" Twing added. "I've seen such a face, right here, right..."

But its radiance did not save me from the world I came back to. It was as if I was being tested, and this radiant face was taken away from me by the very people I showed it too, they felt I had stolen something and did not or could not see the transcendence in it, they saw that it was missing an eye, a gem of starlight and they thought I had taken it. I was put in darkness, in the lowest dungeon, where its radiance became a memory, an inner glowing...

Twing, where are you?

When my door was opened again, great upheavals had occurred, the land was filled with agony, a great sickness, a plaque, the wrath of God, had spread throughout the countryside, villages had emptied of the living. I went deep into the forest and lived a solitary life for many years...

Twing?

They are calling you. We don't have much time. I lived with the memory of that radiant face and I began to see it in the people I met. Over the years some were changed by our meeting and they came and brought their children, in whom I saw a radiance shining even stronger, some of the children stayed with me and helped take care of the garden and the bees, just around here, around here, where it has all overgrown with the years, with the centuries.

Twing leeee...Betsy's voice could be heard through the mist.

*Please, here...Take this...*The shadowed-face with the bent over body held out a hand, growing fainter, *Take this...*

Twing opened his hand...In it was a worn, crumbling leather pouch. He put it in his pocket just as everything turned dark around him. He held up his hands that were now pushing upward, outward, all around him, the earth seemed to give here and there but his sight was now on an opening above him. He had fallen into a cave or a cavern, no, it had straight walls, he felt upward, there were huge roots and logs intertwined across the ceiling. As his eyes adjusted more and more, he saw the interior of a room with caved in walls -- even the remains of a table or a bench of rotted wood. He searched around, feeling his way...

"Twing?" Ben's voice resounded in the cave-like room.

"I'm here...here...down here," he yelled back.

The rustle of leaves, the hand and another face over the opening let him realize he had been found.

"Are you all right?" Ben asked.

"Yes, strangely, yes, no broken bones, I think I've fallen into an old house or cavern, a place that someone lived in."

122

"Let me help you out."

Twing grabbed Ben's hand and was soon up and out of the cavern he had fallen into.

"We must get going. I have been looking for you for almost an hour. Tiger is beside himself. What happened to you?"

"I'm not sure. I simply walked a little way, away from the car, to relieve myself when I seemed to have gotten sleepy, very sleepy. There was an aroma and I was thinking about someone and before I knew it I heard your voice calling me. I'm not really sure what happened except that I must have fallen into that *whole* and maybe gotten knocked out."

"That is most likely what happened. You could have broken a leg. Let's get back."

"We have to mark this spot. I'd like to come back here. Let's cover over the opening and put a marker nearby. Here, this rock should do it." He rolled it near the entrance. "Look at this...This rock has something carved in it. It looks like a dog, a stylized dog -- or a wolf?"

Path Eighteen

Exiled Estate

Twing told his story to Tiger and Betsy, leaving out the details of the hide away he had fallen into, or, as he almost said out loud -- *the time away*. Now they were back at the car, where an agitated Tiger soon had them driving along the Thames again, on their way to the estate of the father he had never known. With the river flowing to the right of them, and before he could think about what had happened, they turned into a lane with a high mosscovered brick wall to their left that finally came to a wrought iron gate. Tiger stopped the car and pushed buttons on his remote. The wrought iron gate opened. They drove through and under a canopy of ivy-twined trees. They drove slowly, until the sky opened to the resplendent glory of an Edwardian mansion complete with wide stairs leading to a grand entrance.

"This is where Twangly was brought up, Master Twing," Tiger informed him.

Twing and Betsy were wide-eyed. "Twing," she said. "This is your fathers? This is incredible."

Big Ben hesitated, but added, "You should have seen the palace he came from -- centuries of power and wealth were in that palace -- centuries of power and wealth were overrun in a few months. We were able to take a few crates and boxes when we evacuated. Twing, you have a ring that was part of the King's ageold jewelry."

Twing lifted his right hand as a reaction to the word *ring* and his memories came back to him -- his mother, his adopted mother, dropping him off at the San Jose airport and giving him a pouch that ended up containing the ring that was now on his finger. The ring had an unusual property that allowed it to emit a pulse from the black stone in the design, a design in the form of a peacock, made up of the smallest of rare gems. His head filled with the sound of that land slide at Blue Lake in the Cascades. He could still hear Mariah's voice screaming out, *Run, run, it's a rock slide!* He and Mariah and Jim ran, but Jim could not keep up and was killed by a large rock. Two radicals also died on that mountain that day. Their tombstones were 30 feet high. He could still hear the monstrous rumbling of the rocks...

"Twing, come, come...Where are you?" Betsy nudged him.

He woke up from his memories and stepped out of the car, only to find several people around him, gaping in astonishment.

"Twing, this is Euphrates and this is Clara, Twangly's nanny, who has been with the family ever since we arrived in England," Tiger said. He continued to introduce the household that had helped bring up Twangly -- none of them knowing he had had a twin brother, who grew up in a very different world, who had been sent away for adoption shortly after he had breathed his first breath, who was now standing in front of them.

They took his bag and Betsy's bags and hugged Ben and they all started up the long stairs, one step at a time, one step, slowly, with anticipation, for at the top of the stairs, in all her regal beauty stood a woman, strangely anxious, not knowing, not knowing what or how to act. In her heart of hearts this was her child, yet, also her pain, the pain caused by her abandonment, which now welled up and permeated her emotions. Only her longtime regal habits kept her from breaking down as she stood there waiting for him, this childboyman. The son, she had not seen; the son, now, coming up the stairs. The same stairs she had walked up and down on, on which she had not giving a thought to the child she had given up. In fact, she had denied that very child all the years he was growing up somewhere else, until Ben called, not too long ago. It was then that she talked to Twing and heard a voice that was new to her; a voice from another world, that sounded as hesitant as hers.

"Hello, Twingly."

"Hello."

They looked at each other, with eyes not knowing what to say and mouths not knowing which way to turn. Slowly, with a deeper knowing, they held open their arms and lightly held each other. He kissed her cheek and she, his. She stepped back to look at him, her long unknown child from her womb and from a father who now lay dying; barely living. *It was her son,* she thought, *so much like Twangly, it was as if Twangly was standing here, but now, it was her long-lost son who was saying hello and Twangly had left…*

"Twingly, your father was not sure about seeing you. It was a shock to all of us."

"Nadjia," a voice came from the opening door. "Nadjia…he has become conscious again. He is asking for Twangly."

"Twingly, do you go by Twingly or Twing?" she asked awkwardly, "And how did you ever get that name?"

"Well, my mother, err, my adopted mother, thought an unusual name would remind her of my unusual origins that she didn't know about, but imagined. She was right about the unusual origins, but the name has been…"

"Nadjia, we should see him," the Doctor advised.

"Yes, Twingly, this is Doctor Highshe."

He looked at him and recognized the very man who had left an envelope on his table at the Cafe Cantata in Boulder Creek, California a lifetime ago, or at least, it seemed that way. So much had changed. Now, here was the very man who had started this wild odyssey.

"Will you go to see him?" She entreated him. "But, remember, he may not recognize you, we must keep him calm."

127

They walked into a domed entrance hall, with skylight light concentrated on the floor. Right where they were standing, the light shone on Twing, momentarily blinding him. Doctor Highshe took him by the arm and they followed Nadjia up a winding staircase, up, up...Until she turned down a hallway, lined with pictures of old ruins; of ziggurats and toppled columns and the relief designs of peacocks. She knocked on a door and waited. A man answered, whom Twing also recognized. It was the doctor's companion.

"Twingly, this is Camec. He is taking care of your father, along with Doctor Highshe. Can we see him?"

"Yes, please, take care to go quietly and maybe one at a time."

The door to the inner bedroom was opened. There, in the bed, with an intravenous connection and with monitoring equipment around him, lay a gray-haired, fine-boned man with glassy eyes.

Twing felt the man's eyes searching for him.

"Twingly, that is your father," she whispered.

"Twangly," came a rasping, hardly audible voice, "Twangly, I want to see you. Come closer."

"Go to him," his mother whispered, "Let him think you are Twangly."

Twing wasn't sure what to think, as he walked to his bedside.

The man, his father, took his hand, "Twangly, I have seen too much, my eyes are gone, do not leave me, you are, you are, I want to give you, I want to give you, your brother, your bro..." His voice trailed off and he seemed to go to sleep, yet his eyes were open and his grip was tight around his hand.

Gently, Twing unfolded his fingers, all the while looking at his face, which was surrounded by the most beautiful garden crocheted onto his bedspread -- a garden of exotic plants with two peacocks spreading their tails. But, now, it was the man of royal bearing that he saw, not the means of life support, not even the garden. Now, he could see himself in the face, in the eyes, in front of him. Now, for the first time, the reality of who he was, where he had come from engulfed him. He felt weak.

128

His knees buckled. He needed to sit down. The Doctor noticed his sway and brought him a chair. A King's son had returned. He sat there, for what seemed like a long time, just thinking of this man in front of him and the world *he* was now a part of.

"You must be hungry," his mother's voice charged the stillness. "I'll go and ask Euphrates to set some dinner for you. Let Tiger show you to your room. Please, Tiger, show Twingly his California room -- In your honor, Twingly."

Riding the Wave

Tiger picked up his bag but Twing would have none of that. He took it from Tiger, "I can carry that, thanks anyway,"

A door opened to a blue painted room, with a sea mural on one wall, of a gray whale bleaching and a surfer catching a 20 foot wave. "*Wow*, I...look...I'm not sure what to think. This is quite a set up."

"Your room, Master Twingly."

"You can call me Twing, and none of that *Master* stuff, thanks."

"Very well, Twing."

"Tiger, I did want to ask you about the...my father, actually about Twangly?" Do you have any idea where he is?"

"We, or at least I, have not heard from him since he left over a week ago. I know his mother is worried about him. We all are."

"Do you think he's in trouble? I mean, could he have gotten kidnapped or...?"

"She has not gone to the police. They are a very private family and do not want to draw any attention to themselves."
"Wh at about the revolutionary radicals? I mean, what do you think? You know what happened to us in Washington, near Blue Lake."

"Ben told me about..."

His answer was cut short by a knock and the door opening wide. Doctor Highshe stepped in and with some urging said, "Twing, I must talk to you, please -- in private, if possible."

"Sure, would you excuse us, Tiger?"

With an agitated glance at the doctor, Tiger left the room. Doctor Highshe closed the door and motioned Twing to sit down. "Twing, your father is dying. He may not wake up from this latest lapse. I fear for the worst, but if he does wake up, I think it is imperative that he sees both you and Twangly. He needs to, if it is still possible, to give you both his blessing. It is an important and ancient tradition for the next heir, but I believe, under the circumstances, it is important that both of you receive a blessing, it would be a reconciling of historic importance."

Twing let him talk while his mind went in search of Twangly, remembering the wild ride they had, in Winthrop, Washington, on the 4th of July, remembering the confusion of Sheriff O'Malley, Twing, Twang. He almost felt like allowing himself a smile but the grave voice of Doctor Highshe brought him back.

"There was a soothsayer, Twing, an old seer, which our traditions still give some recognition to, who told Camec that a reconciliation could occur and intimated that the power of the throne would return. I do not think it can happen without Twangly and your father's blessing. Your mother..." he hesitated.

"What about my mother?"

"I am not sure, but I do not think she…"

"She what?"

"I will be frank with you. When I saw you in California, I gave you the letter that, in a way, changed the direction of everyone's expectations. I fear your mother is not ready to accept the future as it is going: the reality she has to face. She was not happy with the fact that you were made aware of your birth and that you found your brother"

"What does she think?"

"I think she fears you will take your place here, *and this is just my opinion, even though I am not alone in this,* she fears that you

130

might take over the estate, just when she was ready to grasp it. You see…You grew up without knowing anything of your lost past. She lived with it all these years, along with a haunting reminder of a lost child. By denying you, Twangly became her special child with whom she hoped she could share the lost throne with or at least the estate."

"I'm not here to take anything, what do you suggest I do?"

"You, *we*, must find Twangly before his, *your*, father dies, if possible, and if both of you could still get a blessing from him, you could be reconciled and your mother may accept…"

"What if that doesn't happen?"

"I fear for you. There is still a possibility of radical extremism. I still don't know how those two radicals found out that Twangly had left England; left the estate, *and* that he went to Masama in Washington State, unless…"

"Unless, what?"

"Unless there is someone in this household who has or still has a connection to the revolutionary regime."

"*Come on???* Look! I'm not crazy about this. I can leave."

"I don't think you can deny your past any longer."

"Then, I'll find Twangly. He was brought up in this household. He is used to this. We have to find him. Where should we start?"

"Ben has known Twangly all these years, or, at least, known where he has been. There is no place Twangly has been that Ben doesn't know about. It is just too bad that he does not have his ring any more. Ben, however, could get you started. He could take you around, show you where Twangly grew up, but time may be running out. You should go as quickly as possible."

"Then let's go. I'll talk to Ben. Betsy will want to go. When do we start?"

"We can talk to them after dinner. We can take a walk on the grounds."

He glanced at the surfer under a 20 foot wave, remembering his own exhilaration in the Pacific, off Santa Cruz, and finally just fell into a beanbag chair.

"Yea, *wow*, this is wild."

131

Euphrates

"Please, sit down Twing. You too, Betsy. I hope you will like this dish. It's an old recipe, unless you are vegetarian. Twing, I have heard about Californians. Everyone is a vegetarian and does yoga, is that right?"

"I don't think so," Twing answered. "1 was pretty much brought up on hamburger."

"And I serve mostly *good-ole* American food at my cafe. But then, I'm in Washington, California has a variety of reputations that we get caught up in…"

"But I think you took the espresso thing to the *nth* degree," Twing pointed out.

"Well, this is a lamb dish," Euphrates continued, "We are able to get all the spices I was used to cooking with, in London, now. Years ago it was hard to…"

"Euphrates," Twing interrupted her and smiled. "Ben told us about you on our way here. He said you were a great cook, but isn't there also a river by that name. You weren't by chance…"

"Yes, I was named after it, it is as old as time, it is still flowing, I have seen it, in its power, when it flooded the land. This river will flow forever."

"That's why they still sing about Babylon," Twing interjected.

"What do you mean?"

He walked close to her and sang softly into her ear,

"By the river of Babylon,
bah, da dah da dah
by the river of Babylon
that's where I will go.

"Yes, yes, I would like to go back," her voice drifted off and Twing's voice echoed in her reverie,

By the river of Babylon
Bah, da dah da dah
by the river of Babylon
that's where I will go…

"But now it's time to eat."

They sat, in quiet, with the river, the age-old, forever river flowing through them, bringing them together,

By the river of Babylon
bah da dah da dah

Twing could not stop the insistent words and melody, it seemed like he was a part of it, this great flowing river, which had flooded the ancient cities, including the city of Urum, the birthplace of his ring. It had flooded the city of Babylon, flooded the empires that grew and reigned and fell and turned to sand one after the other, like legendary Ozymandis.

By the river of Babylon
where I was born
By the river of Babylon
where I will die

"Twing, you're not eating," Euphrates interjected.

"Oh, ah, yea…It's great, Euphrates, I was just thinking about you."

"Now, now, I'm sure you have many other things to think about."

Ben interrupted, "Actually, I want to take Twing and Betsy on a walk around the estate after dinner. But where is Nadjia? Is she not joining us?"

"She is not feeling well," Tiger said, "And has retired for the evening. She said she would see you in the morning, Twing."

Path Nineteen

Orion

"What about a parachute," Jules suddenly remembered.

"A parachute?" the pilot responded in an incredulous tone. "We don't supply them with our balloons. We are going to be floating, youngsters. We go up with the hot air and come down when it's cool."

"Jules, come on…We're going to go up."

"If you are concerned, we've not lost a balloon in the all the years I've been here, except…"

"Except," they both spoke at once.

"Well, it was before my time, nothing to speak of."

"Oh, Jules, he's trying to scare us. Aren't you?"

A slight smile rose on his face but it still didn't calm their questioning eyes or quell their anticipated excitement or their increasing heartbeats. Like lovers on a long awaited rendezvous, they were ready to fly. Unfortunately, this time, they were with a chaperone, or maybe fortunately, for it was uncharted sky they were going into, at least for them. The chaperone seemed like he had a quirky confidence, serious one minute and in the next, a slight smile would come back to make them wonder. The smile seemed all the more slight because it was under a bushy, walrus mustache that was under a reddish nose that was under a green beret that was all above a woolly, black, turtleneck sweater.

"*In you go,*" he ordered in a strong brogue.

Everything was on the ground. The whole balloon, ropes and all, was stretched out on the ground, and they, they maneuvered themselves around the ropes and into a very large basket, a lifeless possibility they could only imagine. The woolly sweater busied himself with the lighting of the flame as he had done numerous times before...But he couldn't help but notice his young passengers or, at least, give them a thought that brought back his own youth and a love he once had, when he was known as Gerard...when love was young, as young as...

His thoughts echoed in his emotional past. Leylani and Jules were near him -- next to him. He could even smell their growing love. He felt a strange contentment and joy in their joy. It was a change in him. *Maybe, I've crossed a path,* he thought, *Maybe, it will last, I hope it will last.*

"We don't know your name," Leylani suddenly spoke as she noticed him getting ready, "We're going into the blue firmament and we don't know our pilot's name."

"Today, I am Orion -- the hunter. And this is your chariot to the moon."

They smiled, even chuckled, and waited as the flame grew, as the warmth grew hotter, as the balloon began to fill with the heated air. Finally, they were in the destined basket, or *cage*, as Jules thought, surrounded by the ropes of flotation. Their guide untied the connection to the ground, the basket was still, Leylani held onto Jules, Jules put his arm around her. For a moment both were lost in anticipation. The basket began to creak, shake, wobble and roll right off the ground into a buoyancy and lightness that was bearable. A lightness of being that was more than bearable, as they rose higher, five, six, ten, fifteen feet... Instead of looking up, Leylani looked down and gasped, "Jules, Jules, look, everything is becoming smaller, we're growing..."

"It is like King Lear looking down," he responded and continued in his own thoughts. *Perchance to see things...To see the world getting smaller.* He remembered his favorite teacher, the last year at Eton, telling him that Shakespeare's time was a time of personal points of view rearranging the world as one pair of eyes saw it. It was a change in consciousness; a change from the all encompassing wholeness that people lived in for centuries and centuries. He remembered his teacher holding up an old, wooden shield, meticulously painted, with a golden halo surrounding a face, a beautiful face, with a building and landscape in the background. An *ikon* he called it, representing a wholeness, a conscious wholeness. The recognizable images in it all seemed to be on the same plane, in a circular setting of reds, blues and yellows. But it was the gold of the golden halo that he remembered more than anything else -- it seemed to glow with an inner light.

"But how does it maneuver? How are we, how can we float over to the cottage?" Leylani asked.

"With a bit of luck and the invisible hand of Orion, as well as the maneuvering of the flame and the wind currents, we can try to go in that direction."

"Look, Jules," she said, "We are in the house of the gods, this must be the way they feel, looking down on us mere mortals, deciding when to intervene, when to let us live out…"

Jules let her carry on. He was getting used to her excited rantings. He remembered the last time she began a wild tale -- they were looking down from the ruins of Terra Grandeur. Right now, he was enthralled in this view, looking for connections, looking for markings, hills, trees, tors, streams, large stones…

"Leylani, is that the cottage?"

"Yes, yes, It's Aiden's cottage."

"Do you see any other markings on the ground that would mirror the stars, the constellations? That's what we are trying to do, isn't it, mirror the stars that make up the big dog. You know, it's supposed to be the hunting dog…" he hesitated, "of Orion."

They found themselves looking over at their guide and wondering what a coincidence it was? He had called himself Orion. Was it his touch of humor or what…?

"Let's take a look at our star map. There. Look. There's the big dog, and there's Sirius, the brightest star in that constellation, and there, there's the nose star? There are two stars down it's back to the tail, one on the front leg and one for its hind legs."

"Hold it up against the sky…They should be turned like this."

"No, it's upside down. Hold it like this."

"But now I can't see them."

"OK, hold it, let's…"

Their fumbling and fooling around brought a laugh from the woolly sweater, "Why don't you let Orion take a look. After all, I reside in those parts."

He took the star map, flipped it over and said, "Now, everything is backwards -- just imagine it backwards -- on the ground. Here is Sirius…It's on the collar -- other stars are also reversed."

"Look, there's the cottage and there's a larger hill, that could be Sirius"

"All right, do you see any other signs for the back, the tail? The hind legs are back that way.

"There's a hill and another and where the last star of the tail should be, there is a stream."

"It looks more like a tail with the stream than a star."

"That's it. It is a tail. Then, where are the legs?"

They were getting excited now, with Orion leading them on this terra-cosmic hunt.

"Legs should be on the opposite side, towards the West, towards the sea."

"See that outcrop of rock, look left, there's another and another and further out another, it's possible."

"Can we go higher?"

"It looks like there's a mound around one of them, covered over.

"Look, Jules, there's a path, you can just barely see a path between them, it looks like paths between all of them."

"The paths go in and out and around the rocks…It's, it could be a giant…it could be an incredibly huge maze…

"The wind is picking up," Orion interrupted, and made them realize they were still floating *and* being directed by the hands of unseen forces… or by the Gods…

Path Twenty

Secret Things

Maybe it was jet lag or the after affects of a meadow's magic but, like a wipeout in the surf, Twing crashed in exhaustion and asked to be excused. Ben accompanied him to his room and, again, emphasized the importance of searching for Twangly.

"I agree," answered Twing. "Let's go after breakfast. Please talk to Betsy tonight. We're going to need all the help we can get. If anyone knows where he's at, it's you, Ben. He grew up with you."

"Yes, I have already started to map out the possible directions and places. We can look at that and go to the most obvious places first. Also, we should check with his friend Rushdie. He may have made contact by now, but..."

"What is it?"

"Let us detail our plans when we are in the car."

"OK," Twing responded and went into his California room and plopped onto the bed. He was too tired to go back on the surfboard, too tired to undress, too tired to sleep. He lay there wondering about his life and the turns it had taken. Not too far from him was his father -- dying -- he couldn't believe it -- *dying* -- He had not even known him. He did not know what to think. His emotions ebbed and flowed like the waves on his wall. He thought of Angelina and the wild run in the meadow, *If she were here, if only she were here, or if I were there, man, my life would be so much easier, yea, but think of it, I met her because I was looking for Twangly, so one thing leads to another, and one connection makes another and we end up going around in circles or going down some road for reasons I don't know, with an outcome I don't know, if she were here...if she were here...*

I'm just a lonely boy, lonely and blue
I'm just a lonely boy, waiting for you,

He sang to himself,

What am I doing here, lonely and blue
Da dah da da da dah, thinking of you.

The thoughts of her lifted him up and he even allowed a smile to come on his face, *She fed me a mushroom, a field mushroom, she said her mother makes soup with them, wow, where did we go...*

Remembering the bent up, bearded man and his strange story, he put his hand in his pocket and pulled out a crumbling leather pouch, *Can't be,* he thought, but here in his hand, in his open hand was a very old, crumbling, leather pouch.

This is unreal, he thought.

He didn't want to touch it for fear it would crumble into nothing, but his fingers felt it. He pulled it open. He let the contents fall on his bed. In the quiet of his room he felt like he had come across a long, lost treasure. *Wow, this has got to be the way explorers feel or archeologists when they find something.*

As he looked at the objects, he noticed the ring on his finger. He had been given the ring by his mother, his adopted mother. This, he had realized later, was older than most artifacts in the world, it was from the city of Urum. *It was at least 5000 years old* he thought. *It was from his father's palace jewels; his connection to a very old past. Now, he had it in front of him.*

On his bed were the contents of the old leather pouch -- things that came from an old, bent-over, bearded man...*No, I was dreaming. It all just happened to be in the cavern I fell into. I found it there…I must have.* He convinced himself as he picked up a flat, round piece of metal about one and one-half inches across. It was greenish, like old copper. He turned it over and rubbed the patina. He could see lines incised in it. They were in circles. It looked like a map or a maze with the symbol of an animal in the middle.

"*Wait a minute!*" he gasped loudly and jumped up. *This is like the carving on the rock, the rock I moved in front of that hideout. What is it? A dog? A wolf? and…it's in the middle of this labyrinth, this maze-like design…*

He looked beyond the metal in his hand and picked up a small, bleached bone, carved with letters -- old letters. He could barely make out the carved inscriptions. It looked like an N, a vertical line, a curved line, two lines, a circle, a line, more lines and then, too obscure, too worn. *Some kind of name*, he thought, *Maybe N, I,* but his eyes were closing, closing to the mysteries in his hands and he was swept away by the waves around him, this time the waves of sleep.

Morning came too early. His body was still on west coast time but the commotion outside his door was already noticeable. He could hear voices, "Shall we wake him?"

"No, he needs his sleep."

Twing turned over and realized he had fallen asleep with the artifacts around him, the metal coin with the labyrinth, three bones and finally a button, probably made from a bone, with a plume symbol burned into it. He put them in the pouch and the pouch into one of the pockets of his backpack. Finally, he took off his clothes to shower in a bathroom the size of his bedroom in Boulder Creek. As he was dressing, someone ventured a knock on his door.

"Master Twing?"

"Yes."

"It's Euphrates…Will you be joining us for breakfast?"

"Yes, I will be down. Give me fifteen minutes."

"Good morrrning, everyone." Trying to sound upbeat and awake and with a touch of old Jim Bridger, the mountain man of the Cascades. Twing sat down in the chair Euphrates had pulled out for him at the end of the table.

"Well, Twing, how was the royal bed?" Betsy asked.

"Actually, I felt like I was back in Santa Cruz with that ocean next to me."

"He has a wall-painting of a surfer in his room."

"And a whale."

Their morning banter gave them some relief from the tension in the house but it was short-lived and a different mood entered with Nadjia. Her *Good morning* made them apprehensive. She looked at everyone and finally said, "Twing, please, sit next to me. I want to hear about your life in America."

Twing took his coffee to the other end of the table, next to his mother.

"How is my, ah, er," he cleared his throat, "How is the King doing this morning?"

"He is still unconscious, Camec is with him. Please go and see him this morning. Maybe your presence will…"

"We want to leave this morning."

"This morning?"

"Yes, we want to try and find Twangly."

"Well, that is sudden, but I understand, I am, I…" She was on the verge of…

Twing could see her strong will, her face visibly shaking in the fight for composure. He took her hand. She recoiled, not wanting to show weakness, or…recognition…

"Is there anything I can do?" he asked.

"I must go lie down. Please, please find him."

She left the room with Tiger following her, leaving the inhabitants of the dining room in a state of wanting to help and not being able to, and inwardly, resolving to do everything they could do to put the family back together, if that was possible. They ate their breakfast in silence, letting Nadjia's loss linger. Ben finally broke the stillness by asking Euphrates to pack some lunches for them. They would leave after breakfast.

"OK, I'll just grab my backpack. I have something I want to ask you about, that is, once we get going."

"Do we know where we are going?" Betsy added.

"I have some ideas," Ben said, "We are going to pay a surprise visit to Rushdie in London, at least to his family."

They proceeded to finish their breakfast, thanked Euphrates and went to their rooms. On the way, Twing stopped at the bedroom of his father, hesitated and knocked quietly. Camec came to the door.

"Can I see him?"

"He is still unconscious. Come in."

Twing opened the inner door. Immediately, his eyes went to the bright bedspread. He followed it up, until he saw the face of his father. No sound came from him...Just the eyes seemed to entreat him. *We'll find him, father, we'll find Twangly*, he quietly vowed to the piercing eyes. He closed the door and slowly readied himself to leave, keeping that face and those longing eyes burning in his memory.

Journey

The next time Twing looked around he was standing on the steps of the mansion, across from a mermaid spewing water from her mouth, waiting for Ben to bring the car around. They packed up, settled into the leather seats and drove towards the wrought iron gate that had the outlines of two peacocks welded into them. He had not noticed these two sentries before, whose beautiful tails had let them in. Now, the iridescent, bluegreen plumes would let them out. As they drove through, he could barely hold himself back from all he wanted to tell them.

"You know, Ben, Betsy...I want to let you in on something. I'm not sure how it all happened but when you pulled me out of that hole in the ground yesterday, I was given something, actually, I must have found something there..."

"Found what?" Betsy was getting interested.

"I'm not sure *what*, for sure, but it was an old leather pouch. It's pretty old...It almost crumbled..."

"Do you have it with you?"

"Yes, it's in my back pack. I can show you. But I, also...It seemed like I dreamed about it, when I was in there. It was, as if, someone gave it to me, an old man. He didn't tell me his name. They're objects or artifacts -- a few bones. Two of them have letters carved in them."

"This is getting exciting. Twing, I remember the last time Mariah and Jim -- *God, I miss him, our mountain man, as old as the hills* -- anyway, the last time they came by the cafe in Masama, they were looking for Twangly...that seems like a long time age."

"I was also looking for him, and I was also tracking him on the global locator," Ben added.

"Deja vu, Twing."

"Yea, in some ways, but this is some other connection. I'm not sure what? There was an old coin in the pouch also, with a map on it, or I would say, a maze or a labyrinth or something like that..."

"Mazes are a part of the ancient cultures around here. I think they are from the Celtic times. The designs are very intricate," Ben added.

"Let me see, Twing?" Betsy asked, as Ben continued, "I have walked through a garden maze -- or tried to. The hedges were taller than I am. But I think, there is, also, a difference between a maze and a labyrinth. A maze has dead ends and paths that you have to retrace in order to find your way out, or go farther. A labyrinth usually has one continuous path, a long circuitous path. If you stay on it long enough, you'll reach the center and then you can take it out again."

"I've heard of the labyrinth in Chartres Cathedral, in France," Betsy said, "It's one of the most famous ones and was probably used as a meditative path, or a path of initiation."

"There's also a Greek myth with the minotaur," Twing said, as he remembered the story from his high school mythology class. This half bull-half man lives in the center of a labyrinth, or maze, mostly likely, and he destroys anyone who finds their way in, except for one, I forget his name..."

144

"Actually, it's a gruesome story," Ben interjected. "Every year the beast is sent seven boys and seven girls to eat as tribute -- until a hero comes to kill it."

"I think it was Theseus," Twing remembered.

"Yes," Ben said, "It was probably a maze-like labyrinth, because he trailed a string behind him so he could find his way out again. He did kill the beast and he did get back out and he was a hero. But if I remember right, it was a bittersweet victory for him, because, as he was returning home to his father, Theseus was supposed to change the black sail on his ship to a white one, which would have let his father know he had succeeded. But he forgot, probably in his heroic celebration, *he forgot*, and when his father saw the black sail he thought his son had perished and as a result committed suicide."

"That's a horrible ending, Ben," Betsy said.

"Yes, but these stories are supposed to tell us something about ourselves," Ben answered.

As they were talking, Twing had taken out the old pouch and taken out the contents...

As he picked up the old coin, he said, "What's interesting, is that there is a picture of a dog or a wolf in the middle of this labyrinth design, in the middle of this coin, as if it were a kind of beast or minotaur. Even more than that, and this is what is so weird, there was a rock above the entrance of the cavern with a similar design carved into it."

"What are you saying, that's where the beast lived? *Or lives?*" Betsy asked. "I don't know, why did he give it to me?"

"What do you mean?"

"I, ah, I mean...Is there some warning here? or..."

"I think the mystery to be solved concerns your brother, Twing? And right now, we don't have any leads *what so ever*."

"Well, we are going to see Rushdie's family." Ben interjected. "They live outside of London. Rushdie and Twangly became close friends the last years at Eton. They both loved the theater and were in several Shakespearean productions. Before they went to American they were in *A Midsummer Night's Dream* together. I think they were living it when you met him. It was a

145

dream they were playing out in America, in the wild Cascades instead of in an enchanted forest."

"Did you see the production?" Twing asked.

"I did see the last performance, just before they left. Twangly was great, he played Oberon." He continued to tell Twing about the world of his brother, the world his brother had played in, lived in, grown up in. He told him about the time Twangly had gotten into trouble, when he spray painted *T-Rex* on the local bookstore and almost got caught. He told him how he had watched Twangly, from a distance, always from a distance…

As Ben talked they were all looking back now, also from a distance, they were all traveling on the road back, to a past that was new to Twing and Betsy. Yet they all knew that they had radically changed since Twangly's last performance in that garden of make believe. It grew quiet in the Mercedes as they reflected on these changes, until Betsy brought them back into the present, "How about lunch. Anybody hungry?"

"That's a pretty good idea, Betsy," Twing added, "We need your kind of place, you know, local."

"They're called pubs around here, Twing." Ben said.

"OK, do you know any that Twangly might have stopped at? High school kids can go to pubs around here, right?"

"There are actually a lot of local pubs. They even brew their own brews, beers, ales, dark brews. We could get off the main road and travel on the side roads for a while. I know a few pubs. The names are what attracted me years ago: the Pig and Whistle, the Iconoclast, the Plough and the Sword. *In fact*, the Plough and the Sword is not too far from here." Suddenly he gestured with his palm hitting his forehead, *"Why didn't I think of this before?* It's in a village where Twangly was in one of these summer Shakespeare festivals. It would, actually, be a good place to start our search…"

"Well, let's do it then…We need a diversion. We don't know if Twangly is at Rushdies, anyway." Betsy said. "And besides, we're not going to find him on the thoroughfare…"

Hoo bah, hoo bah, came a honking sound from behind them. Ben pulled over to the left and let them pass.

"Man, they're in a hurry, " Twing responded and noticed an elderly man with a woman sitting next to him. "They have a classic horn on a '48' *Rolls.*"

"How do you know that car?

"Just interested. I worked on cars a lot, not necessarily Rolls. In fact, I don't think I ever saw one in Boulder Creek, but I've seen enough pictures of them.

Wellborn-on-Avon

They were now on the country road that paralleled the main road. For a few kilometers, they could still feel the buzz, the speed, of the traffic of the main thoroughfare until their road turned south and became one of those hedge-rowed country lanes that seemed to enclose them. In the distance they could see a square tower. "I believe that's it, that's the village, the village of Wellborn-on- Avon," Ben said, "That tower marks it. Usually it's a steeple that points out a village, but around here, towers seem to break the horizon. Maybe they were trying to copy the Tower of London and have someplace to put away the town drunk. That's where the pub is and, also, where they produce two or three plays in the summer. Twangly has been in a play there -- with other students."

It was a typical countryside village, still lying in the bosom of the past, surrounded by the fenced fields of history. What was once an overnight stop for the traveler, the soldier, the itinerant merchant, the theatrical troupe, the minstrel, was now the accumulation of many generations of those who stayed and those who continued to pass through, leaving their questions and their answers and their influences...Somehow, one young traveler, overwhelmed by his past, his lost brother, his dying father and his future, couldn't help but remember a song -- In the back seat of the Mercedes, from out of nowhere, one more young, searching traveler sang quietly, *do not forsake me, oh my darlin, on this our wedding day*...Singing silently, out of context, *da da duh dah da da da dah da, it's either my life or hissin*...

"Twing. Hello. Where are you?"

"I, ah, ah, er I was just thinking."

"About what?"

"Well, actually, an old song."

Betsy just shook her head and said, "You have a way about you, Twing. One song after another, no matter what you're doing. What song was it this time?"

"It was that song by Frankie Laine, from one of those 50's films, *"Do not forsake me, oh my darlin, something, something, something, it's either my life or hissin…"*

"It sounds like a moment of reckoning," Ben said.

"I suppose so."

"Maybe that's what you're thinking about."

"Yea, but where? Or what?"

"How about here?" Betsy added, wanting to bring some positive possibility into the discussion. How about here? In this seemingly quiet village of Wellborn-on-Avon.

"Let's do it," Ben said, getting caught up in her hopeful anticipation. "Remember, we are also players in this ongoing drama."

They drove slowly through a Main Street that wound its way along thatched roof cottages, some with shops, a bookstore, a tobacconist, a bakery, a park with a statue of what may have been Shakespeare. Next to that -- a pub -- with a strange sculptural work over its door. That turned out to be the Plough and the Sword, which gave Twing a clue as to what the sculpture might be about. It looked like a sword turned into a plough. An old idea resurrected time and again. This time it was over a door -- to a gathering place of words, good ale and camaraderie. Ben parked the Mercedes a few shops up from the pub.

"Did you say that Twangly spent some time here?" Betsy asked.

"Yes, he was in one of the summer productions, before his senior year. I believe it was Twelfth Night. I actually spent some time in this pub, waiting for him to finish his evening performance."

"Well, shall we spend another hour?"

"That would be appropriate. In fact, it would be a good place to start. I could ask the proprietor if he has seen him. He may not remember him but we could begin here."

As they walked, in conversation, towards the pub, Twing barely noticed an antique shop along the way, but noticed it enough to stop at the window. A number of old books were propped up in one corner. One of them, with a torn leather binding, simply said, *The Labyrinth of Terra Grandeur* in old English, with a faded, carved picture of an old castle, built on a hill, with a path around it. "Labyrinth," he thought, "the path around the hillside leading up to the castle." He thought of his coin, the picture on the coin.

"Twingly," came the voice of Betsy from the front of the pub, "We are thirsty."

He caught up with them and they settled down to an outside table in the back garden of the pub while Ben went inside.

"The Plough and the Sword," Betsy said, "That seems to describe this place. They probably had battles around here. Maybe some of the knights stayed and turned their swords into ploughs and settled here, do you think? Beautiful country…It's a bit like the peninsula in Washington. They must get a lot of rain… It's so green…"

Twing interrupted her, "Where did the sword into a plow idea come from, anyway? Do you remember?"

"It's from the Bible. In one of the books."

"Of course, the old Testament. My mother, that is my adopted mother, used to read the Bible, almost every day, she always had it open to a page, a verse…"

"How is she?" Betsy inquired, looking into his face. "She must be…how is she taking this?"

"I called her when we arrived. She's amazing. She has this sense of humor that blows me away. I mean, she said that she always wanted a son who was a little unusual, that's why she gave me my name, right, so she told me to be careful of what I wish for, that I might just get my wish."

Betsy just laughed, "Boy, did she get her wish."

Twing shook his head and with a serious look said, "I think, though, her Bible reading has helped her. She really started doing that after Dad died..."

He caught himself, "*Wow*," and just sat there for a moment, remembering where he was: seeing his real father's face in front of him.

"Twingly, are you OK?"

He started, "Yea, yea, I was just...I was..." Trying to catch his emotions, he finally said, "My mother even quoted me her favorite verse, I think it's the 121st Psalm. I've heard it enough times."

"How does it go? Do you remember it?"

"Yea, it's something like this,

I lift up mine eyes unto the hills,
where, oh, where does help come from?
My help comes from the Lord.
Both the heaven and earth he created.
He will not allow my steps to slip
and he sleeps nor slumbers not,
the holy Guardian.
He is my keeper.
He is a shadow over me.

He is a shadow over me.

He said, again, slowly, not sure of the words or, more precisely, not sure of the word *shadow*...but let it go and continued...

He will guard me,
in my leaving and coming,
from now on,
to eternity."

"It is beautiful, I mean, if that's your mother's way of handling this incredible situation, she, at least, has something to hold on to but, but, really Twing what are *you* going to…"

Ben's charged arrival, with three pints of dark brew, changed their moment of intimacy.

"Here we are, local ale. I also ordered some fish and chips."

"Thanks," Twing responded and feeling relieved to be thinking about something else. "Did you ask about Twangly?"

"Yes, but no luck. Even if he remembered him, he doesn't recall anyone with his description, coming in lately. I also called Tiger. There has been no change in your father's condition."

Path Twenty One

Nadjia's Lament

Tiger, don't leave me just yet, I am not well, I cannot bear this any longer, please...

"Nadjia, I..."

Please, forgive me, but I'm afraid, Doctor Highshe told me he is not improving, he is just staying there, not improving. I'm not sure what to do. Twangly is gone, where is he? In heaven's name why is he not here...

"Nadjia, you must prevail."

Tiger, you have been my most trusted friend. The doctor has always cared for the King, but you, with you, I have always been able to share my most intimate thoughts. The doctor opened up my past, I do not understand, he swore to me he would not reveal that past, why did he? Why? Why? Why did he bring this boy, this Twingly, back to life? Why did he bring him back into my life? Why did the doctor do this to me? He is driving the very heavens against me.

"Nadjia, Nadjia, please calm yourself." He took a step towards her, to calm her.

She fell into his arms. *I have... I was...I've brought up Twangly...I've been his mother, I tried...I tried...*

Out of the years of backed up guilt and the anxious present, an emotional trickle of sobs and moans and words gushed into the arms of Tiger. He held her, for the first time in all these years, he held her, felt her, in her pent-up outpouring he was at last, long last, with her. He had waited so long, so many years in her presence, near her, waiting, waiting for the time to change.

He will die, he thought, *And now, here, in her sobbing and crying beauty, was the Queen -- here -- a woman, like other women.*

Nadjia, he thought to himself, *I've come to love you, you were always close, yet a lifetime away, your presence alone has kept me here...all these years...*

Tiger, I'm ashamed, she stepped back, stepped back into her role of composure, holding his hands, she forced a smile and looked into his eyes, *you will stay with me...*

Nadjia, Nadjia, I will stay, by the heavens, I will stay with you, I will do whatever you ask."

Let us talk more in a while, now I must rest, please, give me your word that you will not talk of this to anyone, and let me know of any news...

Yes, yes, Nadjia," he squeezed her hands and reluctantly let her go. He stood there, letting this extraordinary moment rest with him.

"What is the wish of Allah?" he wondered, but his heart was still with her, *A*nything, he thought, *I will do anything for her.*

"Tiger, Tiger, Ben is on the phone." Euphrates called from the hallway.

"Thank you," he picked up the receiver and talked to Ben -- without telling him of his meeting with Nadjia. Ben asked about the King or any news of Twangly and told him that they would, most likely, spend the night in Wellborn-on-Avon at the Plough and the Sword and gave him the number by which he could reach them, in case there were any new developments.

Tiger hung up. His mind was still absorbed by Nadjia's sobbing, vulnerable presence. He could only think of her.

He must act! he vowed to himself. *Now. He must act!*

Path Twenty Two

Alex

"Mm, mm, good ale," Betsy raised her mug and proposed a toast, "Let's make this the beginning of your new life, and ours," smiling at Ben, "And to your brother, may he be safe and in the right place."

Ben and Twing raised their mugs and they responded with a glassy clink filled not just with ale but with expectations of good fortune. Ben had some ideas, based on his past with Twangly, which included memories of long waiting times. Those were the times he had become like a traveling student, a sponge soaking up details of his and Twangly's surroundings. He had sat at this very table the summer of Twangly's acting debut in *Twelfth Night*. At that time his eyes were still looking for any strange or unusual people that may have been a part of his revolutionary past. But more than that, he had also become interested in the history of these places, the villages, the pubs, the names of the pubs, the way the cottages and houses were kept up, the shops...

"Well, well, well, who do we have here, Ben?" A robust voice came out of the backdoor of the pub. "Are my eyes deceiving me or is this not the young man you were asking about?"

"Almost, this is his brother, Twing. Twing meet Alex, and this is Betsy, from America, from Washington State. This is Alex, owner of this very venerable institution."

"Hello and welcome."

"Pleased to meet you."

"It looks like this pub has been here for a while?" Twing ventured to say."

"It's been in the family since 1777, when some loyalists came back from the colonies, with a bit of money, and settled here."

"Since 1777, *wow*, what a history it must have...And what about the park? The theater in the park?"

"Well, it's a more recent addition. Sometime in the 1800's they built a stage to give Stratford a bit of competition. You know, our notorious -- I mean our esteemed -- neighbor. But, I must say, I remember the production your brother..." He shook his head. "When I see you, I see your brother and it comes back to me, it's partly your birthmark, if you'll pardon me, yes, was it a *Winter's Tale* or, or *Twelfth Night*? Now, A Winter's Tale, that's one of me favorites, I mean, watch out for what jealousy can do, right? But you know, I think your brother was actually in *Twelfth Night*. What a lark. Cross dressing and getting mixed up and losing their identities and regaining them -- lost then found. If my memory serves me correctly, I think he played Sebastian. Oh, we've had some great productions here..."

"But," Betsy interrupted, "have you seen Twangly since then?"

"I cannot say that I have, I see a lot of young people come here, come in, especially on the weekends, but I would have remembered him, now that I see his brother, amazing, amazing..."

"Amazing, *amazing grace, how sweet the sound,*" Twing sang silently to himself, "*that saved a man like me. I once was lost...and now am found,* and now he's lost..."

Path Twenty Three

Bloodied Awareness

Twing just wandered off wondering, winding slowly through the park.

"Excuse me," he had said.

He could hear voices from the table he left, "Twing, Twingly, *he's taking a tour*, let him, let…"

Like echoes bouncing around outside of him, the words grew fainter as his thoughts grew louder inside him. This song of grace seemed to be the sound that wove through and circled around and encapsulated these last few days, these events…*I, I once was lost, but now am found, found, found, man, what have I found, a mother who never wanted to find me, a father who thinks I'm my brother, a California room in a palatial estate, wow, but that's not all, I fell into a cavern, a cavern, and I've got the reminders of that fall…I was blind and I saw this gold shining face, an overwhelming halo, I can still see it. I can still see…"*

He was looking straight into the afternoon sun, letting the light engulf him, come into him, change him…He could hear sounds, gathering around him, joining his awareness of the sky. He heard people greeting each other, barkers selling pasties and bangers, the smell of heather mixed with animal fat being roasted on a spit, the jostling of finery with ragamuffins in and out of corners between velvets and polished boots. In the midst of it, in the midst of it all, came a traveling theater group with a painted wagon, the back drop of itinerant make believe, came in the forms of animated, gaudy, exaggerated bodies and faces of onceuponatime thespians They were in the throes of an ancient resurrected tragedy. Out of the tomb of expiation came a blind man, Oedipus, the King, who had seen too much. Blind Oedipus wandered in and out of the crowd. His empty sockets were filled with blood. Children hid behind his toga, inside their mother's skirts, some young women recoiled, some young men were fascinated, Twing was mesmerized as this blind seer wandered by him, closer, closer he came...near him...

"Blind, I was blind to the horrors around me, those I was a part of, those I committed without knowing, those I should have answered courageously. Blind, I was blind, but now in my bloodied blindness I can see."

The crowd moved with him. In his royal white toga, stained with the drops of blood, the crowd let him pass until he stepped in front of Twing. He stopped and seemed to gaze into Twing's eyes.

"You, too, were blind."

The crowd hushed as Twing felt his stinging, waking words go deep.

Not me! His voice quivered in reaction to this recognition, *What are you talking about?*

Suddenly, it was even quieter, suddenly, the crowd vanished and he was looking deep into the bloodied awareness of his own beginning, sometime, somewhere, somehow, somewho, who, who had given him birth...was this the legacy of an ancient awareness? Was this the legacy of ongoing, growing, all consuming consciousness, a bloodied birth over and over again, each time separating a little more from the Eden of unconscious existence, when all was blind when the wherewhatwhohatwhere and how was blind and lived in, lived in, lived...

He grabbed for the toga in front of him...

How much more? He half yelled and cried...*How much more of your damned, bloody awareness, I'm weighed down with your whole history, I don't want it, want it, want it...*

"You have no choice," came the hallowed reply.

Man, I don't need this.

"It's not a matter of need. It's a matter of connections in strange, a maze ing ways -- connections to all that is around you, connections to your past. Remember, you are the past whether you like it or not. Memory is not just a childhood reflection or a connection to an emotional upbringing. It is not just a life long accumulation but a lifetime accumulation, lifetime upon lifetime upon lifetime upon life accumulation, not just in your head but your body and the bodies around you. Do you think I'm just a character out of Sophocles' head? Or am I the result of the accumulation of life upon life of memory that manifested in me -- a character in a play, a symbol, if you will -- a character springing forth in a time the world was ready, and since then taking on many variations."

Twing was now sitting on the grass, still on edge, yet beginning to listen, as if a stream was flowing next to him, a stream of words, age old sounds, flowing next to him. He dared not ask a question. He was transfixed in this flow, this murmuring, gurgling flow…

As the hallowed voice continued to speak, Twing opened himself up to every word, "You may find the future holds variations of my visage, my bloodied awareness in ideas, in words, in images, in movement on screens, in holograms right in front of you, seemingly real, moving right into the future." Twing began to imagine words, words becoming images, moving images coming into focus, going from the past into the future.

After a long and apprehensive quiet, Oedipus spoke again, "Let me ask you, do you think this is the only life you have?"

As he heard these words the stage came alive with togas moving in the evening light, ancient moving togas with beards and wizened faces. In between was a youth, a young girl with a mirror in her hand, who came running up to him

There is a new play, in the theater, this afternoon. She held the mirror up to his face. *You are in it.*

He saw himself, in his youth, with his birth mark, beyond his birthmark -- the image shimmered in the sun. It seemed to glow, golden in the reflecting sun.

You are in it, echoed around him...*in it...init...*

Entranced, he asked, "Where? What?"

In the theater...they are coming...the play's still being written...the chorus is coming to define the characters. Come, come, she said.

His mind continued her exhortation, *come* he thought, and he remembered his father so many years ago. The father who looked at him from the mountain top of his shoulders -- so large. *Come, don't be afraid...*

A chorus of voices broke into his reverie and made him turn every which way, trying to see who was speaking,

Our story may delight you or it may bring tears, but you will not forget the plight of these travelers and their fears, after all, they have been traveling for so many years...gather round, one and all, for we have come to the beginning of our...

Behind the stage, in the wings, with all the excitement of the first night, Twing was handed a mask. *We have come to the beginning of our time...our moment on this momentary stage...*The chorus continued in unison and rhyme.

"Hurry, hurry! You're on."

With a shove by the stage hands and the breath of God, Twing found himself out on the proscenium, a scene laden with the jewels of a hundred plundered ships. Disoriented and half-blind from their reflections he stumbled against an empty throne, before he could catch himself he lay in front of it.

"You were born into the wealth of the world, the wealth of generations," a voice resounded around him, "Out of a pure cosmic accident, you were born into wealth and privilege, and yet, and yet, you did not see it, for many years you lived in innocence..."

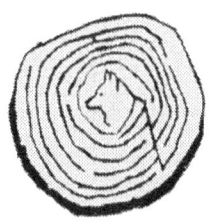

Path Twenty Four

Wolfgang

Twing reached out to the throne in front of him, reaching, until the glitter of the throne throbbed and then it blurred and finally it waned, until the scene changed and the throne became a tree stump, a fallen, broken tree in the midst of a dense forest. In an agile jump, the boy was over it, crashing through the undergrowth…

There he is, over there, came an excited voice. Leanhardt was the first to reach the stump. He, too, jumped in wild excitement, following the sounds of broken branches. Norman set off to the left, hoping to intercept the fleeing boy. He had guessed right. The boy ran towards him after hearing Leanhardt's hoots and howls. When Wolfgang looked up it was too late. Norman caught up with him and held his shirt collar with one hand and his arm with the other. Wolfgang leaned sideways, Norman tripped and they both fell sliding into the pine needle ground.

When Leanhardt caught up with them he pounced on the boy and Norman until they were all rolling, kicking and thrashing about. With dirt and pine needles and branches flying -- amidst the sounds of slapping handholds, grunts and quickened breathing -- Wolfgang began to laugh, "All right, all right, you've got me."

The others were laughing also…In a wild, physical abandon they just let themselves go into spasms of laughter. They rolled off of each other and lay on the ground, spread-eagled on the softness of the sharp needles, the accumulation of seasons and years of growth and decay. Now it was their afternoon of laughter and joy. They just lay there, in their quiet openness, letting a long stillness hover around them. A stillness that abides in a deep forest place, where the very air is alive; where it seems to be waiting for sounds and movement to fill it. Here and there, shafts of light penetrated the dense growth of evergreens shooting for the sky. Below, in the decay and growth, the ground was covered with patches of moss on fertile beginnings, verdurous, soft, sometimes moist moss...*Rat a tat, rat a tat*, a woodpecker intruded in on the stillness, a squirrel scurried up the variegated bark of a majestic pine, bothering a blue jay, whose shrill crackle was like a wake up call...

Aaaah, I'm being bitten...These are biting ants! Leanhardt suddenly yelled out. "I've been lying on an ant nest."

He jumped to his feet.

They all jumped up, danced and gyrated, brushed their clothes off, brushed off the mostly imaginary ants and finally calmed down.

"There's no paradise," Leanhardt added, "as long as there are ants."

"Well, they seem to do all right, here."

"Yes, so do most animals living here."

"Particularly, those chewing on something."

"Like ants."

"Like hedgehogs."

"Like wild boars."

"Like wolves."

"Like, like...Have you seen a wolf?" Leanhardt asked.

"I haven't, but I have seen some wild boars." Norbert answered. "I saw them digging with their tasks, grunting and digging away, chewing up the roots. You have to watch out for them." He made a few snorts, put his head down and started charging at Leanhardt.

"Hey, hey, watch it!" Leanhardt laughed.

When they had quieted down again, Wolfgang said, "My mother's seen a wolf. She told me she saw one the night I was born. She was in the bedroom looking out the window, looking up to where this forest begins. The one we are in, right now. She saw this animal come out of the trees. It went back and forth, she said, and then, it sat down and looked in her direction. She, she almost felt it. That was the night I was born. She said I was born to the howls of a wolf..."

"That gives me goose bumps," Leanhardt said.

"Yes, well, you can see why she named me Wolfgang."

"Do you think it's still here, I mean, how long do wolves live?"

"I don't know, but I'm beginning to feel like it's still around here, watching us."

"Me to."

"Let's go."

"No, let's find a tree and wait for him."

"That would take forever."

"Let's build a hut."

"Yes, and bring some food out for him, we'll put it near the hut, then we can watch for him, or her, if it's a she- wolf."

"Yea, come on. Let's get going."

In a flurry of activity and searching amongst trees and rocks and stumps they found a place enclosed on three sides with an area open to a clearing. Almost instinctively, they gathered long branches that they could angle onto the rock behind them and into the two large trees on either side, then horizontal branches were wedged into the 't's and the crotches of the vertical branches. An opening was left on one side. They could climb in and out of it and plug it up with broken bark. Smaller branches were wedged in and finally the ever present moss was pulled up in chunks and placed over the sticks leaving some holes. It was...it was a house of moss and wood, an enclosed world, for the viewing of a wolf. By the time they had put the last piece of moss on, they realize the sun had gone down and the forest night was descending on them. They ran along their familiar pathway until they reached the edge of the forest, the same edge Wolfgang's mother, Flaxen, had watched from her window when he was born. They ran through the field back to the window lights of the farm house.

Wolfgang, Wolfgang! An hysterical voice cried out. *Where have you been?*

"What's wrong?"

It's your mother, your mother.

WHAT WRONG? He yelled back.

Your mother's been bitten by a snake, a poisonous snake.

WHERE IS SHE?

She was out picking blueberries and was bitten...

WHERE IS SHE?

Old Yeltsin took her into the village, to the doctor.

Without looking at his friends he yelled out, I'VE GOT TO GO and started running on the path to the village. He ran the wellworn path into the twilight, until the forest grew all around him, and in front of him. He ran for miles until he no longer felt his legs, or his aching lungs. He ran with the awareness of eyes on him...and the sound of paws, soft on the pathway ground, running behind him, almost beside him, eyes on him, hot breath around him...He felt this presence breathing into him until it seemed like he was barely touching the ground. He ran like the wind with the sound of his mother in his mouth, *Mama, Mama...*

He ran until he finally saw the lights of the village. He knew the doctor. There was only one doctor. The doctor had helped deliver him and countless other children. He knew his house and ran to the lights beckoning him. In utter exhaustion he pounded on the door, the door opened, the lights fell on him. Out of a looming shadow, the doctor's face and hands met him.

Where is my mama? Is all he could say.

"Wolfgang, Wolfgang," the doctor tried to calm him down. He held him and led him into the bedroom where his mother lay...lay in feathers.

Mama, Mama, he spoke anxiously and as softly as he could, *Mama.* He took her hand.

"She is not well," he faintly heard the doctors say.

With a slow, slight movement her eyelids opened, ever so slightly opened and words flowed on her breath, "Wolfgang, my son, my son, a snake, I stepped on a snake, I stepped on …"

Her breath staggered and no more words came out, only desperate attempts to breathe, her eyes fell back, her hand stiffened around his as if wanting to hold on, hold on…

Mama, Mama! he cried. His tears flowing like a great waterfall down his face, *Mama, Mama…*He threw himself on her feather covered bed and sobbed uncontrollably, forever. He did not hear the plaintive, age-old howl of a wolf in the nearby darkness.

The doctor finally took the sleeping child from the cold bosom of his mother. All day he had cried and slept and cried there, while her floating life surrounded him, becoming ever lighter, ever fainter, permeating the room. He slept in his mother's air until the doctor carried him to a nearby couch to wash her body with the help of Old Yeltsin who had stayed to comfort the boy.

"When her life spirit has loosened and no longer lingers we shall bury her," the doctor told old Yeltsin. "Let's make her ready. Tell the priest to make her grave ready and tell those who have loved her to come and help her soul find its way."

They carefully took off the feather bed, removed her clothes and washed her body. A body, still, in the prime of life, having given birth to one child, by a father no one knew or remembered except in the story she had told her son. Now the story would be buried with her and become a memory to Wolfgang, just as she would become a memory to all who had known her. Her body was dressed in a white gown, taken from the clothes of the doctor's wife who had, also, died too soon. They lay her head against the pillow, closed her eyes, brushed her hair until a soft radiance surrounded her. Old Yeltsin left her and the doctor, went over to Wolfgang, still sleeping, and carefully pushed his hair back with his coarse fingers.

What will become of you? He thought to himself. *What will become of you?*

When Wolfgang finally woke, it was to the sounds of wailing women in the room, surrounding the bed. He had come back to a loosening, lifting groundswell of sound, coming from the depths of those who give birth. The bloodied understanding of life-bringing was now wailing with the final breath of life-taking. Their wailing, vibrations, magnified by every woman, loosed the final boundaries of earthly weight in Flaxen and left her soul free to float in the spirit realms. From these free floating realms she saw her son in the room. He woke up, and felt inseparable from the earthly sounds around him. In the women's earthy tones and overtones and high-pitched voices of wailing woe, Wolfgang faintly, yet distinctly, heard his mother's voice calling him,

What will become of you…?

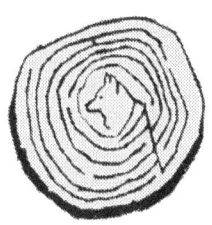

Path Twenty Five

Awakening

From the corners of the rolling stage, out of the surrounding trees, like a fog hovering, the chorus of voices continued, *What lives and what deaths have the ages produced, those untimely and those beyond their time. What have they left in their wake? What lives did they leave in their wake, lost to the earth without awareness of their living or dying, without awareness of their own awareness, only to be born-again...?*

What will become of you? The chorus of voices repeated. *What will become of you?* echoed in Twing's ears...As he turned his head from one side to the other...

I don't know? he answered with an anxious agitated voice. *It's as if, as if...*

Behind him, imperceptibly, out of the chorus of voices, came the young girl with the mirror. *You are doing well. Your depth of feeling is very real. A great performance -- very believable.*

What do you mean? he almost screamed. *I, I...*But he was at a loss to continue.

She walked closer and held the mirror up to him, *You're getting there, look, look at yourself.* He grabbed her hand and held onto the mirror. His curiosity was rough, awkward, filled with desire. The mirror turned...she turned...all turned into a mask in his own hand. A sultry voice, seemingly coming out of the ground, added to this sense of disbelief. His quivering, shaking

body seemed to become charged. *You're on,* she said, *You're on.*
They can feel you.

An Old EP

Again, he seemed to be pushed out, clasping a new mask,
out, out, he heard, until his twisting and turning found himself
sitting in front of an old cabinet, an old brown and antique
cabinet, that someone had left in the house his mother and
father had bought. He had opened it on occasion. Inside was a
record player. The first they had ever had. No one else had used
it. They had no records. It was like a secret room, for him alone;
that only he could enter...But that, he, still, was not sure of
entering. Today, he had the key, a record, an EP record, that he
had bought with his own money. A record with four songs he
had never heard before. He was all alone today when he
entered his secret room, put the adapter on the spindle, put the
record on and fiddled around with the knobs. Everything had to
be right. It began to hum. It began to turn. He took the arm and
the needle. He scratched the needle with his thumb. Chaotic,
scratching static came through the speakers, then silence, a great
silence as he held the needle arm in a timeless moment, like a
pendulum reaching its apex, ready to fall, click, hum...
We e e e ll, I got a woman, way cross town, she's good to me, hoh,
hoh, yea...
His body shivered, the voice, the guitars, the drums, the
beat...It was like a freight train in his gut.
She's good to me ee, hoh, hoh, yea...
It was too much, he couldn't stand it, his eyes were water, his
body was charged, he wanted to move, he began to move, to
gyrate with the beat, he wanted to scream. He heard screams,
uncontrollable screaming, with the pulsing, earth-pulsing beat.
He was one with it now, one with the screaming, pulsing, pelvic
beat, on and on until he was no longer listening, just one with
the screaming, pulsing, pelvic beat...

Then it eased…the pulsing eased…the freight train had gone by and was now barely audible. The sounds eased and he fell down, lay there, lay on the grass, in the secret of his initiation. He was spent, spent like he had never known before.

Sacrifice

A chorus of shadows began to crawl over Twing -- cool him. Togas were flowing like sails around him. Voices were wafting in the air, *What fools these mortals be, to think a moment of ecstasy does not have its counter part in tragedy, and yet, yet, these are the moments that are lived, much more than the day to day doing and controlling…these are the moments that are lived…are lived…*The voices continued, sounding and surrounding him, while, as if on cue, the sails of togas fluttered open, and allowed a space, a place for the evening light to come through, to bath his body in sunset hues of magenta reds and golden yellows.

"*Wow,*" is all he could utter."

Transfixed, he barely heard the girl's voice, *You were incredible. I want you to know this is just the beginning…Take your place in the world…Look…Look at yourself.*

He looked into the mirror and saw himself, a young man with a lean face, eyes on fire, hair in wild propulsion, as if lightning had struck him…And there, there, on his neck, his telltale beginnings: a birthmark in the shape of a guitar.

You don't need a mask anymore, she spoke. *Show yourself as you are.* He stood up in all his radiance. *Show yourself as you are.* He was on the world's stage now… confident…anticipating…

Hey, you! Twing looked over in the direction of the park entrance, *Yea, you.*

"Yes,"

"Who do you think you are? Elvis? We've been enjoying the show, man. You got downright sexy up there. Didn't he guys?"

One tangerine-haired guy and a fish-net girl came up from behind the speaker, "He sure did," Tangerine said. The girl smiled and added, "Yea, quite a dancer."

Twing didn't know what to say. Now he was somewhat embarrassed. He didn't expect this.

"I think he could use a partner. What do you think, guys?"

"Hey, yea, sure."

"Jackie, go up there and dance with him."

Twing answered back, "That's OK. I think I've done enough moving around... Besides..."

"What do you mean, she's not good enough for ya?"

"No, no, I..."

"Well, all right, then, Jackie, go on up there."

"Max, if he doesn't want to..."

"What do you mean if he doesn't want to, I mean he does want to and you better get your little butt up there."

"Hey, it's OK...she doesn't have to. I'm ready to go..."

"He's ready to go, you're dam right you're ready to go, Jackie, show him how to shake that thing..."

He pushed her towards Twing. Twing caught her and tried to balance her and himself.

"Hey, let's help him do the watusi, heh, shall we." They each grabbed for one of Twing's arms but he grabbed an arm with each of his hands and using their momentum kept pulling them until they both hit the grass while Twing did a back roll and was on his feet again.

"Hey, we've got a Bruce Lee here, guys...Let's see if he can do it again."

Max came at him from the front while his sidekick came at him from the rear. Twing sidestepped Max but could not sidestep the other one. He grabbed him around the chest and neck, held him until Max punched him in the stomach.

Twing just barely heard the girl say, *Leave him alone, Max!* But Max was in no mood to stop, he was caught up in the moment, his adrenaline flowing, yet, somehow, something was not right...

From out of nowhere, his fist suddenly became a knife, his face a hairy, snarling, sniveling phantom. Twing lost track of time. In slow motion they held him. He could see the glint of the knife. He pulled on his arms. He kicked, but only managed to kick the threatening teeth of the phantom higher, higher, until they struck his neck, struck his neck in a cutting fury. Twing grabbed the hair of the phantom...Suddenly, there was yelling and a turning of bodies...

"Let's get out of here. Max...Max..."

But Twing did not let go, while the others disappeared as suddenly as they had appeared, Twing did not let go of the hairyheaded, snarling phantom while his neck gushed with blood...

Big Ben had come running and was now trying to hold onto this phantom, *trying to grab and hold a knife* held in it's hand. Twing had been wrestling with a beast with a hairy face slashing with a knife in its hand. He had held onto the coarse-haired head. Where were the others? Had it all been his imagination? Except for this phantom with a wolf's head and the sharp, knife-like fangs, had it all been his imagination? Somehow, it had come into the park, while he was there, engrossed in his theater of the imagination. Somehow, this phantom, this wolf-beast, during the commotion with the others, had virtually pounced on him...It had come from the darkness below the stage. The others, the girl, Max, had all run off. Twing had no idea who or what this coarse-haired creature with yellow florescent eyes was, but had realized the danger, and fought for his life. Big Ben and Alex finally disarmed the phantom and tried to subdue it, but it's fury or the fear of its discovery was too strong for them and it evaded them and ran into the shadows, into the darkness, with Big Ben after it. Twing was awash in blood from the wound on his neck. Betsy had wrapped her arm around his neck trying to stop the bleeding and now he had sat down. She tied Alex's apron around the wound. The knife had not cut a major artery, but had cut the skin that held his birthmark. Like a wild performance, on a once upon a time stage, his guitar birthmark had been cut off, destroyed, and he bled like a sacrificed lamb only to live again...to continue...for his time had not yet come...

And only he could hear the faint, voiceless words of the young girl with the mirror, *You were magnificent, and by the luck of the cosmic draw you did not die, yes, a mature role and you met the challenge, take your place in the world.*

Aftermath

In the darkness, Ben followed, on the heels, after the sounds, of the crashing desperate animal. *Too dark*...The trees of the park filled with shadows, *Menacing*...would it turn on him? Through hedges, he chased it, until the leftover light suddenly showed fangs, and horror-filled eyes. Ben gasped, but momentum and determination threw him through the air, bursting into the belly, into its very taut, tangled belly. He grasped and grappled, but all he felt were the intertwined branches of a bush, part of the hedge, on the edge of the park. He fell into the grass and over him, next to him, fell the remains of the beast, a mask of fangs with fluorescent yellow eyes with coarse hair on the outside and rubber on the inside. The same wolf that attacked Twing, was now, lying next to him, in calm repose.

He picked it up and carried it back to the pub, hoping with all hope, that Twing was all right and *maybe, just maybe*, this mask would be the clue to his attacker. In hurried steps, clutching his hard-won prize, he went back to the pub. Alex and Betsy were gone and the bartender told him, "They *hav* taken the wounded man to the clinic."

"And where is that?"

"Just down the Main Street to Prospero Lane, about four blocks."

"Thanks."

Ben partly walked and partly ran to find the clinic that had an emergency sign over a side door. He walked in and there in the small lobby were Betsy and Alex.

"How is he?"

"He is still with the doctor. I think he's stitching him up."

"They could have killed him -- that knife came this close to his jugular." She held up her finger and thumb with a half inch

172

distance between. "As it was, the knife just sliced off his birthmark, he…"

"Almost fortuitous," Ben interrupted.

"What do you mean?" asked Alex.

"*Well*, look at what I caught up with." He showed them the rubber wolf mask. Alex took it and rolled it around his fingers.

"A wolf mask," Betsy repeated.

"It's very strange," Ben said, "but it's almost like this…this, I mean, why a wolf mask?"

The door to the doctor's office opened, out stepped tusslehaired Twing with a large clean white bandage around his neck. His eyes were a bit dreamy, his manner slower than usual, still, he walked out by himself. Betsy was the first to touch him, hold his hand, look into his eyes, Ben moved closer to him, Alex watched.

"I think I'm okay," came slowly, from Twing's mouth.

"I am so glad, Twing. I can't think how horrible this would have been…"

"I'm glad to see you about, old boy. Doctor, is, was it serious?"

"He is a very lucky man, that knife was sharp and by some stroke of fate just sliced off some skin and it just so happened to be his birthmark. Some people actually have theirs removed surgically. In fact, a surgeon couldn't have done any better than this attacker."

"Do you want to know the strangest part of this? Ben said, "The attacker wore a wolf's mask. Here, Twing, look at this…"

They all fondled the fangs and the hairy exterior, looked at the fluorescent yellow eyes, until Twing just shook his head and said, "A wolf's mask, a wolf -- the sign in the labyrinth coin, the sign in the rock, this is too much!"

"Now we just have to decide what to do," Betsy asked. "Do we go to the police?"

"I think, that, even with all of the strange coincidences, this must be an isolated incident. A nut case…" Ben responded.

Feeling that he needed to explain, Twing pursed his mouth, held his head still and spoke quietly, "It started with a dream, a strange dream that occurred when I fell asleep in the park. Some kids came, actually, kids my age, three or four of them, they were giving me a hard time because I, I was doing a little dancing on the stage, you know, just pretending, I was listening to some music, you know, early stuff..."

"What song was it this time, Twing? Betsy asked with a knowing look.

"*Ahh*, early song, but what happened was that, while these kids were giving me a hard time, something, someone came out of the, came out from under the stage and all the sudden I was looking at the glint of a knife, the blade of a knife coming at me. The kids fled and I thought it was all over with. I felt this sharp bite in my neck, *ahh*, I mean cut on my neck, and I just grabbed onto the mask and his hand. By that time Ben and Alex came, and pulled that guy off of me. He took off and I guess you went after him."

"So what do we do?" Betsy asked again.

"Well, I'm okay, I think, let's let it go." Twing steadied himself and seemed to be looking for the right words. "At this point, my brother is still out there -- somewhere. We have to find him. I think I want to get a good night's sleep. Do you, Alex...Do you have any rooms available?"

"I think so. In any case, we'll find a place for all of you to stay. Let me check with the bartender. He rents out the rooms."

Path Twenty Six

Encounter of Land and Sky

The morning, the cool, clear morning had begun to cloud over, as it unexpectedly did, *unexpectedly*, in the sense, that no matter how many years ago Aiden had planted his feet in the soil of this sea-like, flat-like land, it, still, seemed like the occasional clear morning should stay clear. That was the way he felt as the late morning grew grayer, the same morning he let Annie, or Leylani, as she now wanted to be called, and Jules take his car and drive it to the hot air balloon port a few miles north of the village. Leylani was already floating with anticipation. Jules just barely kept up with her, even though it was his idea to see the so-called constellations for himself. He had heard enough about the nose of the dog, ley lines, bridal paths, stone circles. Now he wanted to get a bird's eye view of these landmarks. Leylani, of course, just fired up his enthusiasm. She even asked Aiden if they could take a camera with them, just in case they saw something.

"Why not?" she said to Jules. "Aiden surprised us with his digital *hammering* connection, so why not put this land over the airwaves, on the screens of all those satelites -- why not show them the secrets of this land? Only the people who were ready for it would make the connections anyway."

At least that's what she thought. That was one thing she had become aware of during these last few years of traveling; that people understood the world at their own level of awareness. She had told people about the energized landmarks and the feelings and emotions that accompanied these outcroppings, these pathways, but few had taken her up on these secrets -- this knowledge. Few had camped with her along the ley lines, sat with her within the stone circles, followed the labyrinthine paths to their sources, their centers…heard her stories…

Why not? she thought. *Why not take a camera…*as they hovered and viewed the landscape, as they wandered and wondered through their own lens, as they made the visual connections that filtered through their own awareness…

Jules, Jules, look, there's mist on the ground, coming up from the beach, from the sea, it's, it seems to be rolling, rolling in, like a circle…"

"It's more of a spiral," he added.

"Yeah, yeah, it's incredible. Orion, look."

But the hunter had not heard her, he was more concerned with lowering the balloon to get out of the seaward air current.

"Jules, I completely forgot about the camera. Let's turn it on -- let it run."

"Point it towards the mist."

"It's whirling…look…it's going around the mounds. You know what it looks like?"

"What?"

"A galaxy…like a galaxy on the ground."

"And it's moving around our stars, our stars on the ground. There's the cottage… there's Sirius…"

"Orion, are we going up?"

There was no response from the sweatered hunter, only a determined movement with the flame. He had not caught a counter current…In fact, they seemed to be accelerating towards the sea.

"Orion, can you get us closer to the ground?"

"Children," he finally said. "We are in the hands of God…this balloon is on its way to the moon."

"Jules, I think he's lost it."

"He must know what he's doing."

"Jules, we're going in a circle."

They were turning. They were following a circular path, a spiral, not up or down, but spiraling. It seemed to be an unusual weather phenomenon. The air currents were going both inland and out to sea, creating an eddy, a spiraling eddy. Their hot air balloon had somehow gotten caught up in strange and unusual air currents. Gerard swore, but it was Orion who raised his hand to the sky. Gerard worked feverishly on the flame, but it was Orion who reached out to his hunting dog, Canis Major, and urged him to leap higher...and higher...until they jumped and flew across the heavens...

"Jules, we're caught in a wind storm."

"Leylani!" Jules shouted above the rearing, roaring powers swirling aroundthemwithinthem and throughout the maelstrom.

Gerard lost his beret. Leylani hung onto Jules.

"We're out of control."

This was Orion's finest hour --with his hands on the ropes he was navigating, no, he was usurping the powers of the heavens. He was after his hound, at a feverish pace, while bounding through the clouds, in a billowing, unfettered choreography of light and shadow. In a chiaroscuro of movement, the balloon flew, turned, tossed, up, down, around, in wild gyrations...

The bansheed cry of Orion broke through the mist and the clouds, *Ai eee, ai eee.*

Leylani's eyes grew in terror and confusion -- her very soul whirling within her.

In grasping desperation, Jules hung onto the side of the balloon, onto the ropes, onto Leylani. Leylani hung onto Jules They were lost, lost, in the hunt, in this wild ride, in this ride...*ai eee...ai eee...*to the moon...

Whirlwind

"SC, we're getting a strange transmission from the cottage, from Aiden's place. Are you tuned in?"

What's up, another afternoon chat?"

"No, it looks like a weather report."

"What you mean?"

"Well, it looks like clouds swirling around with a garbled audio in the background."

"I'm getting it. That's some storm. Where is he?"

"Looks like he's in the midst of it."

"Jeannette, can you understand what he's saying."

"Not yet."

"Can anyone? Is anyone else tuned to Aiden's place?"

We are...

out...of

control...

"Did you hear that?"

"Barely."

"Some thing's going on."

"Aiden, Aiden, come on in. Are you there?"

Jules...

Hold on...

"This is bizarre, Jeannette. Where is Aiden?"

Ai eee, ai eee!

"What was that?"

"What was...I heard it, I heard it"

"I don't see anything but clouds, fog, mist,..."

"It seems to be going faster."

Leylani...

Jules...

Ai eee, ai eee.

Suddenly! Nothing...still...quiet...a blank screen in the direction of Aiden's cottage. The silence was deafening.

"Aiden? SC?" Jeannette spoke quietly and let the sound come back and reverberate throughout the satelites, the *hammering* places around the world.

Others joined in. In a maze ment and questioning awe, their voices slowly rising, filling the screen, *Was this real?" What was going on?*

Alfred, who happened to be tuned in, asked, *Was that live?*

Jeanette, who had not moved since the silence came on, was now filled with questions.

SC, feeling somewhat responsible, finally tried to get a hold of Armani, the wizard behind all the technical connections. Armani, his partner, the man who controlled the hammers, the purveyor of this high-tech reality.

Centuries of Sand

Aiden sat quietly, perched on the two legs of his favorite chair, leaning back against the rough, whitewashed plaster of his cottage. It was lunch time and he watched the sky change, as he had countless times before. Today, he was watching for more. He was intently scanning the sky for a brightly colored balloon.

Would they have taken the solid magenta or the blue and white, clouded one or the 60's tie-dyed version? If I know Annie, she probably would have avoided the tie-dyed, too tacky, he thought and remembered her usual disdain for the very things she was usually in the midst of. But all he saw, as he finished his sandwich, a thick slab of stilton on rye that he washed down with a good pale ale from the Devil's Hook, a local brewery in the village, was the sky darkening. Moving, curling clouds from the sea were joining the overcast sky from the direction of the village and the hot air balloon port. The sky seemed to be converging, convoluting, playing out its, *almost*, routine drama over him.

"Was he in for a storm?" he wondered. "Would he have time to continue digging this afternoon, before the rain came?"

He sat up, and in a somewhat excited and nervous manner resolved to dig, as much as he could, while he had the chance. *It's always on the verge of rain here,* he thought, as he picked up his shovel and started to remove the layered sand. Every shovelful, however, seemed to fill back in. He started to laugh. The more he shoveled out, the more sand seemed to trickle back in. He laughed again and remembered the film, the Japanese

179

film, he saw years ago, about the woman in the dunes whose house was slowly being covered by sand, the sand nothing could stop. He couldn't remember the ending, just the fact that the sand kept coming. That's the way he felt right now, like Sisyphus climbing the hill, pushing the rock until he almost reached the top only to have it roll back down again. He kept shoveling sand, but the sand kept filling in until he reached the top of the hill only to find more sand. He felt it was time for a stronger brew but he kept at it, finally making some headway. Finally, the sand was giving way...finally, jarringly, the shovel hit something solid: rock -- rock hard rock. It seemed to be in a particular shape, as if it had been placed there. He dug slowly. One foot down, he saw the possibility of a sand-covered opening underneath. He could now see what he had wondered about, what he had hit. It was a carved lintel, underneath his cottage. He dug furiously, throwing the sand wildly out into the darkening sky. Three, four feet down, it began to look like the opening of a cave. He dug out an opening between the rocks or large standing stones, that were holding up the lintel. The opening became larger, wider...as he continued to dig...

By this time, sweat was pouring off of him and he was oblivious to the ensuing drama high above him. He was digging down, digging into the womb of his cottage. What had been a sandfilled space was becoming a shadowed place, getting darker. The more he dug out the sand, the deeper and darker the space became. He dug all around the inside of the cavern. His shovel would vibrate when he hit the hard walls of rock. His furious digging now came inter spaced with an occasional question, a momentary wondering, *Where was he? What was this place?* He had been living over the remains of an ancient cavern, dug out by who knows who and lived in by who knows what. The darker it got, the more excited he became until he was exhausted, utterly exhausted with his shoveling and throwing up of sand. By now he had to walk to the entrance to throw the sand. He let the shovel fall, went out and got his flashlight and returned. Coming back to an entrance that was now about four feet high. He stooped down, entered, this time with a wide-eyed gaze, his pulse quickening. He felt like he was desecrating something. Now, there was enough space to contemplate the possibility of this being an ancient cavern in which someone had lived or died. *Maybe, it was a burial place?* he asked himself. He had to find out. He started going around the right side, along the hard rock wall, tracing it with his beam of light, up, down, until his eyes traced the outlines of incised lines. He had to get back a little. There, now, the light on the lines, it looked like a figure, two figures, at least two, in the midst of waves, possibly water. *Incredible,* he thought, and covered more wall with his beam. Near the figures was the outline of an animal, a dog or…*a wolf…a wolf, here,* by the sea, hundreds of years ago. His heart was now beating for all of them. He wanted to shout! He wanted to tell Annie. He wanted to tell someone about his incredible discovery. Underneath him, all along, all these years, were the remains of someone's ancestors. Within this shelter, within these remains, were the meager, but desperate beginnings, of some human's conscious expression: images on a rock wall, incised and lost for millennia. Now, they had been found, by sheer sweat and the giving up of centuries of sand.

What is this all about? he wondered. *What am I doing here?*

He finally let go, he needed light, he needed to think, he went back to the kitchen and took out the darkest brew he had. After several long chugs, he fell into his corner chair and just sat there, wondering, a mazed, at a loss for words. It seemed like hours went by, he nodded off, woke, slept some more, his muscles aching but his exhaustion letting him sleep some more. When he finally roused himself there was no light to be seen…It was an unusually dark, deep night that surrounded him, that surrounded the *nose of the dog*. When it was this dark he knew the sky was also overcast. No starlight or moonlight was coming through. He groped for his flashlight but only felt the chair and the floor. He groped, until he felt a sound. He literally felt a sound coming up through the very floor. He was now, on his knees, feeling with his hands and knees, listening to a low moaning, groaning sound. *It was just the reverberations of the cavern space, like a shell pressed on his ear,* he thought. *It was a low moaning, howling sound, a wolf-like sound, sending shivers through him.*

WHERE IS ANNIE? he yelled out. WHERE IS JULES, *that King of Terra Grandeur?*

He crawled over to the door...found the doorknob...turned it...opened the door to the black of the night...to the fury of the night. It was alive with the wolf-like howling of the sounds he had just barely heard coming from the depths of his digging, *ow ohh, ow ohh*...Now it echoed back and it was not just the howling of a wolf he heard, no, now he also heard a wail, the wail of a banshee, *ai eee, ai eee, ow ohhh, ow ohhhhhhh, ai eee*...He covered his ears and went into shock, an overload of gut level, blood level shock in the black of the night.

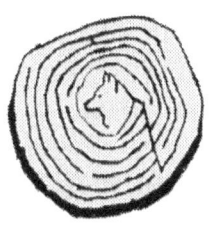

Path Twenty Seven

Armani's Box

Armani had shown himself to be brilliant in the technical aspects of the *hammering* places. He was the *hammer*. He had built the hardware when necessary, refined it, made patent agreements, boxed it up, taken it to remote places, set up the transmissions. He had even taken an office near San Francisco, south of it, in the midst of the digital revolution. He was being recognized and sought after, to help start up other enterprises. SC had not seen him in months, at least not in the flesh. He had seen him, talked to him, even argued with him a few times over the transmissions, mostly at Jeanette's place. They could see each other in the screens, on the screens. He noticed, however, that even the most personal discussions had become public, could be seen and heard by anyone else tuned in. If one was used to intimate conversation, like he was, it was sometimes embarrassing, even infuriating to hear the personal conversations going on around him...

At least, SC thought, *I can turn them off and check into different satelites for something more to my liking.* But his liking, his initial idealism for voices of change in the world had been confronted with a different kind of reality. The *hammering* places had opened up in unexpected ways and places. One was being used as an auction center, to bid on things being sold, others were using the screens to advertise products and services. There was even a casino place that allowed others around the world to gamble -- *live* - - just turn on the screen -- *You are there! You can win!* Of course, the sellers of sex for its own sake had also become a hot part of these transmissions. It was the proliferation of satelites without an ethical context that SC had questioned Armani about, but Armani was reveling in it, and it became clear to SC that Armani had never really cared about what was being transmitted.

Their discussions had, on occasion turned into arguments, open on-screen arguments, about the content, but the proliferation seemed uncontrollable and Armani was feeding the fire -- watching the *hammers* glow in the fire. He was not concerned with the thoughtful considerations of worldwide problems or discussions. SC, however, thought the intimacy of discussions and the awareness of other's *humanity* in personal, yet public settings could be the overriding achievement of this technology.

Instead, he thought, *this aspect seemed to be lost in the overwhelming concern with the advancement of technological products, as if that was the reason for them...as well as, simply, the overwhelming concern with the output -- the mass output -- of the cameras and wall screens and lightboxes -- the hardware -- as if that was the soul reason for them.* "The hardware was becoming the content, the software was becoming the message." He had paraphrased Marshall McLuhan in his arguments with Armani. But the box had been opened... the lid was gone...there was no way to close it.

Others, however, had joined in, making it an ongoing forum. In an ironic way, this was, at least, a lively, worldwide discussion of what these *hammering* places were about.

Halcyon Days

What had happened since those halcyon days when Jeanette's place opened up to Alfred's place in Silesia and then to the *geary gathering* in San Francisco and to Aiden's place on the *nose of the dog*? SC had imagined a worldwide community having interactive, peaceful, cultural contact -- without geographic borders. He had imagined a world wide community concerned with each other, as families were concerned with each other, as they were concerned with the future and how it would affect their children. But now, these ideas, these possible paths all seemed covered with swirling, shadows that cast darkness on what he had, initially, wanted to strengthen -- wanted to realize...

But then, again, maybe, ironically, the immediate interaction, of the screen to screen discussions and arguments, was becoming a lot like family? He was almost forced to realize that it *had* become like the intimate arena of a family and it was there that the most intense feelings surfaced, and also where, sometimes, the most tragic consequences occurred.

Is this part of the larger family? he questioned. *Are these just the dynamics of the larger family of humanity?*

His mind went back and forth in this internal debate.

But his initial vision, did not go back and forth. It was, still, like an *awakening morning* to him...and that is what he wrote in his notebook...

Morning Came, he had written, after his rendevous with that mysterious misty woman, the spy, who brought him into the prescence of a remarkable man...

morning came
after sleepless nights
thinking about the inhumane,
horrendous suicide attacks on innocent people...
morning came
after wandering in the darkness of my own soul
questioning over and over again
the human capacity to act with such cruelty
It is incredible
that the same technology
that extends humanities potential
to do good...
the same technology
that makes our lives easier,
that gives us more potential

185

can also be put to such horrific destructive uses.
Prometheus your punishment was great
but was your contribution greater?
or was it just inevitable?
morning came
after long nights of agonizing
over the proliferation of the
atomic bombs,
the hydrogen bombs,
the smart bombs, the, the, the...
the potential of all of these
to reduce all life,
all cultures,
all ideas,
all values,
to rubble,
to oblivion...
morning came
after all those dark thoughts and realizations
morning came
spreading it's light
it's vision
over the world that was also possible
over the world that could also be seen
over the world that could also be heard
and felt
and loved in innocence
and believed in...
and
had
faith in...

That morning's idealism had not yet wavered.

Now, in the *hammering* places, springing up all over the world, there was still the possibility of making this vision penetrate the varied cloaks of people's realities. *Different voices, different languages, different people could work together on something larger than themselves,* he thought, *they could listen to the sounds of hammering around the world -- they could realize our commonality more than our differences. Here was the possibility of making this vision a conscious part of this world -- his world -- thee world.*

He felt this was still the counterweight to his initial, frustrated feelings of despair and anger and helplessness, this was the thesis to the antithesis. Yes, it was another dialectical movement of history -- out of these *hammering* places -- out of their interplay - - out of their dynamic -- would come a synthesis, in which a hopeful future would evolve...

Path Twenty Eight

Clues and Artifacts

"Twing, Ben and I are going to look around the park and, maybe, the town a bit. Are you up for it?" Betsy asked during breakfast at Alex's.

Without moving his head, he pursed his mouth and halfjokingly said, "I don't feel up to the park just yet."

She nodded, "Of course, that's understandable, we're going to look for other possible signs, but I have a feeling we're not going to find anything."

"It's probably going to be a mute issue," Ben added.

"Unless we go to the police…" Betsy interjected.

"Look, I think I'm OK, we have enough to deal with, what are the police going to do about it, it was a crazy incident. I couldn't even tell them how it really happened, maybe the other kids were in on it? I don't know but I don't want the King, er, my father, or Nadjia to have something else to worry about."

"OK, well, just be careful, if you go out, Twing," Betsy finally said as she halfheartedly accepted his argument.

They left him sitting in a corner of the pub, his neck bandaged, his hair tousled, pensive, with his chin propped up by an arm, eyes wide, his mind alive with what to do. After, what seemed like, a long while, Twing took out the old coin he found, or had been given, put it in front of him, took out the several small bones and laid them in front of him.

"Some more coffee?" Alex startled him and broke his concentration.

Mm, uhh," is all he could answer.

"Sorry, didn't realize you were contemplating the bones."

"Yea."

"That's what they are, aren't they?"

"Yea, they...I found them," is all Twing would offer to him but Alex's curiosity only brought up more questions.

"They look like they have writing on them."

Twing finally realized he had to share these objects with him, *After all,* he thought, *he helped save my life,* and said, They've got some letters inscribed on them or in them. I was able to figure out this one, at least I think it says N I C H O L A S. I really haven't had a chance to figure out the other one...

"Well, let's have a look, shall we." Alex took the one with writing on it and, taking the stance of an investigator, eyed it carefully, turned it around, scraped off some dirt, until he spoke with an excited tone, "I'm a bit of an archeologist meself, you know, loved to dig, ever since I was a kid...you've got an old one here all right, it looks like, and as near as I can tell from the old English, it has the letters F L A X E N written on it."

"Flaxen," Twing repeated.

"That's what it looks like, that X threw me off for a minute but I think it's part of the name."

"Nicholas and Flaxen," Twing repeated. "Two names out of the past, kept alive in the bones, old bones...You know, Alex..." Twing wanted to tell him of his encounter with the old man in the cavern but caught himself and showed him the coin instead. "What do you make of this?"

Alex perused it as intently as the bones, "It's old, this is an old coin. I believe, its got a labyrinth on it..."

"What about the image in the middle of it?" Twing interrupted him. "Would you say it's a wolf's head?"

"It could very well be."

"What do make of that?"

"I dunno, it's interesting," he looked incredulously at Twing and offered a thought, "Is there a connection between this and your attacker…I don't know? I'll tell you though, you might want to check at the bookstore, they've got some books on labyrinths and the…"

"I saw their shop window when we first came into town."

"It's our resident eccentric who runs it, along with his wife…They're not always here, though, take off on a whim, when the moon's full or some other celestial sign. They'll know about labyrinths all right. I'm not sure about wolves, though."

The more they talked the more Twing realized how weak he was from the previous day's encounter and finally said, "Alex, I'd like to recuperate for a few days, I don't want to go back home right now, not with this bandage on me and I don't feel like traveling. Are the rooms we're staying in available for a few days?"

"As long as you want, they're on a first come basis anyway."

Path Twenty Nine

Eye of the Storm

Aiden opened his eyes slowly, the nightmare that had invaded his body had subsided, had ebbed like the tides that washed this flat and soggy land. The effects of a hidden moon on an ancient howling beast, hidden in the stones, the very rocks Aiden had lived over, for over 20 years, had also waned. All was still, as he realized he had fallen asleep, in front of his open door, on the floor. Now he was pushing himself up, shaking his head, shaking off the dregs of darkness, the dregs of an overwhelming black filled night. A night, when the sightless sounds, of ancient fears, had overcome him. He looked around and was surprised to see the morning light, still gray, warming over the eastern horizon. He could feel it. He staggered into the living room, *Where was Annie?* He suddenly said out loud. *What had happened?*

He called out *Annie! Jules!* and waited for a reply. He called again, *Annie?* Nothing. He turned on a satelite. Jeanette's Place. He looked on the screen. No one in the cafe. He looked at the camera and inquired of anyone, "What time is it? SC? Is anyone there?"

"Aiden," a voice resounded in his living room, "Aiden..." Finally Jeanette came into view. "SC has gone home," she answered. "What in heaven's name happened to you? We got this weird transmission last night. Everyone else has gone home. They were up most of the night trying to make some sense of your transmission, trying to make contact with you."

"What do you mean?"

"Well, we heard these wild cries, and your screen was just a swirling mist of clouds or something. It was eerie."

"I had an unusual night myself but I didn't use the camera, I wasn't on...Wait a minute! Annie, Annie took the other camera. The one I had in the kitchen. As far as I know, they are not back yet, wait, hold on, stay there, let me check." He went to the bed room, no one had slept in the beds, no one had come home as far as he could see or could tell. He went back to the living room. "Jeanette, they haven't returned. I have to call the balloon company. They were going on a balloon ride yesterday. Will you hang on?"

"Yes, I'll call SC and try to get a hold of Armani...he had also checked in on this, actually, quite a few satelites had inquired about the transmission from your place, Aiden."

"Let me call the company, maybe, they let the camera run." He looked up hot air balloons and found the listing. He dialed up and asked the first person who answered it if Annie Helden or a Jules...Jules, he did not even know his last name, had rented a hot air balloon?"

"Who is this?"

"This is a friend. They had planned on renting a balloon yesterday."

"They did. They went up yesterday and haven't returned."

"What do you mean?"

"They were to return last night, yesterday. They have not returned. We are on a waiting pattern right now. We're not sure where they are. We're trying to contact them."

"This is incredible. You don't know where they are. This is a giant balloon. You don't lose a giant balloon."

"We had unusual weather yesterday."

"I know that. Are you in contact with the pilot, I mean the person guiding the balloon?"

"We had initial contact and then we didn't hear from him, Gerard, that is. He's the pilot in the balloon."

194

"Well, this is incredible." Aiden took the phone from his ear and looked into the camera. "Has anyone been following this? Annie, I mean Leylani has disappeared, her friend Jules was with her, they took a camera with them. What did you see last night?"

"Slowdown, Aiden," SC had finally arrived and was watching and listening to Aiden transmitting from his cottage.

"SC, thank God! What did you see last night? This is crazy. They might have been sending in SOS."

"We heard, *out of control* and *Jules* and *Leylani* and then we heard a wail, I'll tell you quite frankly, it was unlike anything I've ever heard."

"Are you serious, I heard something like that, also. It was a howlingwailing sound. God, it was like, it was like I was surrounded by...by the Banshees or *wolves?*...Only I was having a nightmare, at least I thought I was..."

SC's eyes widened, "Maybe someone taped it," he halfquestioned and continued speaking to the satelites, "Anyone out there who taped last night's transmission from Aiden's Place?"

No positive responses came from anyone, but more people had tuned in, the screens seemed to be coming alive with interested onlookers.

"SC, I've got to get back to the balloon company. I'll give you a report when I find out something."

"Aiden, maybe people who are tuned in could help. Is there anything we can do?"

"I don't know, I don't even know what I can do, I'm depending on the balloon company..."

Aiden, we'll stay tuned."

Path Thirty

The Olde Bookshoppe

"Where did you come across these?" Alex finally asked after he had studied the bones and the button with the plume carved in it and the labyrinth coin, which he couldn't help but touch and move his finger along the incised lines, circling in and out, in and out…

Twing finally said, "I found them. It was a strange encounter. We were on the way to see my father when we stopped to stretch our legs. I walked around and tripped and found this pouch in a hollow, actually some kind of a small cavern."

"This land is steeped in history, my friend, you never know when you might step into or onto something. I'd say you were meant to stop there."

"I really wasn't looking for anything, in fact, I didn't really want to come here." He hesitated and put his hands around his bandaged neck. Staring vacantly out in front of him he let the words flow, "Alex, I don't know what I'm doing here, I feel like I'm caught up in something, it's all around me, I've lost a thread, a thread that might help me make sense out of what's been happening to me…"

Alex just listened and looked at the tousle-haired youth. He thought of his own path which hadn't veered much since he started working in the pub after his father died. Since that time he had slowly and consistently let go of whatever youthful dreams he might have had. The pub had become his life and he had told enough people, "You end up somewhere in life. This is where my family has roots that go deep. I'm just another branch on this old tree."

He waited for a moment's silence before he spoke to Twing, "You know, I wanted to travel when I was younger, always wanted to go to Egypt, I used to read about the Sphinx and the pyramids, actually, it was in the Olde Bookshoppe, it was there I read about Richard Burton trying to find the source of the Nile and Lord Kitchner riding a camel over the desert, but every time I thought about it seriously, something happened. My father died when I was 20, so I helped my mother run the pub until she had a stroke and I've been at it ever since. I haven't had a chance to go anywhere, but I found out over the years that people came to me...A lot of young people, in fact, have come traveling through here, especially in the '60s. It seemed like everyone was on the move at that time. We had theater in the street. But the point is, I ended up here and, it was almost like, the world came to me. There were kids coming back from Egypt and Katmandu and Tibet and San Francisco. It's been a lot quieter since then but, I'll tell ya, the weekend theater still packs them in..."

"Alex," Twing's voice changed his excited mood, "My father's dying and my brothers disappeared and I almost got killed yesterday."

Alex let it sink in before he ventured an answer, "Look, Twing. Yes, you almost died yesterday. You can thank your lucky star that you didn't, but...but don't you see, every moment you are now alive is also because of that fortuitous event. You could have died, but you didn't...I'd say you have a reason for living. He looked at him, searching his face, "Is there a girl in your life?"

Twing sighed for a moment, his thoughts circled as Angelina's image arose inside him, "Yea."

"Well, keep your future in mind, you've got someone who's thinking about you."

Twing's face turned to a slight smile and with a thoughtful nod said, "I think I want to write a postcard."

He thanked Alex, picked up his artifacts, held them in his hand and walked out into the morning air. Breathing deeply, the air seemed to give life to his step as he headed down the main street towards the Olde Bookshoppe. *They might have postcards,* he thought, and walked until he stood in front of the window he had looked into when they came to the village. He noticed the book on the Labyrinth was gone and he suddenly felt like he'd lost something. *Could they have sold it?* he wondered, and pushed down the handle of the carved wooden door.

Kling-a-ling, kling-a-ling. The tinkle of a bell, pulled by a string, attached to the door, greeted Twing as he entered, *Tinker Bell is alive and well,* he thought, as pixie dust flashed in the streams of light illuminating the covers and ends of olde and relatively old books and objects of all kinds scattered on shelves and on tables around well-worn furniture and Oriental rugs. Twing sensed a strange combination of unpredictability and comfort, as if one could ease into one of the comfortable overstuffed chairs only to have an owl or some other creature swoop by. There was no one behind the counter…There was…

Hah ha, hah he, there's a chance you're number thirtythree, let me see, what will it…

Twing almost jumped out of his shoes. *What!* He looked around…he turned around, looking, looking until he finally saw a short older man with a tweed hat and what looked like a red and white face, with eyes…with eyes that were alive. In fact, when the man's eyes met his there was a wild yell, AYE EE! *It is the King of Terra Grandeur! Moira, look. Come here. Our friend has returned."*

Twing turned around, wondering if he was being mistaken for someone else but there was no one else in the store. "I beg your pardon," he finally said, reacting to the strange greeting. Before the man answered, his companion came in and immediately saw the bandage around Twing's neck. With a mazed eyes, he said, "Jules, what happened to your neck?"

By this time Twing was sure this was all the case of mistaken identity, the King of Terra Grandeur? Jules? Who were they talking about? What was going on? "I think you've mistaken me for someone else," he finally said.

"Mistaken our wandering King? Where is your Queen? Where is Leylani?"

This was getting to be too much for Twing and he finally blurted out, "I've never been here before, I don't think I know you."

"He's lost his memory," the man's companion speculated. "Do you not remember us?"

"I'm afraid I don't."

"It must have been an accident. Can you tell us what happened?"

"You have a bandage around your neck, old sport. What happened at Aidens?"

"What do you mean *Aidens*? I had an accident. Here. In Wellborn."

"And you don't remember us?"

Hey, hoo, this will never do, we've wandered with you, on the tor of Terra Grandeur and the nose of the dog...

"Can I ask you something?" Twing said.

Ask away my King.

"I think you're putting me on, or you've mistaken me for someone else." With his voice rising Twing caught himself and, like the swoop of an owl, a hint of understanding came into him, "When did we go to this tor? Or this *nose of the dog?*"

"Why, we left you at Aidens a few days ago."

"I see, and is it possible it was somebody else?"

"I don't see how, can you not remember?"

"I will let you in on a secret. I have a twin brother."

"No! It can't be. You are one and the same."

"Don't be too hasty, dear, there was one distinguishing mark our Jules had. Do you remember his birthmark?"

"Yes, by Jove, it was on his neck."

Now it was Twing's turn to feel a bit queasy, "I had a birthmark until yesterday, that's the reason for the bandage. I was attacked and it was cut off."

By Jove, what horror…

"You've lost your identity," the woman answered.

"No, no! No," now it was becoming painful to Twing but his need to know was growing, "You met my twin brother, that's the only explanation for this, you met my t-w-i-n brother," he spelled it out. We, I, I've been looking for him, for days now, he's been gone for weeks."

"Dear, this is quite extraordinary."

"You must help me find him. His father is dying."

"Dying, oh dear, this is dreadful…"

"My boy, we were with this Jules and a girl he met, who thought he was the King of Terra Grandeur. We wandered a bit and finally ended up at a place…"

"A cottage on the nose of the dog…"

Yes, by Jove, that's it, we left them there after a raucous night on the telly.

Twing was shaking his head at their unbelievable story and was thinking to himself, *These two are weird, what is going on here?* until he finally asked them, "Can you take me there? It's really a matter of our father dying, he wants to see Twangly."

"Twangly?"

"That's my brother's name, Twangly Rexroth."

"Good heavens, dear, a gentleman."

I say, let's do it, we'll take you there, before you can count to three, hee hee, we'll take you to that place, but you'll have to tell us more…

"Yes, yes, please, but we must stop at the Sword and the Plough, my friends are there and they've been looking with me."

The olde bookseller and his lady friend Moira busied themselves with the CLOSED sign, turned off the tea kettle, grabbed their hats and a *brolly* and were off with Twing. They walked to the pub and found Alex. Ben and Betsy had not returned. Twing was almost beside himself when he told Alex that these two had been with Twangly, had seen him and would take him to the cottage where they had last seen him. Alex just looked at Twing with an old knowing kind of look, as if to say, *See, I told you there was a reason for all of this.*

By the time they talked some more and had a pint of the local brew, Ben and Betsy walked into the pub. Twing literally jumped up and grabbed them, pulled them over to the table, *I've found him!* he exclaimed, *I've found him, they saw him!* They introduced each other but, like a man with a secret past, the owner simply said that he and his wife are the proprietors of the Olde Bookshoppe and as soon as plans had been made, they packed up and said good bye to Alex. Twing shook his hand and thanked him again for his help. He told him he would come back with Twangly, see a play, stay a little longer.

Before Alex had poured a pint to the next customer, Twing had stretched out his legs in the back seat of the '48' Rolls with the old man and his lady companion in the front. Ben and Betsy were following behind in the Mercedes, on the road to the coast, to Aiden's place. "I feel like I've just made a turn on the right street," Twing said to the old man and Moira "What I thought was a dead end has suddenly become..." He was searching for the right word and finally just said, "I've got a lot to ask you, but before I do, will you or would you tell me what happened? How you met Twangly? They told Twing everything that had happened to them, how they picked up Twangly and Leylani, the walk up Terra Grandeur, the jewel he found, the coast storm and how they finally left the three of them, Jules, Leylani and Aiden, after that wild night. They told him about the satelite hookups.

"*Wow,*" was all they heard from the back seat until they asked him to tell his story, which he did, in between villages and pubs. When both cars stopped they all had lunch together, planning the reunion of the two brothers. Twing also told them about the extraordinary meeting with his brother, the letter that started it all, and how he seemed to be on this path, with one thing after another happening to him, taking one turn after another,

"Do you know we heard your horn the day we drove into Well-born?" he suddenly blurted out. That's how it's been. I walked by your store and saw a book on labyrinths and it was one of the reasons to go back there. I was actually going to buy a…" He suddenly remembered Angelina, "The next time we stop I've got to send off a postcard."

The Devil's Hook

They drove until they came to the village close to Aiden's cottage. Twing was adamant about sending a postcard, looking left and right for the right stop. When the driver spied the Devil's Hook, he announced in his inimitable way, *I say, let's wet our whistle at that one, shall we?*

"They may even sell postcards," Moira added, "If not, there's probably a gift shop somewhere,"

But Twing's thoughts were already on what he wanted to say to Angelina…he even allowed himself a slight smile of remembrance, *She's got me,* he thought, and chuckled at the idea of the Devil's Hook…*pretty woman, dah da da dah da, pretty woman…*His head bounced with the guitar accompaniment and he was as close to Angelina as he was to the memory of that old hit song.

Betsy and Ben met them at the door of the pub. She looked at the pub, looked at the olde bookseller and just shook her head, "You sure know how to pick them, mister, mister…You know, I didn't get your name this morning.

"Ha, hah, " he responded with a quick step, "you'll have to guess."

When he said this, Twing and Ben realized they hadn't gotten his name either. They looked at each other and thought about this unusual character with the tweed hat and the plaid face.

Betsy smiled and said, "Is it Rumplestiltskin?"

This brought a laugh from all of them and the olde bookseller, the wee leprechaun, just lit up and did a jig over to a corner table, *I've lost the child...I've lost the child, he repeated, The weather was wild, ahoy...*

Somehow this reference was lost to all of them except Betsy, who ventured to ask again, "Is it a secret? Do we have to spin straw into gold?"

Moira finally ended the suspense, "This is Findhorn, my companion and fellow traveler."

Moira, Moira, you've given me away, hey, hey. He chuckled, *And a how dee doo, to you.*

They smiled, everyone shook hands, and found their way to a table. As soon as they settled in, a waitress came by, "Good evenin, taste of our best?"

Moira was the first to answer, "Yes, please, and menus and this young man wants a post card. Do have any?"

"Well, as a matter of fact we do." She pointed to a plastic case on the wall near the door. "They're free. It's somebody's idea of advertising. We also have our own at the bar."

Twing ordered a Devil's Hook special and went to the case of cards. He looked them over and took out one with a picture of a balloon, a tie-dyed hot air balloon, with the company's phone number and address on the back. He also picked up a couple of Devil's Hook cards and went back to the table to show the others.

"You picked a perplexing one," the waitress said as she looked at the cards and set down the local brew.

"Oh, why is that?"

"Well, there's been some excitement around here." As she said this, she was pointing to the balloon card, "One of the balloons that went up has disappeared."

"What do you mean?"

I say...

The company who rents them is just north of here, I know the owner, comes in here all the time, told me a balloon didn't get back..."

"They don't know where it is..."

"We had some strange weather the other day, almost like a hurricane, it was, clouds a turnin, finally headed out to sea, they think the balloon went with them -- the clouds that is."

"Wow, I'm not sure I want to send it."

"Except now it has a story around it," Ben added.

"What do you make of it, dear?"

By Jove, they have strange weather out here, ha ho, do you recall the storm we had the day we came this way.

"It was frightful."

I met the grim reaper that day, and he almost took me away, hey hey.

"Now don't excite yourself, my dear, I'm sure they will find the balloon."

They continued to speculate on the events over dinner when the proprietor of the pub came over to tell them about a jukebox behind them, one with a screen on it, "It's called a *lightbox*, a local one, the latest," he gushed with pride.

"What do you mean?"

"Well, I'm trying it out. You can get live broadcasts from around the world, sort of like the old radio receiver, ya probably don't remember sitting around those, but I was a *ham* at one time. I'd stay up half the night listening to broadcasts, talking to others just as crazy…"

They turned and looked at the light combinations emanating from, what looked like, a wonderful anachronism, "Looks like my jukebox," Betsy exclaimed,

"Except that it has screens," Big Ben added.

"Yes, exactly, and it's instantaneous, *live* from various parts of the world."

I say, sounds like the screens at Aiden's place, do you recall our astonishment when the wall came alive?

"After Annie's song, that was a night."

"You know Aiden? He's the one who introduced me to this…He said he knew an electronic wizard who, he said, was trying to connect the world. He brought this thing in and connected it. We've tried it a few times…"

"Can we get the news?"

"Oh, you can get more than that, you can go to any number of other satelites. You mentioned Aiden, let's see if he's tuned in…"

"How do we connect?" Ben asked, remembering his own global locator and the unique properties of the old rings of Urum.

"Well, we simply turn it on and talk into it, tell it the name of the satelite and it will either come in or it will let us know if there's any one turned on."

"I beg your pardon," Betsy stated and smiled at Ben.

He put several coins in the pulsing beauty until a hollow voice rose out of the colors, "Satelite, please?"

"Aiden's Place," he answered with slightly more enunciation.

"Number Please?"

"He, *it*, wants a number. Do you have his number?"

"I do, I've talked to him before. Hold on." He took a small notebook out of his pocket, thumbed through the pages, "Ah, here it is, here." He loudly pronounced the number: 2, 0, 0, 5.

Immediately, a living room came into view, *By Jove, that is his place, I did a jig, I did…*

"Leylani howled like a wolf…"

"Aiden, are you there? We're calling from the Devil's Hook. There are some friends of yours here…"

"Look into the screen, the proprietor told them, "The camera's somewhere in there…"

"Aiden?"

With one hand on the telephone, Aiden or what had been Aiden stepped into view, his voice strident and hyper, *Hello, hey, who's there, my God, it's the wee leprechaun, you've tuned in at the worst time, we've got troubles here, you wouldn't believe, I'm on the phone here…with…* He suddenly disappeared, as quickly as he had come into view. The living room turned empty. The sound of a door opening could be heard. The reception blinked, off, then on again, then cut off, a blank screen…

Hey, what! Can we get him again?

"Aiden's Place, 2005, on screen one," the proprietor stated clearly but with no success, the screen stayed blank, "Most strange, we can keep trying but, you know, he's not too far from here."

"It is not like he is half way across the sea," Moira added, "We should carry on."

I say, let's motor on down his way, hey, hey, we've got Jules to find.

They paid for their meal and drinks and thanked the proprietor for the unusual connection with Aiden, intimate and frustrating at the same time...What troubles was he talking about? And why the disconnection? With anxious thoughts they drove towards Aiden's cottage by the sea, on the *nose of the dog*, over the remains of an ancient cave, inscribed with the image of a long ago beast, a wolf that sacrificed its blood for those who went on living, a wolf, whose offspring infused their longing, howling sounds into the very rocks that became their sanctuary...

They drove as if an unseen force had taken over, the road turned and branched off and turned again. The evening light turned the sign posts, the hillocks, the outcroppings of rocks, turned all things, above the low, flat sealand, into long shadows, shadows that grew longer and then receded, as the car turned, almost circled, ever closer to the outline of the cottage, There, finally, in the pale, violet light, was Aiden's place. A bright window was beckoning them, reminding the olde bookseller Findhorn and his lady friend Moira of another night, crackling with lightning and a storm's fury.

There she be!

"Be careful, dear, remember the last time you got stuck in the bog, we had everyone pushing us out."

Ah, hah, here we are

He pulled over to the side of the road. Ben pulled in behind him. They got out and the whole excursion trooped up to Aiden's door. They knocked and with an immediate opening of the door, Aiden stepped in front of them, looking wild, harangued, anxious. *Is there word?* he called out, looking over their heads into the sky, looking, invoking the very heavens above them, *Is there word, my God, is there word?*

I say, old chap, what's wrong?

They were all somewhat astonished and moved back to give him room.

They're lost, my God...they're lost, he repeated.

"Who? What?" several voices asked.

Annie and Jules! His voice froze the names in the air. *Annie and Jules!*

By Jove, what happened, where are they?

They're lost in the sea, lost, I just found out, they've found the balloon, they're lost, they...

He continued but the words had struck them all, like spikes thrown at them,

Twing rushed up to him, *What are you saying? They're lost! Man, out with it, out...* He was caught up in Aiden's anxiety, crazed with a fear of loss that he didn't think he could bear, *Do you mean Twangly? You don't mean Twangly, do you?*

With eyes closed Aiden barely spoke, "I mean Jules, Twangly, Twangly, I don't know, and Annie, Leylani They went up in that tie-dyed balloon and were swept up and out into the sea. They were lost. They were lost and now they've found the balloon, the balloon floating on the waves with no one, no one, no one..." He kept repeating until he just walked back into the house and fell into the nearest chair.

They all followed him except for Twing. He was not going to listen, to hear. He did not want to hear anymore. He simply ran off into the night. He ran and ran, down to the sea, along the sea, along the waves, wailing, *no, no, noooo...one...*until the sound of the breaking waves, the wind, the air overwhelmed him and obscured, even his, agonizing cries...

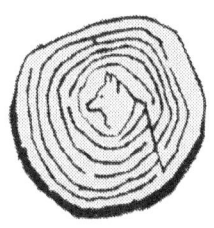

Path Thirty One

Last Breath

"It's a matter of time," Doctor Highshe spoke and nodded his head towards the waiting and anxious Queen, "It's a matter of time. There is nothing more we can do. He is in the hands of Allah."

Nadjia had given her consent to a natural ending for her husband, the exiled monarch, lying in a coma under the peacock covers. The husband she had lived for, and the father she had deceived so many years ago. The man whose life had been in the pursuit of hard truths, whose exile had been a waiting game of possibility. The father who had come to realize that his first born child had been given away and that this secret had been kept from him all these years. Now the Doctor, the same Doctor who helped bring his two sons into the world, had taken him off the artificial life support system. The Doctor had tried to persuade Nadjia to hold on until Twangly was found but her state had become increasingly anxious and nervous.

She needed some certainty, *Where was Twangly? Where was Tiger?* He had not returned, *When will they call? When will they find him?* She had repeated this litany as she went from room to room. Euphrates could hear her coming…Clara could hear her weeping…at odd hours. She was playing out the last act of a tragedy, born in a soothsayer's rantings, begun before their time.

Path Thirty Two

Armani's News

An announcer came on the screen: For late breaking news from the West Country we take you to a member of the search party, "Wesley, are you there? Any good news?"

A variegated greygreenwhite picture emerged on the screen with the insistent choppy sound of a helicopter flying over a wide expanse of sea. A fishing boat could be seen in the distance. "It's a choppy, calm sea out here, the sky is billowing above us, we have a window of light. Wait, I am just getting the word from a coast guard cutter. They have found a balloon, a large balloon floating about four miles off shore. I'm heading out there, stay tuned, maybe…"

Just ask Alice, she's ten feet tall…

"Wesley, what was that?"

"Oh, sorry, that kicks in every once in a while, I've been out here since this morning and I brought some of my old tapes to keep me going, in between reports, that is, we're getting within range now, there, it should be coming into view."

"Wesley, all we've seen is a choppy, churning sea, is there any hope? Have they found anyone?"

"There's no update yet, wait, look, I see the coast guard cutter…"

He circled around, over the cutter, finally a hint of color…

Just ask Alice, who's two feet tall…

"Wesley, you're on *Armani's News*, what's going on, any news?'

The hint of color became a pulsing, surging jelly fish of golden yellow and magenta red and turquoise blue, in and out of the greygreenwhite sea, like a heart beating, up and down. The cutter was getting closer. They were being cautious. Now, they could see the basket floating with no sign of anyone, only the beating of a tiedyed heart on a wayward flight…

Just ask Alice, she's seen it all…

They circled closer, closer, until a hook reached out and grabbed the membrane of this colorful creature, pulling it towards the cutter. Questions rang out. *Maybe they're caught underneath? Maybe they've drowned under the balloon?* They hooked and tugged, pulling the fabric up, up along the cutter until the greygreenwhite chopped surface gave up its momentary heart and the sea was open to the possibility of gasping lungs…but nothing, nothing but the sea was visible.

"We have brought the balloon and basket on board and, so far, have not found anyone or any sign of anyone, no one, in the vicinity of the balloon. We will continue looking, expanding the circle, it is possible they swam towards the coast."

Wesley circled the cutter and also continued outward, circling, circling, further, until he saw the shore line and followed it for any sign of coughed up life. His continuous updating had been followed by satelites around the world. Armani had created and produced *Armani's News*: *instant-live-access* to all parts of the earth. His creation had become immediate communication and this had become intimate living room drama. The extended family, that SC had bare intimations of when he first talked to Armani, had become real. What

Armani and SC had laughed over and convulsed over and made a pact over on that fateful night at the Hotel Europa, had become a reality. The technology had mushroomed, innumerable variations of interactive communication had come into being and into play; from moveable screens on living room walls to interactive live pub *lightboxes* like the one they found in the Devil's Hook. SC was holding Sunday night forums out of Jeanette's Place in Amsterdam, Alfred was holding poetic soirees and historical recollections from his castle room in Silesia, the *geary gathering* had become an odd assortment of bohemian gatherings, with unknown possibilities from chess to watercolors to an arts magazine to the styles of Tarot cards to wading in the cafe fountain.

These and many more satelites around the world had tuned into this drama, off the coast of this sea land, this upside down constellation. This drama had captured the attention of the late night visitors to Aiden's place. When that strange whirlwind of clouds had come on the screen with the vaguely audible words of distress, these visitors became fascinated, curious, questioning…Many of those who tuned in that night were still tuned into Aiden's erratic transmissions as well as the news transmissions from *Armani's News*. Wesley, Wesley Weiderkind, had been intrigued from the start and was out searching as soon as the weather allowed it. He had become a major part of this drama through his reports and speculations and almost fruitful search. The world had been with him when the throbbing colors of the balloon were found. They circled with him and searched the coast and the beaches and the rocks and finally, finally they lay in weariness after a long day of hope was dashed by the finding of empty fabric.

For a few hours, a few moments on this turning planet, many hearts were beating with this pulsing, throbbing, colorful heart on that greygreenwhite sea. But the day was ending and now the colors were fading, falling and finally becoming a moonlit possibility, turning on the hopes and desires of a miracle. With this desire, Betsy and Ben fell asleep, Aiden languished in a bottle of Devil's Hook Dark Ale and Twing lay in exhaustion on the beach. The very beach his brother and Leylani and Gerard might have crawled upon; might have found salvation on, yet so far, were not found on. Only the olde bookseller Findhorn and Moira had driven into the village, they needed some distance from the palpable tension surrounding the end of the day. They needed rest and found an inn next to the pub, which enveloped them and let them sleep; sleep, away the revelation of loss. They talked little but both felt the forces thick in the air.

"We must look beyond the obvious," Moira mused, uncharacteristically, to her companion.

Path Thirty Three

Saltwater Tears

Before his eyes opened, with the sounds of saltwater coming out of his mouth, coughing and barely perceptible, Twing gasped, *Was it a dream? Has he…*Betsy lifted his head, then lifted a shoulder, the eyes opened…He drew back, *Where is he?*

"You've been out all night, Twing. Let's get you back."

They slowly rose and lifted him from the damp, cold sand until he was shivering and shaking between their hands and arms and shoulders. They walked him back to the cottage, around a pile of sand, that was, now, much more noticeable, to the front door. It was open.

"Aiden?" they called.

No one answered. They went in, built a fire, bundled up Twing and avoided his half-crazed inquiries. When Moira and Findhorn arrived, the household had warmed and a kind of calmness had descended upon them.

"Where is Aiden?" Findhorn finally asked, realizing their host had not shown himself. He proceeded to take a walk outside and around the cottage. He had only stepped outside when sand came flying out of a hole, a flare up of sand coming out of the pit, which almost sprayed him.

"Aiden?" he called out, but only the *clang* of a shovel hitting rock, came out of the opening. He descended down, down, through a doorway, which he was able to walk through, until

215

he was within the flickering, wavering light of a torch stuck in the soft seam of the wall. He searched the room and glimpsed Aiden or what might have been Aiden, shoveling sand in a corner. The shadowedshoveler turned to bring a full shovel-load of sand to the opening. They simultaneously saw each other. The plaid-faced visitor almost gasped and for once had no ready words. Aiden's hair was coated with sand. He had not shaved in several days, his eyes reflecting the flickering torch light, like lightning going off and on. Aiden dropped the shovel and went straight for Findhorn, put his hands on his shoulders and with a knowing turn pointed to the incised wall, *Wolf!* His guttural sound filled the cavern, *Wolf house.*

Findhorn nodded his head, as if he had known, all along, what was under the cottage -- as if he had known that an age-old womb had been covered over, over the centuries, until the sleepy, sliding, settling cottage caused Aiden to dig under it, to dig it out.

Aiden pointed again and again to the wall. What had looked like two people were now joined by a third incised figure. Findhorn nodded his head, and with unusual lucidity, slowly remarked, *Leylani invoked the ancient sounds infused in the stones...The word echoed around them...stones...stones...She had*, he said to Aiden, *She has...The mother has reclaimed her own.*

Aiden let go of the wee man, picked up the shovel and with a frenzy began to dig once more, his actions flickering in the torch light. *The sounds of, Wolf house,* could be heard through the sand, *Wolf House, wolf...*

Findhorn listened and watched as seams of sand seemed to be opening and moving about the walls, like sand on a vibrating paddle, creating patterns, moving patterns of moving images, old primordial images of bloodletting and survival: the reminders of generations of people and wolves inside them and out, the reminders of generations of Ngs and wolves.

Klang! Klang! The sounds of shovel hitting rock indicated Aiden's accelerated movements. He was threatening to overtake Findhorn as he moved towards the doorway. In haste Findhorn walked between the rocks and the flickering images. He stepped through, out, around and over the sand dune only to see Twing being brought back between Ben and Betsy.

I say you've found him, come this way, he said, and with his customary quick step, opened the door.

They brought the slightly wet, cold, shivering Twing into the living room until he was settled in front of the fire, buried in blankets. Only then did Findhorn venture to address them and blurted out, *The mother has reclaimed her child, the deed is done, don't weep, don't weep over the setting sun...*

"Please dear, don't speak in riddles, the young man is recovering, he has spent the night with lost souls...He has come back..."

"And he will go on." Betsy broke in to say.

"And he'll find out..."

"Find out what?" Betsy asked, "Can we please get some news? Can we turn on the screens? Where is Aiden? Can we get some word of Twangly?"

"Yes, but how, where do we turn them on?" Ben looked around for a switch or a remote.

"Just say it, Ben," Betsy reminded him and they both chanted, *Armani's News*! It was as if Aladdin had spoken and invoked the magic words. The door opened. A screen brightened and flashed with the myriad reflections of crystal light, not the stolen gems of the 40 thieves, but the technological outgrowth of the earthly forces that had created both. They stared at the wakening screen, until the silence was broken, and they heard the cadenced sound of an announcer's voice,

"...an incredible outpouring of concern for two young inhabitants and the pilot of a wayward hot air balloon. We have come to know something of Gerard Macleod, the pilot of the balloon and we have had constant but erratic contact with Aiden through satelite transmissions from his place, Aiden is a friend of Annie Helden, the young woman who rented the balloon and Jules, her friend, whom Aiden called the King of Terra Grandeur. The hearts of many, many people around the world have gone out to this tragedy in the air and finally the sea, Wesley Weiderkind brought us reports of the recovery of the tie-dyed balloon and the hopes that were in that discovery. But it was not to be a discovery of the three unfortunate balloonists. They have not been found and the sea, the sea that took them is silent, a silence broken only by the whirring of helicopters in the air or the churning of propellers in the sea and the heartfelt communication between all of us.

Now the engines are silent, the communication is ending, the searchers have gone home, Wesley, I'm sure will sleep. He has been up for two days and Aiden is out of touch, too distraught, I believe, to give us any more thoughts or reports.

The miracle we hoped for is, still, in many people's hearts. This is where it will stay...at least for now...Good night..."

The silence in Aiden's living room weighed heavy, Twing was bundled up in front of the fire. Ben was sitting next him, looking and waiting for any reaction. Moira had busied herself in the kitchen making tea for all of them. Betsy was not yet ready to give up, her face showed determination and the look of anger. "They can't give up!" She pushed the words through her teeth only to have the words sink into the stone floor.

When Findhorn returned from Aiden's encompassing lost world, he felt the weight of the air and attempted to lift it, *By Jove, it is the silence of death in here. It feels like the grim reaper has been here. It needs the sound of singing, of voices raised to those children, passing from a good life, to a better one...*

They heard him but continued as if dazed.

Moira finally spoke in the kitchen, "We need a song, we need Aiden and his whistle."

"Aiden," they called out, but no one answered, *we...need...your...music...we...*Each word echoed in the cavern. They waited in silence until...until the high pitch of a penny whistle floated through the door way and the walls and the floor. It fed them and changed them. After it had filled the room, the ragged, upheaval, of what once was Aiden, filled the doorway...He had a crumbled piece of paper in his hand.

"This is a poem, actually a song, I wrote for Annie, once upon a time." He straightened out the paper and began to read, with a kind of singsong recitation, the words to his long ago love,

I called her Annie, my love
yes, she knew how to please
with the wink of an eye
and the toss of her hair
she took my resistance
yes she took it away
well, she took my resistance
and blew it away

and the earth is within her
there's strength in her touch
and some lay upon her
that need her so much
and the earth is my lover
she gives and she takes
for a night or a season
with a rhyme and a reason
I am with her
I am with her

she says she's transparent
with nothing to hide
well, I want to believe her
yes, I want to believe her

and some crazy evening
when I was a little bit high
I told her I loved her
that I'd stay by her side

and the earth is within her
there is strength in her touch
and some lay upon her
that need her so much
and the earth is my lover
she gives and she takes
for a night or a season

for a rhyme and a reason
I am with her
I am with her

When the words had stopped their ringing, he took out his penny whistle, again. He began to play the familiar tune Leylani had sung, on that fabled night, when they all found their way to his door. Moira could not keep herself from being touched by the haunting sounds of the chorus and joined Aiden in their remembrance...

wah oh oh ah oh aaa
wah oh oh ah aaa
wah oo ooo ooo
wah oh oh ah aaa

Betsy joined in, even Ben...The sounds reverberated throughout the room until the bundled figure of Twing began to hum, louder...until he, too, wailed with them. Eyes moist and flowing, he joined them in the crossing of the threshold. He joined his brother, whom he had searched for, whom he had found, *found* and now must let go. He joined Annie and Gerard, his brother's companions on that fateful journey. Overwhelmed with emotion he joined them all, Twangly, Annie, Jules, Leylani and Gerard and Betsy and Ben and Moira, and his father, and the father who had died when he was a youngster and the mother who waited for Twangly and the mother who waited for Twing and the young woman who waited for him...

wah oh oh ah oh aaa
wah oh oh ah aaa
wah oo ooo ooo
wah oh oh ah aaa

Findhorn, the leprechaun, moved slowly and the tears flowed until Aiden floated, floated out of the room, back to his

220

sanctuary, now filling up with the salty tears of the sea. He picked up the shovel in blind, grasping desperation and tried to halt the incoming tide, but he had dug too deep. The salty tears began to fill the room. In desperation he called out, *Annie…Out* of the stones came the guttural sounds of *wolf…wolf house…*

No camera had recorded that night, no live electronic transmission had been seen and heard over the thousands of satelites, no wall screens or lightboxes were tuned into Aiden's place that night. No. Only the thread of primordial loss and the dying connected them to the rest of life; life that continued on, in it's diversity and complexity and emotional intensity. Life that continued with the underlying thread of *knowing…knowing* of death too soon, too painful, too tragic…And that knowing; that connection would take them out again. Out from the cavern, filling with the salty sea; out from the pit of the beast, the minotaur, who had torn them to pieces. They were all floating now, on the salty tears of the sea, the sea that had bubbled up and met them. Those who held onto the thread found their way out…and continued…and continued…

Postcard

The night ebbed and the morning slowly came back into their world. Now, they were on the way home. Ben and Betsy had said good bye for themselves and then said good bye for Twing, who had quietly settled into the back seat of the Mercedes. Moira and Findhorn were taking another route. They said they needed to windup, rollup and dry out before they went back to the Olde Bookshoppe. They were all hesitant to leave Aiden, whose cottage was beginning to crack and break up on its way into the sea and sand, but he reassured them over and over again that this was meant to be and he would see it to the end. The authorities wanted to ask more questions and he insisted that they all leave and let him handle it. That was how they left. Now they were on their way to the estate, to the father who lay dying, to the mother who was waiting for her son, to the household who had known Twangly.

In his cloistered space, in the back seat of the Mercedes, Twing sat with a spent contentment. All anger had been washed out of him. He let his thoughts go to places that he pictured behind closed eyes, *the apple orchard on Mariah's farm, running with New Shep, her collie; biting into a crisp, freshly picked apple, hearing the engine turn over in Evermore, his World War II jeep, riding with Twangly into the Washington countryside - there was nothing they couldn't do - seeing the sky light up on the 4th of July with Twangly and Angelina..she, she was the thread of his life...*He rummaged around in his pocket for the postcard he had not yet written, not yet sent. "Can we stop for a coffee," he spoke out of the arched hollowness of the back seat. Ben and Betsy were both surprised at the sound but were only too happy to hear him, "Twing, God, it's good to hear your voice. Yes, let's do it."

Next town, old boy.

He mentally began to compose the short note he would send to her and was lost in his thoughts when Ben pulled into the parking lot of a bakery cafe.

We're here, old boy, let's get a pastry.

"And some tea, and some coffee for our recluse."

"Uh, yea, I guess I deserve that."

They all entered the cafe, sat down, ordered and let Twing open up. He put his card on the table, the picture of the balloon, which was noticed by all of them. He turned it over and he began to write,

Dear Angelina,

It seems like I've been gone forever. Many, many things have happened. The picture on the front is the balloon that took Twangly home, to the next life, that is. He was lost in the sea along with a friend and the pilot. We had a wake for him and celebrated his passing. Now, we (Betsy and Ben and I) are on our way back to the estate. I miss you so much. Say hello to your mom.

love,
Twing

The coffee and pastries came and the pen was put away. The card was turned over, again, for them all to see. From a not too distant past came a voice, *You've picked a perplexing one.* And then it flew away.

"Is there a post office near by?" he asked the waitress.

"Yes, down the street, on your left." He finished his coffee and told them he would be right back.

Betsy nodded with an empathetic smile and when he had gone, looked over at Ben, "You know, we've been in our share of pubs, it's almost a relief to be in a coffee shop, except that the coffee could be better."

"Don't forget this is a tea culture over here."

"Well, they could use some of Seattle's best, just thinking about it makes me want to have some of my own coffee, or a cappuccino in Winthrop."

"To think I only had tea in your cafe."

"Ben," she paused, "What do you want to do?"

"You mean, with Twing, how to help him, how to let Nadjia know about…"

"Yes, Ben, that's part of it, but I was thinking more about us. What are we going to do? I don't have to go back. I could sell the cafe."

Ben wasn't sure what to say. His loyalty for many years had been to the King and his work. His reason for staying with the family was to help protect Twangly as he was growing up. The irony of that was not lost on him and he shook his head and said out loud, "All those years I helped protect him and *now, now the grown boy has left us,*"

"Ben, he is gone, and we can only do so much for Twing. This is his moment."

"Betsy, I am not young anymore, I don't know how much I can change…I never thought I would go through so much with a woman, I've grown close to you, closer than anyone, I never thought I would…"

"Ben," she took his hand, "I could stay with you."

His feelings welled up inside him. He looked at her, reached out and gently touched her hair. Their touch was the door, the opening they had not anticipated. Now they continued to open up to each other, allowing themselves to trust each other with feelings they had put aside, until they were in a world of their own, their closeness creating a veil around them. They were talking, feeling dreams building out of two lives that had settled into their own separate routines.

"Ben," she said. He smiled at her. And she, too, was filled with feelings she had almost forgotten. "Ben," she said again.

"Betsy, could we...would you... he answered with his eyebrows arched. His face was a question she understood.

"Yes," she said.

Surrounded by the warmth of intimate sharing, they had not noticed Twing come back. Nor did they know how long he had been gone, until they heard a voice getting louder...

Every day it's a getting closer,
going faster than a roller coaster,
love like yours will surely come my way,
a hey a hey hey...

Finally, they realized it was Twing, hiding behind them, making like an *oldie* from Betsy's jukebox.

Betsy broke into wild laughter and Ben sheepishly smiled, as if he had been caught at something. Only this time it was something he wanted to do. They loved this young man. They were in love...a hey a hey hey...

"Twing, we, we're going to get married," she just let it out, "I'm going to stay here."

Wow, is all he could say.

They had their coffee cups filled again, they toasted with the dark caffeinated brew, to their good fortune, their future and to Twing's...to Twing's...

"You have a lifetime ahead of you, Twing." Ben stated, more loudly than he needed to. As if he was trying to override the inevitable reality that Twing would have to face. A reality they knew was weighing on his mind, in deed, weighing on their minds as well,

"You have a lifetime ahead of you," he said again.

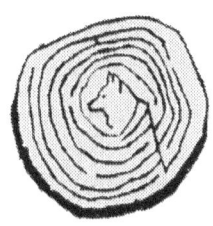

Path Thirty Four

Twilight of the Peacock Throne

By the time they reached the estate, the horizon had turned into violet grays with storm clouds gathering over them, the shadows from this premature darkness made Ben wonder why the lights over the wrought iron gate were not on. He pushed the buttons on the remote and the peacock sentries slowly opened the gates. No lights could be seen in the direction of the mansion as they drove, slowly, under the ivy-covered, tree-lined lane. Betsy was the first to notice a wreath of flowers, first on the left, then on the right, one or two, then more, until the sides of the lane were like a flowered honor guard.

Coming to the turnaround they noticed flowered wreaths and bouquets all around the fountain, now quiet, with no water spouting to keep the flowers alive. They stopped the car, got out and without a word Betsy let the fragrance engulf her…and let her mind wander…*until the palms swayed and the water burst from the mermaid's mouth, bringing color to the twilight until each flowered wreath blossomed and each flower grew in colored intensity. Children ran amongst the trees and over the grass strewn about with blankets. Tie-dyed magenta reds and golden yellows and turquoise clothing covered the flower children, who were making garlands for the visitors of this once upon a time wonderland. Two stone elephants presided over the entrance and let the visitors come and go…*

"Why are you doing this?" one of the visitors asked the garland-makers, "Aren't you a little old for this?"

The answer came in a custom made garland from the flowers of the garden, "Here, put this over your head, add beauty to the world, revel in it, the shadows come soon enough, play, before the flowers turn to the dead and dying."

And, like a portent of things to come, the fragrance of this garden, quickly, all too quickly, wore off and wafted by her. The wreaths began to dull, again, to indecipherable browns. The fountain grew still again. Until there was no need for her or for any of them to say the obvious. Betsy and Ben knew and Twing knew what had transpired, while they were gone.

Why didn't I call? Twing thought and began to berate himself but he, too, was caught up in the fragrant honor guard of wreaths, that had met them; the fragrant, dying beauty that was all around them. He walked up to the door, pulled the iron peacock tail and hit it hard upon the iron plate,

*Bang...bang...*the sound reverberated and broke the stillness...

The hollow clang suddenly reminded Ben of another time, when he was known as Ali Ben Abend and had just come to London; when the tolling of Big Ben saved his pride and his nickname became Big Ben. The sound here, though reminiscent of a moment in his life, was of a different kind and it's tolling rang down the stairs and over the estate. It rang inside the doors, with a hollowness, that made them wonder.

*Bang...bang...*he hit it again.

"Is there no one here?" They began to ask themselves...until a latch sounded and a door gave way.

"Twing, Ben, I..." the Doctor answered. "Please, come in, come, come...we could not wait for you, that is, for Twangly, that is, Nadjia..."

Ben was the first to interrupt and bluntly asked, "When did the King die?"

"Shortly after you left that pub. What was it? The Plough and Sword. We did not hear from you. I called and the proprietor said he was not sure where you had gone except that you had word of Twangly and that you left in a hurry. Did you find him? Is he with you?"

They let his questions of Twangly linger until Twing spoke, "Did he, that is, did my father wake up?

"No, not again. Your mother instructed me to take him off the life support system. He died in the night. Tiger found him the next morning. We waited for three days...Nadjia was with him, so were Euphrates and Clara. We did not hear from you. Somehow word got out -- the news traveled -- flowers, wreaths and wreaths of flowers started to arrive. You see, he still had many admirers, many followers, after all these years. A radical revolution did not obliterate all the good the man did. We buried him today, that is, this morning. But tell me news of Twangly, did you find him? Where is he?"

Twing finally took the Doctor by the arm, paused, looked him in the eyes, and with a deep breath said to him, "Twangly...Twangly is gone. He died. He disappeared and drowned along with a young woman and the pilot of a hot air balloon they were in..."

The Doctor grew pale. He started shaking. Twing sat him down in the nearest chair. *No, no, it cannot be...*He muttered more to himself than to them. *It's not possible. I don't believe it, it can't be,"* he repeated.

By this time Camec had joined them and when he heard he immediately went to the doctor, they held each other, without restraint. They could not hold back the tears. First it was the King and now it was his son. *Twangly, gone...Twangly,* is all that was heard in the great entrance hall of the mansion...

...The same entrance hall that had heard the first words of the young Twangly, had heard the running of his small feet on marble. The hall that had heard his laughter resounding around the domed interior, had heard him being pursued by his father in a game of tag, had heard him making the sounds of animals as he roamed around the halls dressed in animal costumes, had heard the whistle of a train chugging across a vast expanse, from the library to the dining room, only to have Euphrates jump up when it came out from under the table. The years of joy were all there, in the walls and floors and chairs and the bedroom and bed of the growing Twangly, all there, all there and all gone now. Like any child who had grown up, it was all there for those who grew up with him...

When the train whistled again and, like a ghostly reminder, came out from under the dining room table, Euphrates jumped and ran into the entrance hall. She found Twing and Ben and Betsy with the Doctor and Camec still holding each other. She had heard enough sobbing over the last three days that she was, for the moment, happy to see them back. Happy, until Betsy put her arm around her and told her of Twangly's passing. She went into shock. She couldn't believe it. *My Twangly*, she muttered, *My Twangly*. She began to sob, not hysterically, but with sadness, a deep sadness for the child that had been as much her child as any child she might have had.

They stayed in that great hall, asking questions, between the sobbing and the quiet pain of their remembrances, telling each other what had transpired, between the time they left until now -- until they realized the Queen would have to be told.

"Where is the Queen?" Twing asked Euphrates

But she could only utter, *In black, in black*.

The Doctor told them the Queen had gone into mourning, as was the custom, and would be in black until she felt ready to come back. She had been in her room and only came out for the burial this morning. She was covered in a veil and did not talk to anyone. Euphrates had been serving her meals and just left them in the outer room. He hesitated for a moment and finally said, "Tiger is the only one she confides in and he has not confided in us."

After hearing this, Twing felt they should wait before going to see her. Also to wait telling her about Twangly until she was ready, until she asked for him. Until then, they would settle into their rooms and let the sleep cover their cares and let their dreams bring them together again.

Phratee Cat

The Doctor accompanied Twing to his room, asking him, again, how such a thing could have happened to Twangly, when he noticed that Twing's birthmark was gone. In its place was a slight, straight scar.

"What happened to your neck, Twing, if I may ask? Your birthmark is gone."

With all the events of the past few days Twing could not even remember when he took the bandage off. He had not thought about it, but now, the Doctor had noticed. "It was cut off," is all he could bring himself to say.

"When did you have this done?"

What's the point, he thought to himself. *If I can't tell the Doctor, who brought me into the world -- Who can I tell?* And proceeded to tell him the whole story, even to the point of describing the rubber wolf mask.

The Doctor listened intently and with a hint of curiosity asked to see the mask.

"I believe Ben has it. They, Ben and Betsy, were trying to find out more. I just let it go by." As he said this, a stillness came over them and they both thought about the strange and almost tragic events that had occurred. Until Twing's eyes lit up and he, excitedly, said, "There is some good news, Doctor, Ben and Betsy are going to get married."

"That is something to celebrate about. I must congratulate them. Please, Twing, I am at your service, if there is anything you may need." With this moment of recognition from the Doctor, Twing, slightly smiled and nodded his head. They both said good night and the Doctor decided to make one more stop before turning in. He walked passed the Queen's bedroom and heard silence. He continued down the hall and down to the floor below. In front of Ben's room he heard voices and decided to knock.

"Yes," came Ben's familiar voice.

"It's Abriham, I hope it's not too late."

The door opened and Ben welcomed him in. "I hope I'm not disturbing you but I did want to congratulate you. Twing told me you were getting married."

"Yes, yes, he is right, thank you. Actually, we were just talking about when and where."

"Why not here. In the entrance hall. It would be a good antidote to the losses that have invaded the family."

"Twangly's loss is a terrible one, Ben. Do you suspect anything? I mean, the King has died, Twangly is gone, now I find out from Twing that he was attacked, attacked by someone with a wolf mask. He said you have it."

It was in Well-born." He almost chuckled and shook his head, "What irony. Well-born..."

He searched through his open suitcase and pulled out the rubber wolf mask, "Here, this is what I found as I pursued the beast. I did not see him or her, if it was."

The Doctor held the mask and his face seemed to grow more serious, "I don't like this, Ben, this is, this may just be a wild coincidence...He stopped. His face became contorted in contemplation before he continued, "Twangly used to have animal masks. You weren't in the house, but I remember him playing wolf, howling like a wolf on occasion, he had a mask similar to this..."

"What do you mean, they probably sell these by the bushel."

"Yes, but Euphrates would probably know, maybe she could even find the old one, I don't think any of his toys were ever taken out."

"Ben, I know it's late but I just feel an urgency to this, can we see her?"

"We will probably have to wake her, she was very distraught."

Ben knocked on the shower room and told Betsy he had to go with the Doctor. He would not be long. Taking the mask, they proceeded to walk to Euphrates' quarters when Tiger met them in the hall, "Tiger, how is the Queen?" Ben asked, as soon as he saw him.

"She is in mourning, still very upset. Do you have news of Twangly. She keeps asking about him. It would console her."

"I have news, and I would like to share it with her when it is appropriate," Ben replied, and added, that they were on their way to see Euphrates before it became too late. "Could we see each other in the morning?" he asked Tiger, while holding the wolf mask.

Tiger' face went pale when he saw it, *Is this…Are you…* he stammered, *What are doing with that?*

"It's a mask, an old rubber wolf mask, we found. It's a long story, but we're trying…"

Trying to do what, scare the Queen?

"No, no, no, we're taking it to Euphrates."

You're trying to scare her?

"Tiger, this mask was on the head of someone who tried to kill Twing." Ben finally said.

Tiger was visibly shaken but incredulously smiled, and said, *With that, how did that happen?*

"We can't relay the whole story right now, we want to see Euphrates, please, let us know when Nadjia is able to…"

She will most likely visit his grave tomorrow -- in the morning, Tiger answered.

"Good night then."

Good night.

They continued to walk the long hall to, what once were, the servant's quarters, but had long ago changed to Euphrates' Quarters. When they arrived at her door, there was no sound. They knocked quietly. Waited. Just as quietly, the knob turned and the door opened. Euphrates face, with moist eyes and the redness of loss, barely said, "Yes."

The Doctor spoke in hushed words, "Euphrates, your pain is ours also. Please, could we see you for a moment?" She opened the door wide enough for them to enter. "Euphrates, we, that is, Ben and I have a strange request."

She did not look up but sat with her hands folded, as if she was invoking the right words from her visitors, words that might dispel her grief.

"Euphrates," Ben began, bringing the wolf mask closer to her, "Euphrates, have you seen this before?"

Ahh, she jumped back. *What is this?* she cried out.

"Please, Euphrates, it is just a mask."

"But why?"

"Euphrates, did Twingly have a mask like this?"

She blinked and thought, blinked again and, out of her stillness, finally said, "Yes, he was a wolf, he was a lion, he even dressed up as a dragon, yes..." Thinking back, she repeated, "He was a wolf..." Then she saw him stalking in the corner of the kitchen, sniffing the lamb roasting in the oven. She knew he was there, but pretended not to know. He jumped out. She jumped onto a chair. He laughed and took off his mask, *It's me, Phratee, look it's me...*

Phratee, he called me. *Phratee cat.* Her tears flowed and yet, the doctor dared to ask her,

"Is this, or was this Twangly's?"

Through her tears she saw it and took it, "I don't know, it was years ago."

"Where did you put his toys, his costumes?"

"Many of them were put in the attic."

"Can we go there?"

"Now?"

"Please, Euphrates, we feel it is important."

She got up and led them up the stairs, up, up the attic stairs, to the attic door. She opened it and they waited in the dark, until Ben struck his lighter. The dust of years flickered in the flame. She walked over to boxes -- the stacked boxes. Several were open.

"We put his toys, the train set, bears, in boxes, year after year. We put his costumes up here, after he had grown out of them. He was the only child. How could they bear to part with any of his things? They had left too, too much already. Look, here's his lion mask and the body, he loved the long tail. This is where the wolf would be. We put them all in there."

She rummaged through the opened box but could not find the wolf's head, "Here's the body of the wolf, see it, the head should be right here…"

Ben and the doctor looked at each other, "Who knows about these toys, Euphrates?"

"Everyone in the household, I think, they were not a secret."

Again, it was Ben who dared to ask the question, "Would Tiger know about these toys, the wolf mask?"

"He helped me bring them up here."

"There is something rotten in Denmark!" the doctor said to Ben.

"And Tiger saw the mask in my hands."

"His loyalty is to the Queen, Ben. He has been loyal all these years, waiting, waiting for his chance."

"Or he has been loyal to the regime, a radical in the midst, waiting, also waiting for his chance. I don't believe he knows about Twangly yet, but I will bet he was the one who let the radicals know that Twangly had left England and gone to visit America."

"When Twing came into the picture, it was a surprise for Tiger, too, not just for the King and Queen,"

They had forgotten about Euphrates or where they were. They were speculating, wondering, putting the possibilities together when Ben finally said, "He must know that Twing is the rightful heir to the estate and, and he's been the confidant of the Queen, over the years, the Queen…" He stopped. He did not want to go on with his thought. He did not want to think it. He could not bear to think that the Queen may have known about…about…

The Doctor took Euphrates by the arm and led her out of the attic and back down. Ben closed the door on the boxes and toys and a child's animal past. A past that now held a tragic secret, which had been discovered. He was not sure what turn this would take, he was afraid and literally ached inside.

If this was a maze of events, of paths, they had taken a wrong turn, he thought, *opened the wrong door.* All he wanted to do was shut it again, cage the beast.

But, he also realized the wolf had been out all along, waiting in the shadows, waiting for years and it had gone all wrong, wrong for him and, now, he was desperate. Even the King's death was now suspicious. If Tiger knew that Twangly was dead, it would be all the more important for him, for them? (it was unthinkable) to be rid of Twing...

He walked and ran down the stairs and through the halls painted with murals, the images of an ancient glory. The colors formed into ziggurats and many people, a gathering of servants, slaves, peasants, farmers, all paying homage to a God on earth. Paying tribute to him and a royal family. This had been the King's hallway and on a royal throne sat an ancient ruler, with the fluorescent blue green feathers of two peacock tails, on either side of him. For a moment the colors and spectacle of it dazzled him, dazed him...

Bow to the Ruler of the Heavens and the Earth, the realms of the Peacock Throne. The voice rang like a gong struck in a massive arena. He looked around and all around him were people bowing, prostrate on the ground. He stood out and someone whispered,

Get down, fool.

He knelt and looked, the Ruler, in a trailing robe of peacock feathers, with armed men in woven tunics and iron swords, were weaving through the crowd. It was a spectacle of beauty and might. A spectacle that transcended the years, thousands of years. With thousands of variations, from the Peacock Throne to Caesar Augustus to Louis XIV to Queen Victoria to the Tsar to the Kaiser. From the petty rulers of an unknown tribal kingdom to Edward the II, to the great cataclysmic overthrows of history to the court intrigues. Played out in the royal tragedies of Shakespeare -- the Hamlets and the Lears -- Now it had all come home, had become decoration, paintings, in a hallway, images of past glory, momentary, almost forgotten, almost...except in the minds of the Queen and Tiger.

Ben had almost walked past, almost ran through this hallway, but the colored images had stopped him, dazed him and now, after being caught up in them, they, too, lost their allure. He went on, on, remembering the present and this realm of exiled royalty. He came back to the time he was in, the danger Twing was facing.

He finally came to the doctor's room -- Breathlessly knocked. No one there. He went up the stairs to Twing's room. He heard voices and knocked. The door opened. There was Twing…and the Doctor. The Doctor had told him everything.

They looked at each other. How much more would heap upon Twing -- upon them? The night seemed to last forever. When would sleep come? They, all, in their weariness and their determination to come to terms with the world, could not stop. Like drunken sots thrown out of a bar after last call, they could not stop -- did not want to stop. They were determined, to stop even the interminable movement of the clock. They were not going to let this disappear into the quiet, noiseless, dream world of those sleeping. They were not going to let this…they were not…going…to…until they all just simply found a place to sleep, sleep, like the earth, Erda, they just wanted to sleep…

The morning found them, not wanting to get up, yet, knowing they must. Their heads were aching with the leftover night. One by one, they rose and their habits took over. Somnambulistically, they washed their faces and straightened themselves out, until the Doctor spoke, "Shall we face this?"

"As early as possible." Ben answered.

"Let us all go, or else there will be no end to it."

"Let *us* go," the Doctor said to Twing. But Twing would have none of it,

"I've got to do this," he said, "Or else, I might as well not have come. The King, my biological father is dead, I had no contact with him, I have had more contact with my adopted mother and the father of my memories. I've had to face a lot since I came here -- only weeks ago. My birthmark is gone. I have lost the connection to my twin brother. He is dead. I have lost the connection to my mother, this woman, who is the Queen. And this man, Tiger, tried to kill me, for his own reasons. But I think I need to face him…for my own reasons…"

Both the Doctor and Ben were somewhat astonished but not totally surprised at Twing's outburst. Ben had seen him at his physical best that moment at Blue Lake in the Cascades, when he threw the Radical revolutionary, who wanted to kill him, on the rocks. Since then, he had seen him grow and mature through situations and events many people could not imagine. The Doctor could only be proud of this youth who wanted to take on the demons that had entered him, demons that were not necessarily of his own making but seemed to have come from outside of him.

They were, all three of them, going to face Tiger, the man they suspected. They were going to find out the truth. They walked in righteous determination -- down the halls, down the stairs, to Tiger' room and knocked on his door. No one answered. They knocked louder. It was early enough. He had to be asleep. They called him, "Tiger, we want to talk to you."

They waited, but no one answered. They tried the door knob. Nothing.

"Is there a key?"

"Euphrates may have one. I'll get it."

Ben ran to her. They waited. Finally Ben came back. No key.

"Let's break it down." Two of them would slam the door.

"One, two, three..."

They crashed against it, the lock broke and it opened. They saw immediately what one of them, at least, had suspected, Tiger was hanging from the chandelier, his tongue out, a sheet around his neck, a chair on the floor...

Twing would not go in. He had seen enough. He went back to his room and lay on his bed, just to think, to rest, to...

The Doctor and Ben cut Tiger down. There was no need for anyone else to see this. They would have to tell the authorities, his relatives, if there were any. But for now, the weight had shifted, the danger, as it was at one time, had passed. The wolf lay motionless. The self-anointed club had found it's mark. This was not a *wolf house* that would haunt the world for generations to come. The generations had passed, passed with the desperate actions of this man.

There was only one tragic figure who would cry for this man, a woman, whose selfish act, in the midst of birth, brought about a separation and a breaking of the thread. She is in black and no one, besides Tiger, whose lifeless body lies on the marble floor, no one had seen her face since her husband died. Her husband, the father of the twin boys. If he had known of the birth of *two* boys, would the world have been different? Would the events have played out differently? Most likely. I'm not sure how. I don't know, except that another path may have been taken or would have been taken, another door would have opened or another dead end might have been found…or another door, another path…

All in Black

Nadjia woke up to find her breakfast in the outer room. It was always the same: figs, toast and tea. She dressed in quiet movements. There was no hurry. She prayed to her God. She prayed for her husband. She prayed for Twangly. She prayed for Tiger. There was no hurry. One day was like another. One day had become like another. Tiger would be here shortly. They had seen each other practically every day for weeks. They commiserated with each other at the way life had taken its turns, taken its time. Now, they would have each other.

Her longing for Twangly, the child she had lived for, had, also, grown stronger. Every day she prayed for him. Every day she asked Tiger about him; any news of him. Since the King, her husband, died, she had dressed in black with a veil over her face whenever she went out of the room. This distanced her from the others; all those she had lived with. Only Tiger had entered her secret world.

"When would he come?" She wondered. "It was usually in the morning."

Today, she wanted to go to the grave of her husband. She waited a little while longer and finally decided to visit her husband. Tiger would come later.

Euphrates saw her, in black, in a black veil, leaving her room and going towards the sanctuary; the grove where they had buried him, and marked his grave, with a carved peacock stone, from the garden. A simple grave for a King, once a monarch, whose lineage went back to the ziggurats. The wreaths were all around him and the flowers were dying, just as he had died, drying up just as he was. She walked slowly, as if walking in a waking dream...

Twing, your mother has gone to the grove, the grave of your father. Euphrates wrote on a piece of paper, which she put under Twing's door. She did not want to wake him yet, but she wanted him to know, in case he wanted to see her, talk to her.

Twing, however, had spent a restless night, with the never ending image of the hanging Tiger. He closed his eyes and he saw him. He opened his eyes and he thought about him. What could he do? There was no retreat. The demon had not died. The demon was here. All he could hope for was that his presence would fade, fade...that *time* would loosen his presence or...that others, even angels, *if he dared to say it*, would help him put a shroud over that presence...Or that others, others, others would help him...

He looked around and saw the surfer on the wall of his room catching a 20 foot monster wave, ready to take him into the depths. As he stared, the wave moved, and the crashing sounds of an electric guitar rode over him...the music and the words of a California song rode over him,

let's go surfing now, everybody's learning how, come on a safari with me, mmmm bop dip di dip dip mmmm bop...

It was almost sacrilege, but it was real, the sounds of the surfer rode over him, through him...

dip di dip dip mmmm bop...

Next to the surfer was the bleaching whale in the same ocean, off the coast of Santa Cruz, *Santa Cruz, the smell of hot dogs on the boardwalk, the lights reflected in the bay,* On the beach, the smell of salt air, the sound of the sea lions underneath the wharf, the sounds a whale makes, under the water…Listen, now, listen closely…

uurrrrrooooooooorrrrrruuuuuuuuuuuurrrrrrrrooooooo

Yes, yes, He jumped out of bed. He did calisthenics, *one, two, three, four, one…*He touched the marble floor. He did pushups, *one, two, three, on, on, and on* until he was exhausted. He rolled onto the plush rug. He felt the give of the bean bag and fell into it *Wow*, he thought for a minute, in the concave softness of the bean bag. He thought, *I'm going to transform these things, change them, Tiger has already taken his place somewhere in the world, the whale is singing to him now. Twangly's loss is not a loss, but a memory of many moments, it was at the broken down cabin near Blue Lake when we first saw each other, or when we pretended to be future kings at Mariahs. I sang and he recited from Shakespeare, that's when we saw an angel walk through the door, Angelina, Angelina is there, near Masama, she may be thinking of me, then there is my father, whom I did not know, who was almost a historic figure, on his death bed, and my adopted father, they will take their place in my world just as they will take their place in the transcended world, somewhere in the universe…*He got up, walked to the window. He wanted to see the sky. He opened the window and let the morning air surround him He let the smell of the grass, the flowers, *yes,* the dying flowers of a thousand wreaths, embrace him. *It was all right. It was all right.* He breathed deeply, as if it was his last breath. He gazed over the 100 acre wood, as if it was a picture book come alive. He saw movement in the trees, in the sky, in the morning mist hovering over the grass, in the flowing black of a black coat and a black veil moving, floating over the mist. It was…*my mother,* he whispered. She was all in black, floating through the mist and into an old grove, the sanctuary for those who had died, who had changed, who were now a memory, a persistent presence.

He wanted to go to her now, to pay his respects to his father, along with her. He wanted to bring something; a momento of Twangly that would live with his father *and* that would live for her. His mind wandered until he saw the incised letters on the old bones. *Yes, that's it.* I'll leave Twangly's name on the old bone, along with the bones of Nicholas and Flaxen. They came from the earth, where the wolf-rock keeps watch. He took the bones out of his backpack along with his knife and carved into the uncarved bone, T W A N G L Y. Yes. He took all three and went along the corridor, down the stairs, through the halls to the garden door and out, out, into the misty path, floating like his mother. He went into the sanctuary, deeper into the grove, until he saw her there, kneeling in the mist. No shaft of light on her, yet she seemed at peace. She was one, with the stillness around her, around him, around the father, the husband whose presence was all around. He walked slowly, barely touching the ground. He knelt next to her. She felt him there. They felt each other's warmth. He took one bone out of his pocket and put it on the ground, turning it so that the name could be seen. She saw it, looking, until the letters were clear: T W A N G L Y. He left it there for a long time, until he hoped she understood. She said nothing and he wondered if she knew. He finally picked it up and with his bare hand scooped out a hole, placed the bone in and covered it up. He put his hand on her shoulder and left her there…

He did not see her break down or her tears flow onto the freshly packed soil. No, he did not see that her peace had been shaken. By this act, by these letters, born in her womb, *the son*, she had thought would be her future, became her past. Could she hope that he would come home, come through the door? No. She knew. The act of burying the bone with his name on it, was enough. It just confirmed what she had feared. Now, Twangly, too, would become a fading presence in her life, just like her husband…But Tiger, Tiger, her confidant and friend, her connection to the waking world, would come to console her, just as he had, in her time of grief…

But she did not know that Tiger was gone, gone by his own hand. His presence, still, lingering in his room, destined, eventually, to be released and to wander in the realms of darkness, the underworld, doing penance for his actions. What will she think? What will she do? Tiger, her final connection to the waking world…was also gone…

A Broken Thread

When Betsy heard of the secret Ben and the Doctor had uncovered and how they found Tiger, she sighed, heavy, heavy of heart…

"What more could happen to this family? Did Twing…how is he?"

"He saw, but did not go into Tiger' room. He left, hopefully, he slept."

"Ben, the atmosphere around this house is going to get to me, to say the least, I don't think I can stay here…"

He understood, "Let us go to my home," he caught himself, "Our home. You haven't even seen it. Just remember, I have been a bachelor for many years."

She hadn't even thought about Ben having a home outside of the estate, but suddenly remembered that he had always lived in a separate home, and, in fact, had not been on the premises since Twangly was born, that is, until now, after they had all came back from Masama.

"Let us pack up," Ben said, "I'll tell Euphrates to tell Twing and the Doctor and Camec. Let me get you out of this…it has not been…" He wasn't sure what to say and just looked at her with an understanding smile. "Let us go there, until this is settled or at least somewhat settled…This has been a real life tragedy. I think…not even Shakespeare could have imagined this. Maybe, one day, someone will write this down. Maybe Twing. This is a family caught up…" Again, he was searching for the right words, words that could possibly encompass what had happened, "A family caught up in crises, historical upheaval and personal crises. They came together, the events and their lives came together…"

She was packing up as he was talking, "Ben, please, talk to Twing, if he needs us…"

They were soon packed. Ben carried their suitcases slowly through the domed entrance hall, the hollowness of their resounding steps reminded him, again, of the tolling of the clock tower over 18 years ago. He had also been through the revolution, yet, in his first days of exile, in London, he remembered that he felt like he had a future, like he had a life ahead of him, in a new country. The revolution would not last anyway. They would be going back. The years passed, however, and now, with so much gone by, it seemed, the clock was striking again. *Big Ben* was striking again. He decided it was time to let the *Big* go, the nickname he had had since that first week in London. It was time for Ben, just Ben. He, now, saw himself with another future, one with a companion, the woman walking next to him.

"Ben," she said to him, "let's not get lost in this."

"Betsy, we're not lost, we're found." And he opened both of the huge doors that had let them in. Doors that opened to the fragrance of living, growing, blooming life. The sunlight was so intense, they squinted and slowly opened their eyes, until they could take in the magenta reds, the golden yellows, the turquoise blues, surrounded by the greens of the wreaths and the verdant, growing greens of the grass and the old alder trees encircling the estate. The fountain was bursting again, spraying them with the fragrance of rose attar. The oil his parent's had pressed, and brought into his life. They breathed in the breath of lilacs and heather. Two tie-dyed children came up to them and gave them a garland of white daisies.

"Ben," she looked into his eyes, "We have a world ahead of us."

He put the suitcases in the trunk of the Mercedes and Betsy eased herself into the front seat. Ben went back in to talk to Euphrates, He did not see her in the kitchen. He went back to her quarters. There was no answer there. Finally he wrote her a note,

Euphrates,
We have gone to stay at my home. I will be back. Please tell Twing, and the doctor and Camec. Call me (us) for any reason, anytime, you have my number.
Ben

Now it was the Doctor's turn to do what he had been destined to do. In his youthful days, he had been with the future King, at Cambridge, where they were both just students. They had been long time friends and grew up together in the gardens of the palace. After he had finished his studies, the Doctor had rejected a position offered to him by the radical regime, had turned it down to stay loyal to his friend and King, even in exile. Now, the revolution had come home, had taken its final turns and twists, had taken a path that ended in upheavals and tragedies, in a gated and fenced off estate. The Doctor had lived with the secret of the twin boys for 18 years. A secret, the Queen had made him promise to keep. She had given up the first born, who was adopted by an American couple and became known as Twing. He also remembered the day Camec had come to him, *agitated*, by the words of a local soothsayer,

Because of the Queen's deceit, an ancient curse would be carried out, the power of the peacock throne would crumble. If and when the true line of the ruler is reconciled with the deceitful one a new era would emerge…

Ironically, the Doctor had set up the unraveling of this deceit, when he told Twing, in a letter, that he had a twin brother. Now the King was dead, the favorite and the unfortunate son, Twangly, had died, tragically, in a strange whirlwind. There would be no new era of royal power. There was only loss and grief. The power of the peacock throne had crumbled in ways no one could have imagined. The peacock sentries were rusting, too many tears had been shed. Now it was his turn to pick up the pieces that were left. He would help Twing, but the possibility of reconciliation was over, an historic time had passed, Twing would now have to carve out a new era, on his own, in his own way. The doctor had Camec. There was Euphrates. There was Nadjia…

Euphrates had finally brought Nadjia in. She was stiff from kneeling over the remains of her husband and her son. Euphrates had taken the veiled penitent by the arm and back to her room. Out of her long silence she finally whispered through the veil with a voice of disjointed sounds, as if she was desperately trying to put the words together, *When will Tiger come? I need him.*

"He will come, your highness, please, let me get you into a hot bath and into bed."

A New Era

After she had seen the bone with Twangly's name on it, after she had seen Twing bury it in the very soil that covered her husband; had seen him bury it in the sanctuary of the generations who had crossed the threshold before them, in the grove of trees that were within the encircled estate, after she had gathered up the implications of this act, *something...something* snapped in her, something disconnected inside her, a circle she had lived in, came apart, separated...

It was not just a physical circle. Yes, it had grown through the centuries. Yes, she had formally connected to it when she married the King and, yes, it had almost been a family ordained marriage. Almost, in the sense, that they had met each other as students at Cambridge, recognized each other and realized their families had already agreed on their marriage. There were not too many students from their country, so they had met informally with other students and it was at one of these functions that they had said hello. They all walked along the Thames. At first Abriham and others walked along with them. Abriham, the future doctor to be, Camec, Ben, all students, studying, looking forward, waiting, hoping to make changes in the world, at least, when they went back to their country. When Nadjia and the future king began to walk together he told her of his dreams and she slowly became a part of them. When his father died, his studies became real, he became King. Shortly after that, they were married and the power of the Peacock Throne became theirs.

The new King proposed far-reaching changes to the country. "To bring it into the modern world," he said, but he also saw that dreams did not always coincide with the forces outside of them. Their outside world finally broke apart. Through a revolution, centuries of power crumbled. The royal family and their loyal followers fled to England, where the family lived in secrecy and brought up one child in an enclosed and gated estate, while the other child was brought up in another country, far from an ancient past. Yes, *far from an ancient cultural past*, but close to an ancient past of towering redwoods, living monarchs, that were still reigning after 1000 years. This adopted child was brought up in the innocence, and age-old strength, of these redwood realms.

Like the soothsayer's warning, *the power of the peacock throne would crumble*...Who would have thought it would come apart in such a way. If there had been a reconciliation of the deceived son and the innocent son, a new era might have emerged. It had almost occurred, the two sons had met and become friends, until the most unlikely whirlwind of a storm had changed it all, and Tiger, the player, who was going to carry out a tragic act carried out his own tragic end.

With this act, Nadjia's outer circle could not hold and finally disintegrated. The demons of loss took hold of her. Her inner thread snapped...the beast had overtaken...

And yet, and yet, ironically, and strangely enough, who is to say that a new era did not emerge. The innocent, brought up amid the redwood giants near the great Pacific, searched for a brother, found him, only to lose him again. Twing, the innocent, had taken many paths in this maze of openings, doorways, pathways and dead ends. Twing, in some ways, also died, to be reborn again. He was now, he had now, taken on the future, *deciding...deciding* what he would do.

Path Thirty Five

Armani's Revolution

The entrance of the bronzed glass and steel modern post modern postpost and lintel edifice was stark, clean, exact…exactly what Armani had envisioned when he first thought about the headquarters of his media empire. The lights turned green around the door immediately after he had walked through the DNA detector. The glass opened and he waited for his visitors to also walk through. The hollow ringing of sandals and English leather on an inlayed marble walkway resounded around them. The hallway floor had been designed in the double helix pattern, the mysterious underlying blueprint of life…

"Please, gentlemen, a short tour of our offices."

As they walked the curbing, curling hallway there were screens, wall screens, following them, ahead of them, around them, with *live* transmissions. Some with flickering colors, some with cloud patterns or sand dunes, some with talking heads, some with animated creatures of good and evil. Some with evolutionary images evolving in front of them. There was even a raucous party from somewhere…

"As you can see, we are in the information age, immediate communication, immediate information. We are in the living rooms, the bedrooms, the heads and actions of the world. Whatever, wherever someone does something, looks at something, we are there. We have their history. We can bring it up, on the screens. We know when they have interacted with us, we have what they have ordered, what they haven't ordered, what they have said and sent through the air..."

There were a mazed and glassy-eyed stares from his visitors.

"How did you start all this?" one visitor ventured to ask.

"Gentlemen, it seems like a long time ago, but in this age, even our development time seems immediate. Keep in mind that somewhere, someone is working on the next phase. Let me take you into one of our next phases, into our *future room*. I show you this in all confidentiality and I expect the same from you. But to get back to your question, it was a fortuitous meeting with an idealistic, young singer-songwriter in Amsterdam. He had had some kind of a dream. He said, it was about a place where different people, speaking different languages during the Great War, were working together, *while*, near by, they heard guns and explosions and men killing each other. He called it a *hammering* place because he had heard them hammering the shingles on the two cupolas of this building, almost all carved out of wood. He was so moved by a man, a visionary, who had brought these people together, to work on this building, that he wanted to...this singer-songwriter wanted to set up places, like this visionary. He called them *hammering* places, places for people to gather. At first it was in clubs, even old castles, wherever screens could be set up. And through those connections - we also called them satelites - through those satelites, the world could become an extended, world family, bringing in different cultures. We could bring together their arts and values and their ways of living together...and ways of solving problems."

"All very idealistic, but that didn't create the system..."

"No, gentlemen that was my job, I was interested in the exactness of electronic, digital transmissions, at light speed, but I couldn't just transmit 1's and 0's or just convert information into ones and zeros, I had to have something to connect them to, like the double-helix you're walking on. *I needed content.* Obviously, we have 1,000,000 years, maybe more, of content intertwined with form behind us, and, maybe 100,000 years of meaningful sounds, becoming language, becoming words stamped in clay tablets and carved in marble stele, becoming images, and symbols in stainedglass windows and manuscripts, becoming mass-produced books, on and on. We have a human history of ideas in words and language, in symbols of understanding, all helping to bring about cultural inclusion and, unfortunately, also cultural exclusion. You see, I simply wanted content for my electronic hardware and it was SC the singer-songwriter who, strangely enough, was the catalyst for the intertwining that began, that started in the *hammering* places. First, it was the wall screens that went into the clubs, then the *lightboxes* went into the pubs and cafes. We didn't stop until we went into people's homes and finally into the very walking, talking interactive person themselves."

They followed the double-helix pattern, *until, out of somewhere*, came the raspy voice of an old man,

You have to read the signs, Whirling, understand the signs.

"Yes, master. "

"See that one on the ground."

All lines in the greater pattern are in the smaller pattern, inside the lines are images, symbols...You have to look.

He took his hand and gently moved his finger around the lines that were already there. Slowly, as if uncovering a secret, inside the pattern, was a symbol, The sign of a wolf was made visible, his nose pointing to the left.

"I see it, Whirling said. But how did you know it was there?"

"You have to go beyond the visible, underneath the obvious, within that which is there, but not yet brought into awareness -- brought into consciousness."

The turns of the hallway, with its screens teeming with images and sounds, were, however, becoming disorienting to the visitors. Every turn began to have similar screens, similar images, similar sounds and yet, they were all changing...

"How do you know which way go?" one of the visitors asked.

"Interpret the signs gentlemen. You have to know the signs." Their host answered.

One of the visitors with hair the look of a haystack was getting edgy, "I think I've seen enough, I'd like to get back."

"Stay with us," Roland said, "You'll just get lost and we'll have to find you."

They continued to follow their host, a man with oiled hair, whose three piece suit was now covered with a flowing cape. They were disoriented, reaching out, even daring to touch the walls of screens, they crackled and luminous colors showered around their touch.

"What is that?" Haystack asked in an agitated voice.

"Mr. Armani, wherever are we going? This is like a maze in here, a labyrinth with no end."

"We're not through yet, gentlemen, but look, feel, touch the screens..."

The shower of sparkling light that came from their touch moved into a pattern, a circle of light...

"Wait, watch," Armani said, as he voiced the magic words, *Open Future World*...An ancient future becoming the new mantra. The wall screens, surrounded by light, seemed to open. They walked into a place filled with people, glowing people. The sounds of a penny whistle could be heard, and the tinkle of a bell, as well as the thumping of feet, in tune to lively music...

Path Thirty Six

Virtual Celebration

By Jove, Aiden you've done it again, hey hey, the longer we dance, the longer you play...

"Now, dear, watch your feet, there are others dancing out here."

But the feet of the driver, the olde bookseller, Findhorn, the wee Leprechaun would not, could not stop. The music was infectious. He was all over the floor. The tables had been pushed back and as much room as possible had been made in the remodeled bookshop. What was once a living room area had become a cafe. Guests, who came in through the Olde Bookshoppe entrance, still had to walk around the overstuffed chairs and past the screeching owl perched on the counter. They could still meander around the piles of books; old and olde ones. The tinkle of Tinker Bell was still heard when the front door opened, but this private party, this intimate party had opened itself up to the world. Over a red glow, in a mist that seemed to hover under them, Whirling moved in amongst the dancers, through the dancers, and said in astonishment,

"Nicholas, Roland, we are inside them and they are inside us. *Hey*, look at Haystack, doing a jig with that Leprechaun."

They smiled, laughed, they were real and yet they were not real. They danced together...

"Armani," Whirling called out, "They are here, yet we can walk through them, dance with them, hear them, move through them."

"Yes, Whirling, this is the future. They are here, in this futuristic crystal ball, if you will. They can see us on *their* wall screen, *but we've gone beyond that!* You are now in the *future room!* You are privileged to behold this future. They, the whole party, the whole wedding party is coming from Betsy's Coffee Cafe and Olde Bookshoppe in Wellborn-on-Avon. Yes, they can see you, gentlemen, on their wall screen. That is, if they look at the screen that has been transmitted from here, from the *future room.* Yes, they can see 'you' Whirling, Nicholas, Roland, Mr. Haystack. But *they*, all of them, the whole party from the Coffee Cafe, are in our *presence* here. You could almost say, they are guests in this room. They are present in this room, through their electronic presence, through the miracle of holo grams, holy grams, if you will; spirit grams, electronic spirits, glowing spirit bodies from Betsys' Coffee Cafe and the Olde Bookshoppe. Walk through them, dance with them, look around, see what Betsy and Ben have done to transform this place..."

Haystack stopped dancing and looked around the Olde Bookshoppe...looking, looking...until he shrieked at the sight of a wolf mask in a corner. "This is like the wizard's room." he said. His eyes continued to fix on the wolf mask with the yellow fluorescent eyes. He wanted to touch it, to feel it's coarse hair, it's fangs...He even thought about getting it and putting it over his head, for a moment, but there were too many oddities in the way. He let it lie in the corner and looked elsewhere.

Roland went to join him and passed a suit of armor. He beheld its shimmering metal, beautifully engraved with curlicues and paisley patterns. Its upheld arm was holding a sword over an olde chess set.

Haystack noticed a music stand with an open book on it. He looked at the olde English lettering on the two pages that were spread open. On the left was the title, *The Labyrinth of Terra Grandeur*, with an intricately designed initial *L*. Underneath the title was a pathway encircling a hillside, a rocky tor, leading up to the ruins of an olde castle. He tried to read the lettering on the right page…

…from the time he stepped on the path of the labyrinth of Terra Grandeur, to his apprenticeship, to his adventures on the eastern steppes, to his imprisonment, to his wanderings, to his hermitage, the Wolf House, where he took in and cared for children, orphaned by the plague, the scourge of death…

Haystack wanted to read more, he began to turn the page, his hand went through the book, like everything else, it was there and it was not there. He walked over to the knight and into the knight's armor. He looked out and saw a screen, a *lightbox* screen, from the olde Bookshoppe, projected into the *future room*, with all his friends in the *future room*…He saw himself…

Hey hey, come this way. Let's celebrate Ben and Betsys' day. Findhorn was in his element. *Moira, let's raise the glass, don't let the good times pass.*

They raised their glasses of the Devil's Hook Special Wedding Ale. The music from Aiden's penny whistle faded. The dancing came to a stop. The party room, where the tables had been pushed back, opened to two people. They were holding hands, within the colored light coming through the stained glass, of an old arched window, behind them. Smiling, this was their day, their wedding day. They had waited for this day and for unknown, yet compelling reasons, they had decided to settle in Wellborn-on- Avon. Betsy wanted to open that good coffee cafe and Findhorn and Moira had offered her and Ben the possibility of combining it with their Olde Bookshoppe. Moira and her longtime companion were getting older and not always at the bookshoppe, but they did not want to sell it. As a result, this had become a marriage of old and new, romantic and literate, joyful and wistful, an historical collaboration with a future world. Betsy had asked Aiden -- who had moved into the village close to where his cottage once was, close to where that fabled *nose of the dog* once was, close to the cottage that had slipped back into the sand and sea -- Betsy had asked Aiden to help make their cafe into a satelite cafe. Aiden had contacted SC, who had contacted Armani and Armani had created the future out of what was to be their new satelite. Unbeknownst to them, he had put several cameras in the Coffee Cafe and the Olde Bookshoppe, unique cameras, cameras that could create the holy grams that they were now seeing, as well as the microphones that captured the sounds they were now hearing. It was all, now, being transmitted to his headquarters, to the *future room*, halfway around the world. He wanted to share these holy grams with the visitors who had come to see him. These pilgrims, who had come to this room, from other places, other times. He wanted to share the future with these visitors, who were, now, being initiated into this state of wonder...

Thus, the new satelite was born. This was the inauguration and the wedding party all in one. Other, older satelites, from around the world, were tuned into the party. SC was watching from Jeanette's place, which had changed from its stark DeStijl into festive decor for the day. Alfred, from his castle in Silesia, had set up candles around the room and his tapestry seemed to glow behind him, seemed to come alive. It was almost as if new adventures were being woven right into the old fabric. He had written another poem, for the newlyweds. The *geary gathering*, from San Francisco, had even bought a carafe of red wine to celebrate, while a watercolor was being painted by the local artist, especially for the couple. The Devil's Hook Pub had rented a large screen for the occasion, even Alex, at the Plough and the Sword, down the street, had bought a lightbox for his customers. Satelites were turned on, tuned in and people had dropped in from all over the world. Armani and his visitors were ready to raise a glass with the virtual crowd in the future room. He passed out glasses and opened up a bottle of champagne. *POP!* The sound brought attention to the screen that Armani, Whirling, Nicholas, Roland and Haystack were being projected on, viewed on, by a million satelites around the world. They were the timeless visitors and their champagne-filled glasses were ready. They were all there for the world to see, but especially, for the newlyweds...Ben and Betsy, however, were not looking at that screen or any other...They were looking at each other...

Findhorn, however, saw the bubbles coming out of the *future room*, looked at the visitors, recognized Nicholas, from books, or from dreams and realized they were in the presence of different times, yet, he wasn't sure what time. Everything had simply become a part of his present consciousness; the past had become a *persistent presence*, a *persistent presence* that pervaded...

In his exuberance he welcomed them to this timeless celebration, *A hearty welcome, to those who have come a long way, please stay, this is their wedding day, a hey, a hey hey*...He raised his glass, and who knows how many others raised theirs with him, while he sang an olde Irish blessing,

> *May troubles be less and blessings be more*
> *and nothing but happiness come to your door.*
> *And may you have luck where ever you go*
> *Your blessings out number the shamrocks that grow.*
>
> *May wind be at your back and sun be over head*
> *and friends be at your side where ever you are led.*

When he was through, a great klinking and klunking and clattering of glasses could be heard throughout the the room and throughout the world.

SC took the microphone at Jeanette's place and sang a love song he had written for the couple. "This is for you Betsy and Ben,"

> *I've never sung a love song like I'm singing one now.*
> *Don't know where it came from,*
> *but it sure did somehow.*
> *I've sung the old songs,*
> *made up my own songs,*
> *but never sung a love song like I'm singing one now.*

255

You two were meant to be,
I just want to say,
you two were meant to be,
how long have you known
that you've felt it so deeply?
Surprised at how freely?
You two were meant to be,
Let me sing it again...

You've never been so taken like you're taken right now.
Don't know how it happened but it sure did some how.
You were contented,
single intended,
yet, you've never been so taken like you're taken right now.

As if on cue, the bright sounds of Aiden's penny whistle came in to play the chorus and Findhorn the leprechaun clicked his shoes in time, while SC began the last verse,

I've never seen two lovers like I'm seeing right now.
Don't know where you came from but you sure did some how.
You've chosen romance.
A crazy slow dance.
The one and only lovers, yes, the one and only lovers

You two were meant to be.
It seems right to say,
you two were meant to be,
How long have you known
that you felt it so deeply
Surprised at how freely?

You two were meant to be,
Oh, I want to sing it again...

You two were meant to be,
Come on, let's sing it again...

And they sang it again and again…Until finally shouts and whistles resounded, glasses clinked once more, others got up and gave them their blessings.

Alfred's Gift

Alfred stood up, becoming a presence in his castle room, with the candle lit reflections flickering upon the stone walls and the medieval tapestry, which was now focused on two riders, a young man and a young woman riding like the wind across the great steppes of the east. They were lovers of old, waving to the new, in new bodies, not young, but young at heart.

To one side of this grand woven epic stood a suit of armor with a green plume on its helmet, shining in the candle light. Alfred stood next to it, adjusting a cape draped over the steel shoulders, a cape held together with a safety pin, the button had long ago broken off.

Alfred looked at his paper, "To your happiness, Ben and Betsy…I hope the meaning of this is clear,

Sometimes,
you are so far away,
when we are speaking;
and yet, so near,
when we, in silence, sit
close by the fire,
and when we are dreaming
of times gone past,
and of times to come,
we feel the thoughts
as if they're beaming,
radiating to our heart.
We wonder,
when words are spoken,
if we are receiving
what's really being said,
with an open mind

or without a doubt
or without deception.
Words can be bent,
they can hurt and cut,
if they are spoken wrong,
we can get a different meaning.
But if the spirit
of love,
and good will
presides,
then the right meaning
will grow,
in talking,
or in silence;
and it will always be
redeeming.

"Your meaning is very clear, Alfred, we will keep your words in mind, thank you so much…"

Gift of an Eye

It was a wedding of two people united, in the world, for a moment, united in the world…Someone said, "Speech, speech."

The two lovers broke from each other's gaze. They looked up beaming. They looked out, all over the world, and yet, yet it was intimate, as if it had only been with their friends. The Doctor was there with Camec, who took the moment to give them a small gift, which they opened. It was the keys to the Mercedes. "Something to get you back to the estate once in a while," the Doctor said with a wide smile. Aiden was next and handed Betsy a small box, "Something I found when I was cleaning out the cottage, before it broke up completely."

She opened it and they both saw the star amethyst which Twangly had found in the ruins of Terra Grandeur and had left in Aiden's living room the night before his fateful ride.

"Aiden, this is too much, please…"

"No, no, I think you should have it."

Findhorn and Moira both saw the gift, the jewel, it dazzled him with the memory of something, something he had come across, which was now sitting, hiding in the Olde Bookshoppe, *Moira, it is a jewel with a star, I know the place, it is not far, hie, fie, bring me the face that has brightened our place…*

Moira looked at him, and was ready to tell him to stop the riddles when she remembered what he was talking about. "Yes, I know the face, dear. You bought it from a professor who was more interested in pounds than sense." She went into the Olde Bookshoppe, moved some books from a shelf. Behind the books, somewhat dusty, hung the shield, the *ikon* with the haloed face. When she brushed it off, a golden glow slowly returned to the halo around the face, the face with the one eye. The glow warmed and moved through the room as she brought it to Findhorn. In the future room Nicholas was transfixed by the glow and walked with her. They walked past the armor with the raised sword. Moira took it to Findhorn, whose fortuitous purchase had brought this moment about. He showed it to Betsy and Ben.

Look, by Jove, it is the missing eye of the haloed face, Findhorn, the magician, said in a maze ment.

Betsy took the jewel and put it into the hole opposite the other jewel. Nicholas was next to them, inside them, around the golden, glowing shield, the very shield found in the charred remains of that horrible massacre, where he had met Flaxen, the very shield that saved a knight so long ago, and yet, almost yesterday. When the late afternoon light came through the arched, stained glass window and shone on the beatific face with the eyes of stars, Nicholas' face ran with tears. He held his hand over the shining, glowing face, he reached out to touch it and his hand became one with the light and the jewels and the stars.

Findhorn said to them, *Somehow this has become whole. Please, take it and treasure it.* They realized they could not argue with

259

him and thanked him profusely and said they would treasure it always.

Now Euphrates came to give them her blessing. She had left the estate and brought Clara, the nanny, with her. They were both sobbing with joy. "I can only give what I have," she said, and brought a basket of fruit from the garden of the estate, along with bread they had both baked.

"Euphrates, Clara, thank you, " both of them said, and held them for a long and tender moment.

In this moment, their thoughts were, not only on the joy of the present, but also on the presence of the young man they had loved and still loved, their Twangly, who would always be with them. They held him in their thoughts just as they held Ben and Betsy...They held him in their bittersweet joy...

There was one person, however, left at the estate, one woman, who would not even find the *bitter*, of the bittersweet, today. There was one woman, who had a recollection of a husband and a father, the father of Twangly, her son, in whom she had put her future, but no remembrance of Betsy or even of Ben, who had been a friend of hers, from her student days. There was one woman, who was still cloistered in her own world, who walked the halls asking for Tiger,

He promised me he would come...he said he would come...he said he would come this morning...

Euphrates had left her today, talking to her imaginary guests, as she had gotten into the habit of doing. Practically everyday Euphrates had helped her set up a tea set, around the parlor, for her guests. Nadjia insisted that only the best spoons be used, from the silverware with the peacock design. The only set they had been able to carry away from the palace, on that far away fateful day. Euphrates had left her on the estate, in the palace of her dreams and her past, with her favorite son, Twangly and her husband and Tiger, who had finally come to see her. She served them all tea and cookies and made sure their cups were filled. When Euphrates came back to check on her, the door opened slowly and Nadjia put her finger to her mouth, *Sh, sh, they are resting.*

The mother of an ancient empire had lost too much and was no longer able to come back...

Speech

There was one other dear friend whom Ben and Betsy had hoped would be with them, who they had hoped would share this day with them and it was to him that Betsy raised a glass to, "I'm not a speech type but I do want to send a toast to a very special friend, a young friend of ours, who, in an unusual, I'd almost say strange, way, brought us together…"

"I would very much say so," Ben added.

"To put it into the vernacular of the history over here," she continued, "this young friend of ours has been like a knight out on a quest. A Knight who went through one trial after another - being attacked and literally fighting for his life, dealing with the death of his brother and his father…finding the inner strength to deal with all of this and still…"

Ben interrupted, "And still come up with a song."

"That kid has more songs in him," Betsy added, "So, here's to you, kid. Here's to your spirit, Twing…Keep singing."

They raised their glasses again and this time it was with a wistful, joyful recognition of the young man who was in their thoughts…but not in person.

Twing had left the estate to the Doctor and Camec and Euphrates and Clara. *Take care of my mother, please,* he had told the Doctor. *I trust you with her. Do what you can for her and the estate. The estate needs you, it needs all of you, until we know what to do with it.*

He had left, after enough practical matters had been dealt with. He had taken a plane back to America. *It was time,* he thought, *for a much needed change.* It seemed to him he had wrestled enough for a while. He would take a Concorde back to New York, from there he would take the train across the country. He wanted to see the country roll past him, think, read, even write, catch up on his journal. He smiled, *Catch up on my journal, are you kidding, wow, I've got an epic to write, where is Tolstoy when I need him.* With those thoughts in mind he had left the estate and said good bye to all, before Betsy's Coffee Cafe had opened and before the wedding plans had been made.

But made they were, the day had come, and when the popping ceased and the bottles had turned over, when the champagne had celebrated enough, Armani finally said to his group of guests, "Gentlemen, we've seen the future and it is just the beginning. Wait until two future rooms are connected. We'll send each other through the air. They will be here and we will be there, all in one place. We will be able to talk to each other, see each other, walk through each other…"

He let that sink in. Whirling, was more and more astonished and fascinated with the possibilities. "Can we think about a joint venture, Armani?" he inquired, "That is something I have been thinking about for a long time."

Armani did not answer right away and led his group of visitors back through the pulsing, circular lights, *Close Future World*, he said and took them all back down the hallways and corridors of screens. The echo of their footsteps followed them and filled the curved space ahead of them.

After they were, again, reflected in the long hall of mirrors, the long curvilinear tunnel of living screens…After they were, again, brought into the timeless presence of their long-ago past, Armani finally spoke, "Whirling, you have a long and venerable reputation, I would consider it an honor if we merged our knowledge and our resources and brought this orbiting, blue orb into the future,"

That was all he said, until they walked around another corner, into the lobby of his headquarters. The DNA door was opened and Armani thanked them for coming,

"We'll be in touch," he said, with a sly smile. *We'll be in touch.*

Everyone walked through the door with the green light around it, *except for one…* One, who had stayed in the future room, in the future with the others. The party was not yet over and he had found the shield once again, He had wandered for years, looking for it, until he found it in the children. Now the children had grown and he had found the warmth of that light, that golden glow, again.

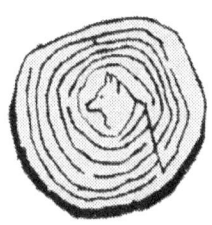

Path Thirty Seven

Homeward Bound

After Twing was seated in the window seat of the Concord and finally in the air, he thought of his brother. He imagined him in a wild whirlwind, blowing around in the clouds. He missed him. *Everything, that happened to me, would have been easier,* he thought. *We could have lived through this. We...*He touched his neck. He felt a slight, straight line, a scar where his birthmark used to be...*That was the we,* he thought. *We both had the same birthmarks. Now he is gone, passed away, and I, I am here, flying...*

He looked out the window, they were above the clouds, the sky blue enclosed them and yet seemed endless. When he first left Boulder Creek on his way to Seattle he remembered looking at the clouds and wanting to jump into them. Now he waited for the window light to change. He was resting, dozing, when the sun began setting over this wondrous, bilious world. Long shadows began to emerge, darkening the clouds, underneath them, around them, making the golden yellow of this blazing, life-giving, setting sunlight, even more contrasting. He opened his eyes and let this striking brilliance blind him...Suddenly he was with the old man in the cavern, with the glow of that haloed, shining face. It's radiance sweeping through him. He bathed in it. He let it warm him. He let the eyes, the two jeweled stars look at him -- through him. He looked out. He saw the face, looked at it, saw it come alive, looked at it and saw a birthmark on its neck...He could feel the upwelling of his brother, the presence of the brother he had just gotten to know.

After landing at JFK airport, he found his way to Grand Central Station inundated with the sights and sounds of New York City. He stopped for a Coney Island hot dog, *Mm mm, what a snapfresh hot dog*, he thought.

For the trip across America he had bought an Amtrak ticket with sleeping accommodations, his own room, with a shower. Not like the last time, when he rode coach...when he rode coach and...*Why couldn't he let go of that?* He remembered the warning tape on his seat, *This will be the end of your line*. That was all he remembered...all he wanted to remember of the two revolutionary radicals. Their threat had come, partly, true. Twangly, the one they were after, was gone. They just didn't know he had a brother, a twin brother. Even he wasn't sure at the time they were chasing him, and now...He gently nodded his head, sighing, until his thoughts brightened again...He did want to remember the little girl, who laughed at his tousled hair standing on end, as if he had been struck by lightning. He chuckled to himself, even laughed at the sight of himself in the mirror. The train slowly pulled away from the station. He let it go and closed his eyes, until his window was filled with the forests of upper New York State, rolling westward.

"I'm taking reservations for dinner."

"Sure. What time?"

"Is 6:30 all right?"

"Yea, sure." He could hardly wait.

Dinner was a salad and a hamburger steak with mashed potatoes and a great gravy. There was even a table cloth and cloth napkins and silverware. He knew Amtrak wasn't the Orient Express but they, at least, tried and he was comfortable enough. Before he could turn around he had settled into his private sleeper, fading, in the hands of the engineer guiding them, fading into the rhythms of his dreams.

The days went by. Time seemed to slow down, every mile of rolling grassland and endless corn fields soothed his nerves, his aches, his soul. Every river crossing, on old wooden trestles or new steel-beamed bridges, brought the flow of the water into him. The rivers were wide, the land was even wider. On and on he rolled. Slowly, and, without being conscious of it, the land of the gatedcountry estate and the cottage and the sea that had taken it, began to fade. Even the persistence of those he had lost and left behind began to fade. They all began to take their place in his memory; to begin to be outweighed, *strangely enough,* by the lightness of what was ahead of him. Like a teeter-totter from his childhood, he was going up, getting lighter, brought up by the weight that was on the other side: the weight that was behind him. He sat in the club car thinking about Masama, thinking about Mariah's farm, thinking about Angelina, *Was she still thinking about me?* he wondered. *And what was she doing? Right now?*

The land was beginning to slope upward, *It must be the Rockies, the great divide.* he thought, *the great divide, yet we're still connected.* He let out a *Rocky mountain high iiiiiii…The great divide, it's just that water, streams, rivers run eastward on this side of the divide and run westward on the other, all off the same mountains. That's my life,* he thought, *the old and the new, the past and the future. They run off the same mountains. Only with me, the mountain is always moving. I'm always moving, changing, yet, still the past rolls off and the future rolls off. I'm just in a different place."*

"Reservations for dinner?"

"Please."

"6:30."

"Sure, OK."

Well, we have to pass over somewhere, he thought. *I wonder where the pass over the northern Rockies is? I should look on a map.* But he really didn't want to, had no intention of doing so. He wanted to let his body roll with the land. He wanted to let his mind flow with the contours, the undulation of the land.

In the mornings, he ran in place, did calisthenics, *one, two, three, four,* not enough room for push-ups unless he went out into the hallway. Why not? It was just barely wide enough and room enough, until breakfast time, when the aisle came alive.

Now it was down, down to the flat, sagebrush, flat land of eastern Washington State. Soon, too soon, the train would come into Wenatchee. This time he would not hitchhike. *They will pick me up there, Mariah and Angelina...Angelina, I wonder what she looks like, if she's changed, it's been a while, she's probably, well, she couldn't look much better, I mean, she is an angel...a moon child, as Jim Bridger called her, yes, she is all of that and more...*

The last night on the train, in his sleeping car brought dreams of what was to come, the past had faded, slowly faded over 2500 miles, faded, all, but for the occasional thought of a wedding, that he remembered, was going to take place, about the time he reached the farm.

Path Thirty Eight

Thread of Life

Wenatchee, next stop.

He got his bag and waited by the door. The train slowed down and finally stopped. With a little trepidation he took that first step, was almost afraid to look around, in case there was no one waiting for him...took that second step, "Twing, Twing, " the sound of an angel surrounded him. He looked and saw her running to his railroad car, hair like the wind, running to him. He dropped his bag and put out his arms and she, she filled them up, the sweetness of her touch was overwhelming to him, they held each other. Mariah came and held them both...he had come back...

They rode home in the old pickup, bumping, swaying, touching, so happy to be together, close together. She drove along the Columbia. He did not notice. They turned and followed the Methow River. He was enthralled by her face, the smell of her hair. They drove through Winthrop and past the gold-panning cafe. He was listening to her and talking and listening and they were all talking when they hopped out of the pickup.

He just stood there for a while and smelled the air, the smell of sage. He looked beyond the farm house and the orchards to the sky around them. *When had this horizon ever been so wide, the sky ever been so, so...vast, so big...?*

He took his bag inside. Angelina and Mariah showed him to the room he had once stayed in, there was a new watercolor over his bed, he noticed it right away. It was an expressive, radiating movement of colors, of golden yellows and magenta reds with turquoise blues. The more he looked at it, the more radiant it became.

"Mariah, I'm glad you didn't put a gray wash over that," he said to her, "or try to bring it into form." He was remembering the last time she continued brushing on one wash after another, until the forms that emerged became a *portent* for the tragic ending of her friend, and the godfather of Angelina: Jim Bridger.

She smiled at him, "We'll let you clean up, get unpacked and then, we thought, we would go to Betsy's Cafe for lunch. What do you think?"

He wanted to say yes, but held back, "Betsy's…Betsy's? What do you mean?"

"Merryweather opened it up and she's doing a pretty good job. She didn't want to change the name."

They left him in thought, while he unpacked, showered, changed his clothes. He took everything out of his left pocket and put them on the dresser. He checked his right pocket and took out the old disintegrating pouch, which barely held the objects, the artifacts, the *secret things*, given to him in a lost moment…He rolled the incised copper coin between his fingers. It was not the usual size coin with the usual historical figure or eagle's head on it. No, this is one coin he would never forget. This one had the symbol of a wolf's head in the middle of an incised pathway, a maze, a labyrinth, a symbolic pathway. He felt he had traveled on it. It was a pathway. No! More than one pathway. Many! Many pathways, fraught with dead ends and dangers, circling in and out…he had gone forward when possible and backward when needed. Where had the blueprints been, the maps? He had taken one turn after another. He had confronted the mythic beast. He had almost died in the clutches of the beast. The archetypal demons had roared with ferocious mouths…the loss of his brother and his father, the forlorn path of his mother, the guilt-ridden death of Tiger. *These demons had eaten well…*

But for him, for now, a way had been found; a way to go on. A pathway, now, guided by the experience that came from wrestling with these demons and guided by the knowledge that was gained in that wrestling. It had all became a part of him, his outer and inner self, his undivided self. He sensed his inner world had become clearer, brighter, *better yet*, he felt a warmth of light emanating from within, a light that did not come from the outside -- not from the vast sky of a Washington morning or from a brilliant sunset streaming through a Concorde's window, not from Brother Rubens' *ikon*, the shield with the golden, shining halo that had saved Sir Waldundstein…No, he felt an emanation growing from within; an inner golden, glowing light that had helped him find the way to go on…

He moved everything else out of the way and put this coin, by itself, in the middle of the dresser, as a reminder, just as a reminder…

"All right, I'm ready," he half yelled out of the bedroom door. "But not until I make one phone call. There's about eight hours difference between here and Wellborn-on-Avon and they are ahead of us. The party must in high gear. He dialed the number of the Olde Bookshoppe. It rang and rang…

Hi dee, ho, please join the show…

"Helloooo, this is Twing, calling from Mariah's, I think I've reached the right place. How are you, Findhorn? How is the wedding celebration?"

It has been a splendid party, hah hah, he he, they are in rare form, as well are we, ho ho, hee hic.

Can I talk to the married couple?"

Twing just held on and smiled at the sounds of the leprechaun, until the voice of Betsy came on the line,

"Hello, Twing, I hear you, I can just imagine you in Mariah's living room, it's been amazing here. We've missed you."

"Well, I, I want to wish you both well," he stammered for the right words, "I have something for you,"

With his right hand, he had taken two more objects out of the old pouch, two bones with names on them, one had B E T S Y carved on it and the other had B E N…He held them and apologetically said, "I have two bones with your names carved in them. Just like those out of an old fairy tale. Remember the bones of Nicholas and Flaxen. But you will have to wait until I get back…"

"That's all right, Twing. You've been toasted to…and we've had toasts of all kinds, blessings, poems, songs…"

"Actually, I do have something, also a song, "

"I would never have guessed," She put Ben's ear to the phone with hers…

"This is something that I came across, on my way across the States, while I was thinking of you, but…it might be more appropriate for your new coffee shop then, *ah*…but it's going to be your new life, also, so, here's a toast to the new Betsy's Coffee Cafe and to you and Ben, and, here goes…" He half sang and recited, like a troubadour at an old song festival…

You're my Cappuccino…
When I meet you here oh,
early Sunday morning,
early in the morn…

Could be rainin, could be stormin!
like the night we knew.
But no matter just how crazy or how blue we were…
Somethin's sure,

Now,
You're my Cappuccino,
when I meet you here oh,
you know I'm feelin fine
and I want to make you mine…
now now now

Lady Cappucino
let me know what you know?
When you sit there steamin,
when you sit and dream…

Are you thinkin, are you feelin
like the night before?

But no matter just how crazy or how blue we were,
somethin's sure

You're my Cappuccino…
I love to meet you here oh,
early Sunday Morning,
early in the morn…

"That is clever, Twing, it's just like you. We never know what to expect from you. Thank you, Twing, thank you."

"We will think about you, old boy. Come and have that cappuccino with us, next time you're in Wellborn, will you?" Ben chimed in.

"Yes, next time. Good luck, you two,"

He handed the phone to Mariah,

"And from us, too," Mariah added and sent her blessings to them, "When I heard you were getting married, Betsy, I started a watercolor, I think it's going to have the first Betsy's Cafe in it, with Goats Peak in the background and maybe the Masama general store and who knows what else will come up. That will be a belated wedding present."

"Thank you, Mariah, we will put it right in the Cafe, over the counter…"

"Many blessings, you two, until we see each other…"

"And blessings from me," Angelina added, as they hung up the phone.

For a moment, it was the quiet of leftover voices and the joy of their joy that lingered. When Twing finally looked at Angelina, his feelings welled up and he smiled one of those smiles that could only come from knowing something, having gone through something extraordinary that…quite…simply… in this moment… made him feel glad to be alive. He held out his hands to both of them and, with an engaging grin, said,

"Shall we have lunch at Betsy's?"

Acknowledgments

In appreciation and acknowledgment of all those who, inadvertently, or in any other way, inspired the sign posts and markers on this journey - the music, the words, the places, the ideas - the following are a few of them and not necessarily in their order of appearance...

William Shakespeare
T-Rex
Amsterdam
Variation on Blues song
Adler's Museum Cafe
Jacques Brel
Rudolf Steiner
King Arthur's circle
Excerpt from the Kalevala
Novalis
Troubadours/Minstrels
Constellations and the Zodiac
Bridal Paths and lay lines
Louise
Ingmar Bergman
Tarkovsky - film maker
Ikons
Medieval Shepherd's Play
Faustian Bargain

Art movements- Destijl, Futurists, German Expressionism
Scriabin
Kandinsky
Blue Rider Almanac
Karl Orff
Neanderthals
Poets and songwriters
Alfred Neumann - philosopher poet
Bhagwan Rajneesh
Greensleeves
Other states of consciousness
The Lone Ranger
Royal Domains throughout history
Spirituals - By the River of Babylon
Pop songs - I'm Just a Lonely Boy
Beach Boys
Greek Myths
Frankie Laine - Do Not Forsake Me
The Bible
Psalms
1776 Revolution
Amazing Grace
Oedipus Rex
Refugee Camp
Jack London
Eps
Elvis Presley
R&B
Isaac's sacrifice
Bruce Lee
Orion
Archeological history
Silicon Valley
Fairy Tales
Roy Orbison
Jefferson Airplane
geary gathering

Scottish clan
Findhorn
America
Buddy Holly
Flower Children
Radical Revolutions
Radical thinking
The twilight of Royal Power
Masama
Digital revolution
Irish Blessing
Amtrak
John Denver
Cappuccinos

About the Author

Rainer Neumann's life is punctuated with the endings and beginnings of places, relationships and a variety of creative pursuits. Throughout these he has had an on-going interest in the structural environments of out culture.

He has published a novella *Masama* about an unusual family reunion near Blue Lake in the Cascade Mountains – where twin brothers confront destiny and he has written and illustrated *On the Wings of a Swan* an allegory of love transcending the every day. His latest novel is *Goodbye Bolinas we'll see you again* a heart-rending, mind-bending, love-sending paean to a turbulent summer in the sixties.

While exploring the California coast he has made many pastel drawings that have been published in a book entitled *from Pigeon Point to Point Reyes.*

www.ingramcontent.com/pod-product-compliance
Lightning Source LLC
Chambersburg PA
CBHW020606260626
47157CB00003B/885